CIRCUITS
OF THE
WIND

VOLUME ONE

CIRCUITS OF THE WIND

A LEGEND OF THE NET AGE

VOLUME ONE

MICHAEL STUTZ

" ... go find yourself where,
why in the mirror there?"

Confiteor Media

2011

Grateful acknowlegment is made to Scribner, a Division of Simon & Schuster, Inc., for permission to reprint an excerpt from THE GREAT GATSBY (AUTHORIZED TEXT) by F. Scott Fitzgerald. Copyright © 1925 by Charles Scribner's Sons. Copyright renewed © 1953 by Frances Scott Fitzgerald Lanahan. All rights reserved.

FIRST EDITION
Publisher's Cataloging-in-Publication data

Stutz, Michael.
    Circuits of the wind : a legend of the net age , volume one / Michael Stutz.
    p. cm.
    ISBN 978-0-9838558-0-4

1. Internet—Fiction. 2. Computer hackers—Fiction. 3. Internet—History—Fiction. 4. Computer programmers—Fiction. 5. Computer bulletin boards—Fiction. 6. Generation X—Fiction. 7. Coming of age—Fiction. I. Series. II. Title.

PS3569.T885 Ci 2011
813'.6–dc22   2011939257

Printed in Charleston, SC, USA

Cover design by Peter Lutjen

circuitsofthewind

2 4 6 8 10 9 7 5 3 1

Hemisect this heart

to see, tattoo'd inside,

M A R I E

The wind goeth toward the south, and turneth about unto the north; it whirleth about continually, and the wind returneth again according to his circuits.

—SOLOMON, KING OF ISRAEL

Can't repeat the past? Why of course you can!

—GATSBY, GREAT AMERICAN

ACKNOWLEDGMENTS

are made to the gurus, Daniel Frank Kirk and Irwin Allen Ginsberg; the confiders, Aldo P. Magi, Jack Angelotta and Jonathan Konrath; the coadjutors, Peter Lutjen, Adrienne Bashista and Yessenia Santos; the encouragers, Leo Gurko, Steven Snedker, Arthur S. Nusbaum, David Amram, Dean Koontz, Anne Mini, Brian Lobertini and certainly Jack and Aldo again; and also to Jessamyn West for the barn time, Bill Burroughs for the blessing and Matthew J. Bruccoli for the many expectations—semper gratias.

Contents

CIRCUITS
OF THE
WIND

VOLUME ONE

BOOK ONE

THE IMMINENT BIRTH OF THE NET

To know the legend of a world that has been lost, first you must go back. To even catch a meagre glimpse at any cost, first you must go back. You have to take the bow of history, pull it back, project yourself onto an orbic stage with phantom cast; then you will be back.

You'll soon relive the memory of what's gone, the eager step-pings of a fawn. You may hear the brassy ring of horn-note o'er field and dale, taste the sugared weep of spring with its milky rain of hail, and see the lovely bodies—the ones that flitter with such ease before you as they swoon beneath the trembly midnights of the moon. Listen closely for the call that's luting high upon the wand'ring wind and seems to say, "I was there— it had only been a flicker and a flash inside the darkness of the past, but I was there."

Of the future it needs desperately to know: Will the flame of sunrise always melt away the darkest shadow? Can the wind ever shake down all the mountains? Does the weepy willow still hang above the river's edge? Is that a dreary sigh that crawls alone upon the ocean floor? And what hope lies there in this tired dusk, when dark time is groaning at the door?

I walk away from this, and still I look for you. I believe, the fire burns, and I must find you.

. . . the air is empty in the pause, and bestilled I cannot wait. In this new moment I pass through antique doors alone, en-treated, expectant, eager, that as seeker I shall find, as thinker I shall know, and as the burning of the love I felt in youth whose memory is now candle-drawn and cold I shall come again, away, alone, in a world that happened somewhere long ago— just as Napoleon has even trembled from his tomb, and in some corner glade a willow bends and weeps inside the alabaster day, whisp'ring out these words of living life upon the lyre of the August wind.

But the square silence of the temple steps is littered with so many mothy questions: What have we ever done? Where have we ever been? And what is it even all about, with these things we carry with us through the densely woven thickets and the dark and endless tunnels? We have tried, valiantly we lived and died, and what remains is the poison of the worm, the spoiled grain we tossed and trampled underfoot, and a sail that has carried firm and gone away—so very far away, alone, and long ago. And what else will it ever be about, and tell us what again have we ever done?

You know their doubt, and here the willow tree's a bulbous cloud, a waterfall all brusque and proud; break a staff and route it into fresh new ground—and soon another willow tree is found. On this very stage the actors play you're able now to say, "There shall come a sprinkled hail from the shaken hyssop, the lifting of a reed against the worm, a dew that sweetens all the earth like wine—and somewhere they will always know the rough and barren cry that fell upon the dusty, sun-glared desert of an isolated time."

You'll have finally found that place at last, a living moment of the past. And when it is you do—it too shall disappear into another moment new.

1

CHILDHOOD'S PROMISE

HE KNEW the telephone early. Where there once had been indifference, when first he'd only noted just an olive-colored blemish on the wall, soon came recognition and finally even curiosity. In time the thing took on a great significance.

It would sometimes shake the room in a flaring jingle, causing everything to freeze, and the lady would rush over to attend to it. It went like this no matter what—the lady would stop everything and run. She'd quiet it, speak importantly around it—perhaps even direct it—and he wondered if she'd set a timer to make it ring, for she seemed to control it sometimes by lifting up the handset while a finger carefully revolved the dial front. She'd stand there for great lengths of time, gesticulating wildly—dictating to, conversing with, nodding toward, or otherwise influencing it, all the while with the handset propped up to the side of her head in what at first appeared to be comedy, but sometimes became a long and tedious routine.

It was some while and not without false trails before he discovered that voices fell from it: there were times when she held the handset to his head, and he was prodded, coaxed, urged to speak, and she'd tell him that these other people could

7

hear him, she'd perform a litany of names; after confused deflections where he convulsively pushed back for fear that it might injure him, the magic was revealed one day when he finally acquiesced and felt the soft pitches of sound tickling the inside of his ear—and to her happy praise he quickly gurgled an acknowledgement.

Once he understood something of its workings, when he knew how it would pitch and jingle and then bring up the soft voices, he thought that it was a connection to the other side of the kitchen wall—he thought that there were adult neighbors sitting back in there, beyond the green and silver stripes of wallpaper, and that they were talking to them through it, summoning them at all hours.

Eventually he came to know that it actually reached out well beyond all that, through long wires, and soon enough he learned that the whole entire world was connected to it, was accessible from there and waiting for him at the end of a phone line. The lady told him this, he saw no reason to disbelieve her, and yet he harbored doubts—for it scarcely seemed possible. He'd stare at this fantastic gateway to the world and soon decided that it'd somehow bring him to his future, this great connecting force that wrapped around the whole entire planet and brought everything imaginable to the striped wall of their kitchen.

They were in the city of Clifton, one of the three-dozen great cities that had been built and blossomed there in the land of America, a sprawling metropolis along the upper edge of that crossroads state they call Sohola, which had the whole of America inside it—the nation ended abruptly at its northern shoreline, where beyond the soft ripples of the inland sea there was nothing but the vague promises of Canada, while if you drifted far down toward its southern border you'd notice that everyone had a different accent, and it never snowed so much in winter, and grits were on all the breakfast menus; it was also the state where New England undeniably saw its final end in those forested hills that tapered off along its eastern sections, where they'd come tumbling down from Ithaca in New York state, and Pittsburgh, Pennsylvania, and other points in that Appalachian highland that cupped the whole East Coast—and everybody knew that it was the place where the Midwest decidedly began, with all that farmland across the loamy plains that stretched all through the bedded night so long into the west.

Clifton pressed up tightly against the cold gritty shores of Lake Catawba, one of the vast and endless Great Lakes, those cool and glimmering inland seas of old America. In its downtown city core it was much smaller than Chicago, but the suburban mass of greater Clifton, radiating out in all directions south along the shore, held a sprawling land mass just about the size of the entire state of Rhode Island.

Its downtown skyline—a dense sprouting of gray office towers, brick warehouses, factories, department stores and big old buildings—was dominated by the solitary Clifton Beacon, stacked up upon the throne of Center Square; it was illuminated at night in a pale yellow light upon the sable harbor, a glow that could be seen for miles out on the sleepy waters to remind you that the city was still there, looking like a miniature night-light of the Empire State Building—and actually in a sense it was, having secretly been a prototype of it, and for a splendid while back in '30 bore the distinction of second-tallest building in the world.

In its basement cavern was the city's great terminal, where trains slowed down in their smooth liquidic way and soon left again to disappear into the far horizon, and during business hours the rapid streetcars spat from their gates in six directions only to pause along the curbs for a dozen miles out, penetrating far into the suburbs and sliding brusquely over their placid empty streets.

The house was in the inner city about a hundred blocks west of Center Square, not half a mile from the lapping edge of Catawba's periwinkle bowl, on a street of two-families that'd been huddling tight together there since at least the century's two World Wars. Most of them were steep-roofed and boxy, with covered porches sweeping shadily all the way across the front of them—stationary giants looking down upon the sidewalks, while a garage that often matched in color and design was like its baby sitting on the ground out back behind. Telephone poles—tall as the homes and smooth, as if they'd been rubbed for years—were staggered along each side of the street with their black wires roped up high. There was one next door. Their house was on the north side of the street, toward the western end, and its exterior wood was painted a cheerful apple yellow. They lived on the second floor. It's there, inside the lockings of those rooms, in the first years of the decade of the 1970s, where he spent bright, whirlwind days of learning through the steady observation of the lady. She attended to all his needs and was the one who fed him, and he was there with her, constantly around her, this long-haired lady who only later did he learn also had a name—now, to him, she was only "Momma."

His waking hours were spent on cushions and soft beds below steep cliffs of avocado green and goldenrod, where he kept himself patiently amused by examining the frills and nubs and edges and tracing all the patterns. He was a big-eyed baby who'd somehow assumed that he was king, and the adults of his kingdom were extravagant aristocrats, all of them wearing brightly colored, complex robes of clothing, heavy polyesters that his fingers pulled at so he could examine. Dadda would sometimes peek down smiling at him with a head of shiny black hair and giant sideburns that were somehow like handles to reach for, but when the head bobbed back it was mysteriously gone for all the sunny, happy hours of the day, which was when he spent all of his time alone with Momma.

In time he came to know the various relations between his mother, father, and the greater family—and it didn't take him long to discover a special phone at his grandparents' house, which was somehow nearby. This one was within reach. It sat ready on a giant snowflake of a doily, atop a streamlined end-table of sunny wood; after some experiment and mimicry he saw that the handset made a noise when lifted. The noise stopped when he carefully moved the dial with hard turnings in the right direction, and if done properly he knew that he'd hear the voices in the handset.

His mother didn't want him touching it, but his grandmother seemed to think that it was clever, and allowed it up to a point. He pushed that point continually, until even she asserted an adult authority and kept him away with a firm unbreakable grip. He wondered with some jealousy how these adults could know all of the white symbols beneath the circle of the dial, how they knew to combine and select them with their fingers to all means of successful ends—he yearned to do the same. He persisted, began to furtively experiment, and then commanded it openly when his turnings were met with good success.

"Don't do that!" his mother scolded roughly, reaching over to take the handset away from him. "You're going to get the operator on the line!"

But that was the very point—and as the handset was pried away he could finally hear the fair voice calling out, in confirmation of his theories: "*Op*erator! *Op*erator, may I *help* you!"

He'd found something that was real and far away from this torpid room in Clifton with its doilies and heavy curtains, and everything around him took on the foggy underwater cast of a confusing, languid dream. He'd found a voice, it was calling out to him, a connection had been made, he yearned to take it further—and when it went away he cried and stomped and turned red-faced with tears and anger.

The wonder of the telephone, so complex and technological and suggestive of another world, had completely enraptured him already at this early age—and he saw this wonder everywhere around him, in a parade of many things that came bursting forth in a steady procession through those years following his naked infancy: he saw it in the Sunbeam electric blender, with a good long panel of buttons, a heavy glass pitcher with complex notchings, and a black lid to seal it like a top hat; he saw it in the big mixer parked up upon the counter, sleek and white as a moon rocket, with a wide turning knob at the end labeled with serious instructions and the beaters that whirred throatily when it was on—their curved steel fins were shaped to him like rocket ships, one slender and the other slightly pudgy for good variation, a fact he'd idly contemplate when he got to lick them after his mother's baking; he saw it in a plastic measuring cup whose rows of numberings and complex red arcs and lines along the side were of some scientific import, possibly for use during the exploration of space and sea; and he saw it in all the other objects kept in deep cupboard tunnels of the kitchen, and even in the smaller cupboard tunnels of the bathroom, which had their own style and flavor and were vaguely dangerous, similar to what was found in the doctor's offices where it always smelled sharply of rubbing alcohol and there was the constant fear of pain and needles.

Then there was the console television on the living room floor, a giant toy whose glowing, moving screen could be controlled with a panel of buttons on the side, including a big round one that would click in friendly advocations as you'd turn it; there was the console record player with its moving robotic arm and spinning platter; there were countless radios with serrated dials that were good to turn, and some had nice buttons with stars crowned in the center, or a mysterious red indicator wand that moved, backlit by a pale evening sun that glowed sadly like the final hopeless moments in the dying world of dinosaurs.

He saw this wonder in all the hidden pockets of their house, and in the house of his grandparents, which he'd freely roam, exploring and taking inventory; he did this everywhere that he was brought, and in strange buildings he often saw the wonder and the way—it was inside all the stores and their complex paths and mazes, it was marked on all the doors and handles, and was reachable somehow by all the buttons and the machinery that moved; the entire world he lived in was a single vast and complex city, connected with these buttons and latches and switches, like the command post of a giant ship that was ready to take off somewhere into space, and he spent so much time examining its wondrous aspects—crawling under tables, pulling open drawers, looking at the lights, pressing buttons, tracing paths, touching and experimenting and seeking more of this great wonder that was out there and everywhere around him.

And then in the bright warmth of a summer's day, when he was almost three, the family moved. This happened quickly and without warning. He was taken to the suburban outskirts, to a freshly built development in a town called Roman Valley that was somewhere south of the old and bustling crowded city, tucked off safely near a highway ramp. It wasn't so worn and rusty and so grim and heavy-shadowed here—the new house was a giant box of white aluminum, trimmed on the sides and bottom edge in smoky orange brick, a brand-new colonial full of black-shuttered windows, with a long recessed porch and a dark black eagle of molded plastic mounted regally above the center of the attached garage. The house kept guard on a corner lot at the foot of a new development that'd been built out of a quiet forest near a farm house. It'd been the "model" home, he later had been told, one of the prototypes for all that was going up behind it and available for free inspection by all potential buyers—but now it was theirs, sparkling heartily, fresh and ready for all their days of living.

Happily, there were many more great, compelling wonders here—they were in the orange-glowing cyclops eye on the new automatic coffee pot that would stare down at him in bold authority and even seemed to blink of its own volition, in the roly-poly face he saw on all the electric sockets with its open mouth agape and sadly drooping mime-eyes, and in the color television that he now had full access to, a complex robotic box whose outer limits were unknown. It was wheeled readily before him on a metal cart with plastic casters, and he sat before it for many hours of the sunlit day, and it became an early friend. He drank in its soothing endless views into some futuristic Elsewhere, far away from Roman Valley: of calm, pastoral places that were shown with the sporadic punctuations of pleasant music, of mad scientists whose lives of deep experimentation seemed to be a good and valid option, and of a talking horse named Mr. Ed.

He believed in this distant world, longed to be a part of it, and came to love the big electric box that provided him the windowed view. He constantly experimented, and with the television knobs he soon discovered ways to change all the tints and colors, raise the volume, make dark shadows and sharp silver fuzz upon the picture, and even summon a horizontal stripe—black like licorice and banded with lines and colored dots—that poured and fell fast down the front of the screen and whose true importance was unknown, but that always darkened the mood of his parents whenever it came racing into view.

And there was much exultant wonder in the greater world where he was being taken now: he saw it in the three rectangular windows on the front doors of homes they drove past in the car, staggered like the slits in paper punch-cards, and in all the pleasant stampings that were on good garage doors;

he saw it in the tube-test stand at the dime store, with rows of special complex outlets, deep black wells that formed snug connections to the right glass vacuum tubes and made a light glow warmly in affirmation, as he witnessed when adult men carefully approached it; he saw it in that cold metal plate they had at every shoe store, lying on the carpet tucked beneath a chair—he sometimes got to step his stockinged foot in it while the salesman carefully touched his heel and adjusted levers along the side and read the numbered markings; there was the elaborate message system at the department store downtown involving pneumatic suction, where workers placed their paper messages into a cylinder, and by opening a gate into this great tubed network where the air would howl with heavy suction it'd get eaten by the pipes, and he'd carefully watch as it shot quickly to the ornate and crusty moulded ceiling, went fast around a bend and then shuttled far back into the inner depths beyond a wall, where according to his parents another worker would receive the message and know just what to do—and he decided then that one day he would build a house with such a system in it; and he always happily anticipated the cashier's change machine at the Pick-N-Pay grocery store, knowing of its wonder: with the pressing of a button on the register, the proper change would be spooled out from their receptacles and spill down noisily into a metal bowl for your convenient taking, a bowl like the ones for holy water inside the doors of all the churches—his mother sometimes let him scoop the change, and this meant so much to the young child, knowing that he had a valid role in keeping everything running smoothly.

He figured that all adult living, in fact, was a duteous taking-part in the complex operations that kept this entire system going all around him, a vast unending game played ultimately for the benefit of the common good. This was his earliest conception of Civilization.

And that's how the life of Raymond Valentine begins: a boy's enchanted with the wonders that are everywhere around him, and somewhere else a wind is whispering far among the willows. He was enthralled by all the happy joys and mysteries of these wonders that hinted at a greater life, and all through childhood he saw them everywhere he went. They called out to him, mesmerized him, and these fascinating wonders—with all their possibility of a vast and unseen reach, of a power and effect, of work and operation—began to haunt him. He knew that there was somewhere to go with them, somewhere far beyond us here—that there was something real and living to be had among the brilliant magic. He had to find it.

2

MAD SCIENTISTS AND ROBOT BUILDERS

SOON THERE were others in his world, faces to relate to, children with whom Raymond played and at times also deeply conspired. Often, these contemporaries were also charmed by all the wonders that were out there, and towards the eventual mastery and domination of these things they'd share experiences, compare notes, brainstorm. This happened so quickly that all ideas of remaining in the friendless hold of long, impatient days in those second-story rooms were discarded and forgotten.

The first to have come into his world, just beyond the naked stone of infancy, had been Linda, tall and powerful. A brilliant young woman who could think in many languages, and speak them quickly, she claimed him as her young prince. She was much older, and was consigned to watch over him at times. Raymond came to love these moments. She'd scoop him in her outstretched arms and raise him deliriously high above the warm city pavements, above the thick wall of bushes and the summer backyard flower-beds—she was something like a princess, with her orange-freckled face and luxuriant, river-parted hair, a soapy odor on her tender flesh that hinted prettily of roses and chrysanthemum, and eyes whose woody irises were alive with vigor and exuberance and life. She loved her time with him, and when he saw these flashes of her joy he felt their spirits dance. His mother beamed happily in approval and she proudly called her his "girlfriend"; perhaps one day they would be married.

Then there'd been a boy his age, whose name was Jeff, and who came running down a back alley from the sooty row of homes behind Raymond's grandparents' house. He was always ambling over in a soiled undershirt, eager to play, his face of chubby cheeks and dirty mouth crowned with buoyant blond locks—but after a few visits he was strangely discouraged to return by the stern commandment of Raymond's grandmother.

After the move to Roman Valley, Raymond discovered almost immediately that there were children in the wheat-brick ranch that faced the side street and hovered low in the lot directly behind them. He watched carefully out the kitchen window at them, looking nervously with big brown eyes and a sad face as they ran wildly across the front swath of their lawn with loud callings, and he felt an excited terror—he knew that he'd eventually encounter them and have to deal with them. He discerned a plump and black-haired boy who seemed about his age and had a coal-dark, penetrating gaze, and there was a younger boy who was sandy-headed and still in diapers.

In time they met, when both sets of parents stood at the property line and talked one day—the boys peered between the legs of the adults, ran around them all in wide circles, and then became quick friends. They had a yellow ball and chased it wildly around the yard with guttural snorts and hollers, and all the tension fell away—but Raymond wondered anxiously about everything that was to come ahead.

That first successful meeting soon drifted into a steady friendship; Raymond played easily with the older boy, whose name was Joey. They played with blocks and balls and quickly formed new games of their own. Raymond and Joey were the leaders and controllers; the younger brother, Toby, sometimes tagged along, but was frequently the victim of Joey's sudden whims and cruelties.

One of their favorite games became the making of "formulas," just like the scientists they knew from good television movies—they'd commence play in one of their garages, and with an old bottle tightly in hand they'd pour into it a little from any of a half-dozen containers and chemicals, and tincture it with random samplings to see what it would do: Prestone automotive antifreeze tippled from a large yellow plastic jug, foul-smelling potent amber liquid poured from a tiny glass bottle of Malathion pesticide, slick fumy gasoline drizzled down out of the spout of the red-painted metal gascan, a sprinkling of tiny white fertilizer beads taken from a ripped but immobile giant paper bag of them, and a squirt of heaven-blue Windex spray for balance. They'd watch the colors change with each addition, smell and note the odors of the formula's development. Sometimes there'd be hair-like rainbows spiraling on the potion's surface, or loud alarming odors wafting forth, or the liquid would settle into discrete striped layers, like sedimentary beds of the prehistoric earth.

"This one smells good!"

"Maybe you should taste it."

There was a moment's consideration. It did smell good. "No, give some of it to Toby—he'll try it."

Of course there was nothing even remotely scientific about their ways: no charts or notes, no careful samplings, no hypotheses or recorded observations, and no reason. It was all just spurious indulgence. They'd mix whatever chemicals or substances looked interesting, in whatever amounts they happened to feel were good. Then they'd test the concoction on a flower or a weed, pouring it on a gathering of potato bugs or a colony of ants, sometimes rain it out upon the dense webbing of a spider's nest. Untold numbers of nature's minions perished at their hands this way.

And as the five o'clock sun swabbed its bright imperial gold near the horizon and slim, cloaked shadows cast long and low about the yard, Joey became filled with a wild impulse. He took the open-mouthed, glass baby bottle containing this latest winning serum, a thick, rich maroon mixture with dark ponderous purple speckles, and cackling demoniacally he chased his younger brother with it, scrambling over the sloped stripe of lawn alongside their house. They ran madly with screams and shrieks that echoed out in summer lanes; Raymond followed curiously behind. In Joey's fever he splashed it out at Toby, and some of it hit—wet gobs of the dark potion dripped down the back of Toby's shirt. He cried and ran into their house, while Joey's laugh only subsided with the irritated call of his mother barking out from inside its inner depths.

The game sometimes commenced with a mere suggestion.

"What do you wanna do?"

"I dunno, why?"

"My father just got a new bug spray. Wanna make formulas?"

"Arright!"

They made formulas often, and Raymond would demonstrate the game to other boys he met, who in turn passed it on through the networks of childhood.

Raymond and the neighbor boys enjoyed discussing all about the enraptured wonder of the living world, and they'd explore each other's properties together, marching up and down and noting all their finds: there was the gas meter, connected to the side of the house with all its thick bent tubing, a bulky sculpture of green iron boxes riveted together and with moving dials inside a glass window, which provided a good command center for their imaginary submarines and spaceships; a tiny hole in the sidewalk at the end of their street was the home of a warty green troll, and then later it was decided that it'd been made by the builders who'd constructed the neighborhood, through the use of their powerful tools, and it went all the way to China—and at night if you peered down it long enough you'd see the sunlight from the other side of the world; the elaborate garden that Joey and Toby's father Mr. Malvicino was building in their backyard—with fiberglass dividing walls, wire trellises and fences, and a rusty-white tin shanty—provided hours of enjoyment, wandering the mazy paths with all their flavors and discoveries: there was the sweet and juicy fragrance of fermenting fruit; the bountiful grape vines whose stringy Indian gum, like thin purple worms, they picked and chewed at for the momentary sharp tart thrill; the grassy outer path along the back where they'd pluck and swallow cool, ripe gooseberries; there was the warm seedy richness of the figs, the fragrant forest odors of humus and decomposing leaves, and the sunken prickly smell of tomato vines in heat.

Legends were everywhere, in everything. Their lives were settled deep within them, had been borne inside them. Joey would tell Raymond long, entangled stories about his family, and how his father Mr. Malvicino had known the world of Italy long ago, and had ridden a motorized scooter there; Raymond imagined it and saw Joey's stout unshaven father with his tan shorts and black knee-high socks scooting past the piazzas and fountains of Rome, and he somehow knew that the scooter was colored a happy citrus orange. Raymond knew very little about his own father's past, it seemed more fictitious dream than real—whereas every house around them held deep secrets and intrigues, and all the people were fascinating characters with long, complex histories that swept wide around the world. They learned from an old red-faced man who spent his days inside the cavey shade of his open garage, wedged in an aluminum lawn chair, that the development itself had been built upon a forest, which had once been Indian ground; for verification they looked beyond the wavy lawns to the bare, exposed areas of raw earth along flower bed and under bush, and they saw that all the soil there was riddled with buried treasures and broken petrified artefacts from these lost and ancient civilizations.

Outside on summer afternoons they saw the wonder in the airplanes that gashed the open azure skies, shooting out in slow fuzzy fumes, which with their frothy comet-tails were like boats slicing over smooth glass seas, and to their minds they were often rockets that were daringly on their way to conquer other planets.

As they observed the skyward territories they'd always be on the careful lookout for airships of interest: seething helicopters, fat lolling blimps, tiny specks they knew were far, distant dirigibles—and there were military jets with pointed missiles on their wings, slender space rockets out on advanced top-secret Moon missions, and, of course, the UFOs: and as magic once, just when they were out there in the backyard discussing this, they saw an alien craft that very moment, shockingly they'd looked upward to the deep heavens and yes! it was! and they pointed at this thing, a circular disk with black windows on the round control deck spinning, just like in the old movies: the thing moved smoothly along in the upper atmosphere, and they ran across the length of the backyard pointing and staring and shouting out in summer bliss until it receded in the giant sea of sky—and yet Raymond's mother, who was on her knees weeding alongside the house with her garden gloves on, took little heed of their profound and historic discovery.

In time they developed a new game, coming from further investigation of the devices and the fascinating objects that were around them. They sought to master these things, to make them work like in their dreams, and they began to sneak in sessions of experiment surreptitiously on the family stereo set and on any other electronic hardware stored in the home, sometimes leading to the painful cry of loud electric sounds and the awakening of lights in heavy blinks.

On the Valentines' back patio one sweltering July afternoon, while Raymond and Joey Malvicino were easing back on the flower-print cushions of the cedar lawn furniture, slurping and licking at Popsicles, Raymond casually mentioned between frozen bites that his mother had a good transistor radio that they might be able to take apart. Joey grew excited, his dark eyes glimmering, and with a last wet gulp he took the empty, orange-stained wooden stick from his mouth.

"I can get a screwdriver," he offered eagerly, showing an orange tongue. "I know where my father keeps them!"

"Okay," Raymond hushed quickly, sensing the onset of an important plan, "how 'bout you go get one and I meet you here with the radio?"

So Joey tumbled off, and when he returned they began to operate on the transistor radio. The disassembly was accompanied by a new boldness that even Raymond was aware of and he attributed it to his advancing age. Once it was laid open on the patio table, its innards exposed and hanging, the wires in their bright casings and all the electronics with their colorful stripes and markings revealed, they looked and touched and pecked with all the insatiate intensity of hennish old women locked together in a huddle.

"Oh, so *that's* how it works!" Joey blurted happily, finger tracing golden paths.

"Maybe we can make it do something else—maybe we can make a new invention!"

When Raymond said this, he felt as if it were the dawning of genius. It was a ripe idea: yes, perhaps by simple rearrangement they might find new functions, invent new ways—it seemed entirely possible—and this game of Making Inventions, a careful dissection of anything electronic, with attempts to bring new functions and extensions by altering what they found, became their favorite pastime and hobby. This was a clear advance over Making Formulas.

He considered volunteering his father's electric adding machine for the game, with its long spools of paper and dark screen of numbers glowing wintry blue, but he dared not, fearing the terrible repercussions—when the radio no longer worked his mother wailed dolefully, and he knew there'd be irremediable trouble had she even suspected that it was a result of their experimentation and tampering.

Other friends had also settled in his life, good familiar faces who shared his passions to various ways and degrees. These occasional playmates were the Kristos brothers, Stephen and Teddy. Stephen was Raymond's age, and somehow it seemed that they'd always played together; since infancy they'd been brought together in what had been a staggered flash of many moments. The Kristoses and the Valentines were close, longtime friends, the parents had known each other since their youths, since somewhere late in that smooth pastel decade of the 1950s, and Raymond knew that the Kristos family was somehow intertwined with his own family and were bonded as relatives—there were many photographs attesting to this and the Kristoses were always there at the large holiday get-togethers with the people of Raymond's mother's family; he grew up through the years with them.

So during childhood there was always a visit to the Kristos house on Christmas, which meant seeing all the fabulous wonder of the suburban city grids awash in white winter at a time when all the nation's homes were lit with colored lights and garnished happily with Christmas decorations, and the Valentines would travel in the car and drive past all of them, which

Raymond would observe in a long and endless wonderland, seeing illuminated Santas waving on the way, fat snowmen in the yards, all the sloping roofs of ranches that were patted down with heavy white quilts of snow, and the tight growths of icicles that hung down sharply from the sides, and there would be the bright gaiety of the lights in all their hues and palettes that traced out the front gutters and climbed the rooftops and filled the bushes and the trees of the many houses, and there were silver twinklings of garland and colored wreaths upon the doors, and he saw so many decorated trees of every variation and variety bursting from the inner darkness of big front windows with a thousand shining gems, and there were the warm glows of window-lights that cast down upon the long white stretches of crystalline front lawns, which meant that families were gathered together in the warmth inside—and when the car arrived at the Kristos house, they'd walk out in the crisp purple air to explode in the brightness of a happy welcome at the door, and then into the warmth they'd be pulled, to become a brilliant happy glow of radiance themselves for all the other winter passerbys outside.

That year at Christmas when the kids were alone for some moments in the family room, the younger Teddy showed Raymond the special wonder of the colorful lights strung around their Christmas tree—they had diffuse wreaths of plastic over each of them, which circled all around the light with a row of pointed tips, and they made spectacular glowing rings of color play along the dark branches. Teddy was proud of them, his father had recently brought them home from K-mart, and with great excitement he showed them now to Raymond.

"This one's the king," he said, fondling a blue one, "and this one's the queen." The queen was pink. He explained that all the others—green, yellow, orange—were knights in the royal court, "but some could be princes."

"Boy, that's neat," Raymond said lusciously, with absolute approval and understanding, and he stared in joy and wonder at the magic patternings of light they all gave off. They cast beacons deep into the dark inner cellar of the tree; he observed the bright, blaring colors as they lit through that heavy copse of shadowed branch, around thick bending walls and twisted tunnels, brightening everything with their gaiety.

There was a deep connection forged there, between the children, in the secret sharing of this winter wonder of special lights upon a tree. For this wonder was part of the endless enchanted joy, there seemed to be an infinity of them, and during the Christmas holidays with all the lights and rush and colors, new doors were opened into other worlds for little Raymond—in tinsel, garland, and the glimmer of the lights; in ornaments and wreaths, and in the calling out of carols in the frosty night; in a tall, tinkling Christmas tree at one of the shopping malls, that actually spoke, that observed you from up high and listened to what you wanted for Christmas (Raymond told it "a record player"), and then it boomed out an answer (Raymond was too awed and scared to note its words); there was a happy old man named Mr. Jing-A-Ling, hunched back with thumbs out in his suspenders, wistful silver sideburns that hung down to his chin, a Clifton legend who had connections to Santa Claus somehow and who held keys to an elfin kingdom that was stationed at the top floor of a downtown tower, in the bright labyrinth of an endless department store, where commemorative photographs could be taken among the snowy piles of cotton sparkling magic and the glittering candy canes and those tall, fine-formed elf-blooded women who were only there to sparkle beautifully, bend down and assist; there were the legends of the kindly fat Frosty the Snowman who came to life on children's love, and Rudolph the Red-Nosed Reindeer, that unfortunate outcast who perseveres at righteousness and finally is appreciated by all the doubting others who'd been so cruel; there were the songs and carolers and snowy sled-rides; jingling bells, the pungent, curling smoke of hearth fires, and a bright merriment that hung in the air, in all the public spaces, because Christmas was coming, and everybody knew it; there were those big bursting bags of gaily-wrapped packages and soft red stockings that nice ladies always had for them, filled with chocolates or little plastic toys; and of course there was old St. Nick himself in felted red, that snow-bearded man with sooty boots and elfin twinkle who chuckled fatly and appeared constantly in the convivial, hearth-warming joviality of the season—and this was all part of the magic enchanted wonder that would come to Raymond every year at Christmastime.

Two years of sporadic preschools had concluded and Raymond started Kindergarten at the public elementary school, whose roofline looked like an outstretched accordion and where the windows were bordered in thick black panes. It was a daily ritual which he immediately thought was a waste of time—his attempts at reading in the school library were thoroughly constricted, while long stretches of the morning were wasted on coloring the empty backs of scrap paper that kind local businessmen had donated to the school, and playing on the ground with large cardboard boxes that were printed on like frosted bricks. Once Raymond watched a tall, skinny boy named Tony—the popular boy of the class—kneel down with his hands on the ground before a fortress wall of bricks while four girls carefully piled more bricks upon his back; he then rose up erect, on his knees, toppling all the bricks, his arms reaching out of their grey acrylic sleeves up to the ceiling in unstoppable victory while behind him all the girls kneeled back with mouths open in perfect little ohs, and it all played out like the theatrical choreography of a musical that was put on just for Raymond's idle observation.

Raymond found that his own place was at the outside edges of the class, where he was the quiet sad one in the back and always looking. That's where he met a boy who also knew the wonder and was looking for a way; his name was Mark, and his roasted-nut complexion and ragged cap of stringy blue-dark hair made Raymond think of all the exotic wisdoms and lush canopies of the Far Pacific. They bonded instantly, recognizing in each other a shared interest in all the great legends of the world, and they quickly traded pieces of the secret lore—robotics and electronic power, lost islands, the many types of sea shells, outer space and the saga of the dinosaurs. Raymond sensed right away that Mark had a strong handle on it, that he too had been charmed by all these many things and was after finding a connection and a way; Raymond admired his thinking and his passion for that secret enchanted world, and the two soon became happy playmates.

At school Raymond taught Mark about the game of Making Formulas, and in the following summer they experimented with it on a time-still afternoon at Mark's house. Mark quietly retrieved an empty glass jar of Chock full o'Nuts coffee from a neatly stacked shelf of them out in the garage, and the two boys quickly filled it with a cascade of various items from the clean, bright kitchen, where everything shone perfectly of mint and pearl.

The formula was bubbly and soon had the ill, gut-wrenching wreak of excessive garlic powder. Mark's mother, Mrs. Laynkord, came out from the inner chambers of their house, and Mark quickly dumped it in a flower pot before he could get in trouble; consequently their afternoon play turned elsewhere, to much less exciting matters.

The mothers spoke often on the telephone and during afternoon visits they'd talk at each others' homes as the boys played, and even Raymond's father finally got to meet Mr. Laynkord when the Valentines spent an evening at their house in the wistful end of summer.

At the dinner table beneath the gold-glinting, peach-lighted chandelier, Raymond wondered of the complex histories that had brought Mark's parents together in some foreign place and then to here, a fresh settlement in Roman Valley. While Mrs. Laynkord's dark eyes and long, sultry hair mirrored all the lushness of a distant, Polynesian exoticism, Mr. Laynkord was a tall blond-haired man who looked like someone from the Sears catalog, his hair trimmed calmly with a sharp side part. Eyeglasses shaded the bright blue chips of his eyes, he dressed up for work in his office every day, drove a big Buick, and wore a different set of clothing on the weekends that still seemed, to Raymond, to be fairly dressy.

Raymond assumed from the conversation at the dinner table that Mr. Laynkord was a scientist—one of those men who worked each day at a large corporation to bring us all happiness. Raymond thought that in years to come, Mr. Laynkord would be noted for his doings, that he'd come to be known as one of the benevolent greats who helped guide the course of the space age, having contributed to the realm of rocketry and invention and man's general advancement. Mr. Laynkord was always working, traveling, and seemed to exist eternally on some important mission in some other city, in some other place. It seemed to Raymond that the Laynkords were somehow more real than his own family, that their motions in the living world were more broad and definite and lasting.

While the adults stayed downstairs after dinner to talk in the living room, the boys ran up to Mark's bedroom to see his toys, and when the topic of robots came up for discussion, Mark suddenly grew quiet.

"What's wrong?"

Mark wouldn't answer—he just looked pensively out his bedroom window—but when Raymond pressed again he finally said, "Well I've got a secret, if you promise you won't tell."

"I promise! Tell me."

"I'm going to build one."

"Nu uh! Really?"

"Yeah, really! I'm going to build a robot!"

In confidence, Mark revealed that it was going to be operational "in the next year."

Mark was receptive to all the enchanting wonder, but this would make him an actual inventor—Raymond couldn't believe such a bold pronouncement. Mark was only trying to impress him, he thought, and so he sought to make the truth come out with sharp interrogation. He started with the first obvious question to ask. "Where are you going to get the parts?"

Mark turned again toward the window, and with contemplative eyes he looked out at the front yard of his house. He then told Raymond how he just found them, how some of them he just found outside on the curb—or he'd find parts on garbage day, discarded by mysterious old men down his street. "And sometimes my grandpa gives me parts," he added suddenly, "and my father gets me parts from work."

"Really?" Raymond asked in breathless awe; he knew that these were intricate, advantageous connections, and their contemplation stirred a mild jealousy.

"Yeah, sure," he said quickly.

"Let me see your parts," Raymond prodded.

Mark quietly turned and went over to a tall cabinet, a component of his white modular bedroom set, and on his knees he carefully opened a bottom cupboard. He removed a flat plate of grey metal that had several rows of hard black switch-like objects on it. It looked like you could open and shut the many switches.

"This is going to be the brain," he said, holding it up. It did look impressive.

When Mrs. Laynkord stepped in to check on them, Raymond quickly seized the opportunity.

"Mrs. Laynkord," he asked politely in a sing-song, "is Mark really going to build a robot?"

Looking away from Raymond, over toward the wall, she spoke carefully. Her buoyant, exotic voice was now soft, a sea-breeze whisper after dark: "Yes, Mark has some parts that he says he will build a robot with."

This confirmed everything—Raymond knew that Mark was one to cling to, a fellow explorer, someone to advance with, a best friend to share all the seasons of these years and the unfolding drama of his life with. Later, Raymond told the Malvicino boys about Mark's methods for obtaining parts—and from then on, Raymond and the Malvicinos were always on the watch for the treasures that the wind brought, the little things that might be there at the curbs on their streets, or along the sidewalks held back from their tumbled journeys by the sharp-bladed forest of the grass: tiny springs and clips, bent and often rusted bits of wire, dented batteries, and mechanical parts of mysterious origin, sometimes with electronic elements—surely traces of factories and high-tech laboratories which were undoubtedly nearby; perhaps some even fell from satellites in space. On certain days these wires and parts rolled in with the wind, seemed to be tumbling forth from the outer world just for them, and they patrolled the curbs in the neighborhood to find them. Raymond hoped that he'd accumulate enough of these parts so that one day he'd be like Mark and use them to bring a great thing to life—he imagined it a kind of wondrous living robot, something that would set order to his world, a creation unlike anything that anyone had ever seen, and he believed that its day would finally come. There was a willow shaking somewhere far off by a twisted river-bend.

3

MARK

IN THE rustic autumn of that year, Mark and Raymond started first grade together at St. Bartholomew's, while Joey stayed on at the public school owing to the Malvicino family's recent conversion to the Jehovah's Witnesses. Raymond played with Joey and Toby on the weekends, but he saw Mark in school every day now, and they considered themselves "best friends"—a relation they acknowledged to each other and to their mothers repeatedly.

Together they constructed richly detailed dioramas out of shoe boxes, and worked at a dozen other crafts—they made rockets, rolling up sheets of paper in long tubes and affixing pointed paper cones to their tops, adding sleek fins to the sides along the bottom, holding them victoriously high and imagining the rocket fuel propelling them through deep space in a bright orange burst of lifted arm; then they migrated to paper airplanes, folding them delicately and always seeking the most technical advancements, dreaming of special models made of intricate folds that could travel a mile in the air or that could do special tricks, that when dropped off a balcony would flip in wide loops, some several times, maybe even perfect figure eights, or return to their maker just like a boomerang. Together they shared and developed many legends and ways; Raymond

31

imagined that when they were adults they'd work like this as best friends and world-famous scientists with white-shining labs at their disposal, inventing many wonderful things. They were always conspiring through the school year, sharing ideas, and to Raymond it was an intense collaboration; with each day came a new challenge or discovery, and he learned what he could.

They played with Legos and with action figures, often combining toys and mythologies to make variant worlds that opened into new intriguing depths: the Six Million Dollar Man would be stranded on the moon base of *Space: 1999*, where he had to fight alien monsters from outer-space dinosaur worlds; *Star Wars* action figures were laid supine in tiny cardboard boxes which were space vessels that kept them deep-frozen through the stark eons of time, to emerge in new dimensions in the dense jungle battlegrounds of the Laynkord's backyard; and at Raymond's house a tall white bucket filled with cold water from the garden hose and long, cut strips of paper towels became an outdoor play set for their Lego men, a distant ocean-planet hidden beneath a moon and filled with living white seaweed thick and long like tangled highways.

Sometimes the boys would play at Mark's grandparents' house, a white-sided ranch set far back from the road and with a breezeway of jalousie glass that connected to the garage; it was across the main road at the mouth of Raymond's development and up the steep hill in the old section of Roman Valley, where the roads and sidewalks were shaded in the summer by a long processional of gigantic trees.

Raymond liked it there. One time he'd slept over, and he and Mark each had single beds with low sunken dimples in the middle, facing a wall with two framed watercolors of young men in wooden power boats, flags waving at the stern, foaming the waters of some calm lake. Raymond imagined their sure movements in the wet-gray midnight shadow—and then in the summer morning, Mark's grandma cooked them silver-dollar pancakes on a griddle that was built into the counter, until the air of the pink-tiled kitchen grew warm and heavy with the fragrances of maple syrup and sausage grease.

Mark's grandpa couldn't speak right—Raymond wasn't sure

if it was a speech impediment or if he'd lost his voice in old age, and was afraid to ask; he was always wandering the property in his undershirt, applying pesticides to the tiny grove of fruit trees out back past the clothes line, pointing the thin-wanded nozzle of a heavy steel sprayer can mounted on his belt. They called him Duke. On summer nights Duke slept early while Mark's grandma kept her hair in curlers and read the newspaper at the kitchen table with the crickets jangling and swooning dizzily from out the screen of the back door; she smoked cigarettes, coughed loudly, and scooped out salads of thin onion slices and tomatoes soaked in vinegar—and later, wanting to bring this world back, Raymond had his mother make it for him in a Tupperware bowl at home.

Early on a Saturday morning, Raymond's mother dropped him off there for a few hours of play. Once inside the doorway, Raymond stooped down automatically and began to untie the laces of his shoes while Mark waited.

"Did you ever use a cassa tee-tee?" Mark asked in a passing inquiry.

The name held some intrigue. "No, what's that?"

"You can put sound on it, and play it back later," he explained nonchalantly as Raymond set his shoes behind the door. He told Raymond about how he used his cassa tee-tee to play with his *Star Wars* action figures: he'd record battle sounds, songs, army commands, narratives, and play them back to the action figures, which he'd set up in an elaborate play set world on his grandparents' tiled basement floor.

"Oh, that sounds neat! Show me."

In bleach-white socks they tumbled down to the quiet, cool-aired basement where Mark demonstrated. To Raymond, it looked like just a normal tape player, like the kind he'd seen before and was getting used to in life.

"Isn't that called a cassette?"

"No," Mark answered plainly. "It's a cassa tee-tee."

They debated this. Raymond questioned the correctness of Mark's pronunciation, but admitted to himself that even if Mark were wrong, his name did bring a kind of glamour and zest to it: he liked how Mark often made the mundane special by looking at it from a different perspective—it seemed to be one of the secrets of Mark's approach to life—and after all, perhaps he was right, perhaps this was a special variation on the word. But Raymond wondered.

"Are you sure?"

"Yeah, I'm pretty sure."

"Ask your mother."

She wasn't there and they decided that his grandma wouldn't know, so the question remained unresolved—but Raymond decided that he needed one, that a tape recorder such as Mark's could help him in his own explorations. At home later that night, Raymond found and appropriated his father's battery-powered unit and learned to make it record to a tape, upon which he earnestly sang the melancholy, sentimental song with a heart-knocking melody that had greatly affected him: the title theme to a television movie called "The Last Dinosaur."

Somewhere far away a distant wind was rising. Here, his heart was moving and swaying to all the legend and the lore.

What everyone first noticed about Raymond were his eyes, warm and brown and impossibly big—when he stood there quietly they made him sad-faced, a lost, lonely puppy beneath a perfect bowl of satin-brown and shiny hair. His cheeks were round and full and in happy moments the flesh went rosy. His legs and arms were still a little husky with baby fat, and from the overprotections of his mother he was kept away from sports and most other healthy, boyish exertions—weight would play a boyhood problem off and on and sting him with its consciouses and cruelties—but he had a black dirt bike he was very proud of, and with the Malvicinos he still engaged in plenty of wild backyard running, impromptu games and dangerous explorations.

Beginning in second grade—and specifically that rushed, cold week of Christmas break when Raymond's mother took an overnight hospital stay and then returned with his new baby sister, Sally—he'd become excited about the video games that he'd begun to see advertised on television. They stormed upon the scene of life that season, where they flooded the consciousness of children with their bold, bright presence—and once they came they were everywhere, colorful and blipping, a constant temptress. Everyone seemed to know about them and how they were played, and everyone seemed to know that much more would be coming. Somewhere, adults were working hard to make the whole world magic.

The Kristos boys had a set of hand-held electronic sports games, single games for two players with springs and levers and timers inside of them where the game boards in the middle would be lit cherry-red by peg-shaped lights to show the movement of the ball, and there was a dial counter on each side that you manually adjusted to keep score. They favored the football game, and on long trips with their families together the boys would play these games in the far back seat of the Kristos' yellow Suburban wagon, but Raymond wasn't very good at them—the Kristos boys were becoming active in real sports, they played soccer now and knew the rules of all the games, whereas for Raymond that was all a blurred confusion of scores and points and goals.

But more important were the video games that actually connected to your television—they were computerized and would use the television screen as a graphical display, and tried to be as good as the upright models that were in the shopping malls and were like colorful graffitied refrigerators with recessed screens and where a quarter let you play the game. These home video games, the great new entertainers of the age, only had one name to remember: Atari. There may've been others, but in the winter of '78 it was only the Atari that mattered, the one that everyone knew and cared about. If it wasn't the best, it was ubiquitous—and its sounds and shapes and colors and the names of all its games soon threaded all the young boys' minds. Raymond knew it was the traditional choice, and he had to have it.

He yearned for it, yearned to immerse himself in its many worlds, to enjoy all of its sensations, and—as a good and grateful child—to show his silent toothless grampa all about the wonders of the modern age. Mark had one; Joey and Toby had one; the Kristos boys had one; it seemed that everyone had gotten one for Christmas that year. But it took more desperate months for it to arrive in the Valentine household, and when it did finally come in the drippy green of spring as a reward for his First Communion, Raymond felt that its late arrival took much of the prestige and gloss away from having one: by then it was already considered to be expected and standard equipment.

The rich color paintings in the booklets that it came with, depicting the exciting battles you were to relive when you played the games—which came in black cartridge squares that plugged into the face of the machine—made Raymond think happily of World War II, of his grampa's generation, and he thought that they'd approve of such wholesome avocational pursuits in the young. But the actual games weren't at all like the elaborate pictures: in Combat, the tanks were represented by big colored blocks, snouted, that moved with a gurgly groan, and there were long ragged rectangles for battleships and diving planes in Air-Sea Battle that fought with spurty bleats and blurts, and the ducks and smiling clowns of the carnival game in Shooting Gallery were coarse and blocky.

Newer cartridges kept coming out with an improved graphics and sound, and steadily he accumulated a collection of them, rewards for every holiday and good report card. He knew all the worlds and landscapes of these games, all the places that they brought you, the songs and sounds of them and the patterns on the television screen.

At a Saturday afternoon birthday party for one of their classmates, Raymond sat in the high shag of the living room where it smelled strangely mildewed and he watched a hyperactive, introverted boy as he roughly played with the unattended Atari, sprawled out on his knees before it, turning it off and on quickly with the Space Invaders cartridge loaded. When the boy pulled out the cartridge when the system was still turned on, a fat black stripe was printed down the screen over a pine-green background, and the speaker emitted a constant, high-pitched wheeze. Raymond edged closer.

"Hey whaj'ya do?"

The boy was nonchalant, hunched over, and still moving his limbs in all directions. "Pulled it out when it was on."

"Try it again," Raymond quietly encouraged. "Try it with another one."

They discovered that you could make interesting screen patterns and sounds from pulling out cartridges with the power on, and they saw that if you flicked the power on and off quickly several times with Space Invaders loaded, the game would play with "double bullets," so that when you pressed the button, the gun you fired would shoot out two bullets in quick succession instead of only one.

When the truth of this registered with Raymond, he bounded off to the adjoining patio room, where the main group of boys were patiently examining the birthday boy's new set of Lego blocks below the tall glass windows and a few youngish mothers were distracted with themselves at a round, wrought-iron table in a corner.

"Mark, c'mere, lookit this!" Raymond hissed, excitedly pulling his best friend away from the group, and he gleefully explained his new discovery.

"Well this will make it easier to get to higher screens!"

Mark sat down quickly by the Atari and began to play it with a renewed vigor and interest. The stomp of aliens slapped quicker, laser bullets bleated out with white-hot phosphorescence, Mark's eyes were illuminated beads, his fingers gripped at the stiff black handle of the joystick and his hand moved and twitched with excited passion. But already Raymond knew how he himself liked the colored bands of stripes better than the games.

In the next year Raymond continued to distance himself from the popular games. He became a quiet boy in school, detached and oversensitive, and he retreated to the inner legends and their wonders, the worlds he found in films and books—worlds that he'd known for as long as he could remember, since at least decoding the writings in the first Golden Books when he was three years old, and then as the greatest consumer of the competing Troll Book Club and Scholastic Book Services in St. Bart's when they'd been introduced to him without warning on a dazzle-eyed day in the first grade. He spent long hours reading, alone in his bedroom—which had been decorated in red, white and blue with all the Colonial paraphernalia that had come with the Spirit of '76. He began to read through the Hardy Boys series, which began as a slow, tugging tease in second grade and opened up into a passion over the following year, as Frank and Joe Hardy and their chum Chet Morton became his older friends and role models and seemed to present a good way for living in the world. The fact that there was now a modern television series based on those books—starring Shaun Cassidy, whom all the popular middle-school girls at St. Bart's seemed to be inflamed with—only added to its living veracity.

He also eagerly researched scientific topics, and together with Mark they found a good shelf of books at the library that showed how to carry out your own amateur experiments at home, assuming that every home had a basement workshop—but it seemed that only old people like Mark's grandpa had them now; and there were chemistry books whose secrets could be had with simple chemicals—"to be obtained at low cost from your druggist"—but after weary investigation he saw that they only seemed to be available in expensive tiny vials at the hobby shops; nothing around him was as good as it was supposed to be, as it once had been, and it seemed that all the best books had been written long ago; even movies were always sequels now, or blatant remakes of past hits; still, he vowed to keep the old traditions going, no matter how difficult it would be, and to his overwhelming delight he found many good, older books on learning for young minds, and he pursued leaf collecting and fossil hunting and rockhounding with a new kind of seriousness, keeping a spiral notebook for his catalog and observations, and reading through page after page of experiments for the "amateur scientist."

During Reading hour he found himself advancing far ahead of his entire third-grade class, at first stealing just a page of his reader and then another, holding back until he finally lost control and ecstatically dove inside the worlds that he was finding there, and he victoriously completed the entire book before the last icy winter thaw. Then he gobbled up the stories that were kept in little pamphlets in a crowded box and never shown to any of the students. Something about their straightforward depictions of living people going about their everyday lives stirred heavy breezes in him, and he kept it closely to his heart—the people in these stories had something he was lacking, something real and moving: he listened carefully and heard thunder, strong padding rain, and the soft cascading melody of rustled leaves. He gorged on them; during quiet study time he avoided even his own homework so that he could read further ahead.

Fortunately his teacher, Miss Sainko, never seemed to mind. She was a gigantic, white-haired, pillow-bodied woman who was never angered and who kept her body hidden in loose flower-print dresses that only exposed her giant forearms and heavy lower calves. Whenever she spoke—which was always in a soft phlegmy voice that came out from her hammy, protruding lips—it inexplicably reminded Raymond of those big bowls of tangy yellow potato salad that were laid out for picnics and holidays. She seemed oblivious to his reading and before long he'd gone through all the third grade materials in the box, and then cautiously began the fourth grade booklets, and his pride swelled when in a few weeks' time he'd worked his way through everything that'd been marked as being for the fifth and sixth grades and all the secrets of the overbrimming box were his. He'd discovered another window to the greater living world—the only thing he couldn't seem to do was go there.

Then as third grade had almost tapered off its hold, disaster rallied the placidity of his days: the Laynkords were moving away. Mark's father was being transfered out to a distant city, and they were to leave the moment that the school year was over. Mark told him all about it with excitement in his voice, and suddenly it seemed that he was acting on a stage while Raymond was somehow sealed away from the living world of life. The new city that Mark was going to was named Seattle: and to Raymond this was the sound of a remote world, far across the continent, stationed on another sea, where the skies were always richly smeared a shade of indigo and the air was cooled by brisk clean winds shaken down from icy mountain caps; where giant turtles swam in the frigid deep far beyond the black bulging rocks of shore, out in the ultramarine and foamy waving waters of the sea; it was a whole huge city built up in this higher altitude of verdant pine, rimed distantly by purply snow-capped mountains; where the vastly technological Space Needle rose high upon it in the middle, with its glass observatory that spun round continuously in all the fog and night; a

place of shady moss-eaten walkways and ancient wooden carv-
ings from the Far Pacific, of plush leathers in the hotel dining
rooms beneath the twinkling chandeliers where white cloths
hang limp on waiter's arms and in the mornings on the downtown streets the smells of all the rich and roasted coffees and
wet salmon, crab and oyster permeate the bricks and all the
curbs—Seattle, yes, Seattle, a glinting emerald city set so far
upon the western edge, much further north upon the globe of
earth than almost all the nation. Seattle, a land where all the
streets were sloped and tumbled, and where the progress of industry was happening and fresh. Seattle, where the Space Age
built its rocket pods and blasters, where great barges rocked
the seas, where sleek and shiny dome-topped cars spun wide
rings around the mountains on the smooth new roads—that
faraway, jewel-begotten city of Seattle was the place.

Raymond listened with horror as Mark told him how the
private kingdom of the Laynkord residence would be occupied
by them no more, they'd be abandoning his bedroom and their
clean and gleaming mint-green kitchen—it was already up for
sale, to be inspected at any moment now by unknown stran-
gers—and Mark said that his father was already out there,
out in that distant, glimmering city of Seattle, on a lone adult
journey to procure a new home for the family.

On the last day of school the final bell came quickly, and
from behind the shield of his denim bookbag which was stacked
tall atop his desk, Mark calmly answered Raymond's question-
ing: "Yes, I'll write to you when we get out there."

Soon Mark's bus number was called out on the P.A. system,
and with a tug of his bag he rose and headed out to the ripe-
yellow bus that would shuttle him home. Raymond's bus hadn't
been called yet, but in a sudden impulse he quickly took his own
bag and followed his best friend out the classroom door.

He ghosted quickly down the cavern of the hall, just steps
behind Mark—then past the round atrium in the center of the
building where behind locked panes St. Francis was a cold
white pillar among the fragile little trees and underwhelming
bushes there, a stone-floored courtyard where only wayward
squirrels and resting robins ever ventured. The buses were
parked outside the main doors just ahead, rumbling and shak-

ing with the release of petrolic fumes in their momentary pause along the curb—this was the final moment. Raymond knew that it wouldn't go further, that Mark was leaving the scenery of his life forever, and he felt the grim truth of the moment stab him deeply. He didn't want to come back to this place next year with Mark gone; *he* wanted to be the one to move, to leave this land and go off to somewhere better, far away, out in the living world; the thought of his own life commencing there in the closed and faded story-book of northern Sohola, in the winding residential streets of Roman Valley, in that big and lonely house, was suddenly doleful and dreary. What winds would ever come his way? How to rise, and where to go?

Raymond called out to Mark, as if he could still change it and keep his friend forever—but he knew that Mark was already gone. Even now, with the wash of the courtyard's dusty light flaming at him from the side, Mark looked partially erased, and Raymond knew that in this life Mark would go where he could not—they wouldn't grow together to be renowned scientists and robot-builders after all.

Finally catching up to Mark's side he asked again: "We'll write each other all the time, right?"

Mark calmly turned his head aside and told him yes, and now there was hard duty in his eyes. "You'll always be my best friend," he swore, and then he moved briskly toward the outer doors.

THE TELEPHONE
CONNECTION

ON A BRIGHT late-summer afternoon, when the mellow air hung warm and still, the family traveled far across town to see the Kloppes, friends who lived out amid the dark woods and rolling hills of Clifton's east side. Sondra Kloppe had grown up with Raymond's mother—they were old friends from before their marriages, and Sondra's name was often a part of the common talk at Raymond's house. Although she too was a dusky blonde, the women made a contrast: Raymond's mother was like the long-haired fancy ladies on television, with almond eyes that had been fired in emerald, while Sondra was a wide, heavy woman who moved with slow padding shuffles, always wavered like she might topple, and wore her hair with ragged bangs just like a boy's. She stared with dolorous eyes inset on a blank face, spoke in a thick, glutinous accent, and the great spade of her two front teeth would stick out when she was thinking.

The Kloppes had just completed a renovation on their home, and during the visit where Raymond's mother carried Sally through the large house like some kind of shoulder luggage she was trying on, Raymond enjoyed passing time in the mazelike

43

tour of it all, observing the innards of the many rooms and wishing he could share those observations with his sleeping sister—the strange trims that ran the distances of long walls and the glass cabinets with smooth curios that had a style unlike anything he'd seen before. He was interested in this world of the Kloppes, but he somehow didn't feel close to them.

When Sondra was showing them a bright back room that smelled sourly of paint, Mr. Kloppe came in quietly from behind, carrying a white desk telephone by his wide fingers, with its cord wrapped several times around the base. He went and stood up next to Mrs. Kloppe, who was talking. He was a short man whose trim brown hair was a careful ring around his head's center peak, and the two of them seemed to always hover close together, connected by their own magnetism, and they both gave off the same blank and quiet aura.

Mr. Kloppe had glassy eyes that goggled outward when he straightened his shoulders—and although he was soft-spoken, Raymond thought that somewhere hidden in him wasn't cruelty, but the capability of overseeing it. But now as he straightened up again with a waving of his shoulders he just said, "Here," and with a forward bend he handed Raymond the telephone.

"Maybe you can fix this," he suggested in his fast voice. "It's *broke*, but maybe you can get it to work."

Surprised, Raymond took the phone feeling that Mr. Kloppe had great faith in him; Raymond was proudly aware that he was known as a young experimenter and inventor, someone who had experience working on robots.

He cradled it carefully and with wide, open eyes he spattered out a grateful, exuberant thank you. Looking down at his new possession, Raymond heard Mr. Kloppe speak softly to the other adults: "It's broke, so he can play with it."

Instead of a rotary dial like all the phones in Raymond's life, it had a grey keypad for making tones, and he was excited about getting home and taking it apart on his own time where he wouldn't be scrutinized. But he saw that it also had the new type of modular plug, a tiny plastic jack so unlike the fat four-pronged squares that he was accustomed to, and that they had at home—so as soon as Mr. Kloppe disappeared somewhere with Raymond's father, he quietly asked his mother if he might plug it in.

"Oh," she said absently to Sondra, "can he plug that in, or don't you want him touching that?"

Sondra looked with a turn of her head, her front teeth sticking out, and in her thick, sharp accent that made it seem as if she spoke with a mouthful of food, she said that she didn't think it could harm anything but that Raymond should go use the other plug across the room. "Dat's de sekont line, zuh bizniss line," she explained. "Use zat von. Vee von't get any calls on zat line on a Zohnday."

She pointed to this other outlet, which Raymond guessed was the one that Mr. Kloppe used to confer with his associates, his fellow art dealers and important, fast-talking men in ties.

So he sat on the ripple-pattered carpet before the outlet and he plugged it in, and instead of a dial tone there was a great desert, a land of cold quiet. He turned the base of the unit upside down and saw that to fix it he'd need to take it apart.

"What, get it to work?" Mr. Kloppe asked happily as he wandered back into the room.

"N-n-no," Raymond stuttered out, "I n-n-need to have a look inside."

"Oh!" Mr. Kloppe called out, goggling his eyes, and with his head and shoulders bounding backward like he was avoiding the onrush of some great invisible wave. But he seemed to completely understand: "You need to take it apart? Need a screwdriver to get in there?"

Raymond nodded affirmatively many times.

Mr. Kloppe seemed to be in a jovial mood, and with the patient workings of his borrowed screwdriver Raymond began a careful dissection of the phone to find the wonder that was in it, to get to the very heart of its tickings and switchings, perhaps even to make a new invention. He unscrewed the earpiece and mouthpiece of the handset and placed them down on the soft new carpet. Carefully he removed the screws that drilled into the bottom of the base, and turning it back over he lifted its hard protective shell. It revealed a dense brain of golden relays, rainbow-colored wires, and two large dongs. He traced paths, examined switches, tightened connections. He touched wires. And then, satisfied with all that he had done, he carefully reassembled the device. The mothers were standing in this bright empty room, just behind him, deep into the world of discussion they had spun; Sally was still asleep on his mother's shoulder and his father had walked off again with Mr. Kloppe. Raymond plugged in the telephone and lifted the handset off its cradle—and in a bright blast came the cherry-ringing victory of a dial tone. He felt his face bend broadly into smile as a magic expectancy flooded his spirit.

A whole new world awaited him through here—the living world that was out there on the wires. He realized with a sudden soothing brook that this was so much better than robots or video games—this was a way to make a real connection to the greater living world. He could dial any number that he wanted, there was a hive of wires that tangled all the earth, and with this handset he could pass through all of them—Mark was reachable from here, the whole world was waiting for him here, the entire hidden land was his to roam through. He savored the thought of making all these endless far connections; but first, he should make his victory known.

He carefully placed the handset on its cradle, and with quiet glee he interrupted his mother's talk to make the glorious announcement. "I fixed it!"

He was alone in his glory.

"I fixed it!"

Sondra's front teeth shone; she and his mother both looked down toward him across the room.

"I fixed it, it works!"

"Did you *really* fix it?" His mother's voice held strong doubt—it was rattling its cage.

He was angry at her public scorn of his ability. "Yes, it works, try it!" He was so glad that he could keep it.

"Maybe Mr. Kloppe will want it back," his mother quickly suggested, to Raymond's stern disapproval and shock at such complete betrayal.

"I sink he might vant it, yah," Sondra said absently, her eyes glassily focusing somewhere on the carpet by the phone, and her teeth briefly coming out to touch her lower lip. "But he can play viss it vell hees heer."

Raymond was stabbed and punctured by an ice-white bolt, but he hid the anger that flowed into him with expert precision. At the calm guidance of an interior voice he kept very still, and when he stared at the phone there was a blank and dead expression on his face.

Raymond grew much more conscious of the telephone that year—of its procedures and all its capabilities and dreamy possibilities. He was allowed to answer the phone at home, albeit under adult supervision, and the first time that he lifted the receiver and spoke a tenuous "Hello," he waited breathlessly for the reply, knowing that a great long future was ahead. He understood the concept of long-distance calling, and how it was performed by dialing a 1 and then an area code before a number, and he knew that there were astronomic charges for every minute you were on the line. He'd taken a telephone apart, he knew the roads and contours of its interior. He grew in confidence. He answered the phone at the Valentine house even when his parents were home; he could use the phone book; he knew how to make calls now; he grew accustomed to freely calling Joey on the telephone; he found the extension jack on his bedroom wall, which was hidden away behind the walnut desk of his Early American bedroom set, and he requested a phone of his own for it.

"That's not for a telephone," his mother said plainly.

"Yes it is, it's just like all the other ones!"

"No it's not."

"Sure it is!"

"It's not connected."

"How do you know?"

"I just know."

"Well let's try it!"

"Not right now."

"Why not, I want a phone!"

He developed a gallery of stories and theories that filled his time: telephone numbers ending in special suffixes such as 1234 meant something important to the telephone company, or were secret "fun" numbers, set up to entertain you with a recording or a song; phone numbers were assigned to houses along the street incrementally, so if you dialed a number one digit away from yours you got your neighbor; if you got a busy signal you could just stay on the line and you'd hear it change right to a ring as soon as the other party hung up their phone—and he had to quietly apologize for all these theories when reality would come and strongly contradict them; he'd retreat ponderously, and sometimes develop alter-theories.

His mother became a good source of information on the subject. She'd lived in the days that Raymond had only known through books, and was familiar with all the concepts that he read about—telephone operators instead of dial tones, black and white instead of color, a world where houses were built with dumbwaiter shafts and secret passages and there were rich people who had butlers and chauffeurs. He took to quiet moments gaining insights about the past from her, as she dazzled him with stories about her youth and explaining old concepts like "party lines," those telephone lines that were shared with other families in nearby homes.

"You mean you didn't have a phone of your own?"

"No, we shared with someone else on our street."

Raymond quietly pictured this.

After a moment, his mother added more detail. "Sometimes you would want to use the phone and you would pick up, and the neighbors would be talking on it, and you would have to wait," she said. Raymond thought of the inconvenience and was horrified. "They would *never* want to get off when you needed it. And sometimes"—this was added with a cheerful air of alacrity—"when you were talking, they would even listen in."

"Really!" This was a question, asked in a scandalous hush.

"Yes. You could hear them pick up, and they would try to be quiet about it, but *you* knew that they were listening."

Sometimes, she explained, two-family homes would share a line, or a household might share with someone just down the street.

"Well what if you got a call? Would both homes ring?"

"No, the operator would know which one to ring up. But they could still listen in."

Raymond dwelled on this world from long ago, when the

telephone lines were more expensive and less necessary than now, and the phone could be shared with neighbors, and operators working in a telephone office somewhere in the neighborhood would connect and control them at all hours. He'd seen old movies where this world was shown, where telephone numbers all began with words like Maple or Grand for the exchange instead of only numbers like they did now, and you'd pick up the phone and tell the operator what number you wanted instead of dialing it yourself. He pictured how it must've been, the living days of life in homes like the one his grandparents had lived in—he saw his mother young, wearing a pair of horn-rimmed glasses made of the same thick black Bakelite as the telephone she used, her hair bright blonde and buoyant—and in all of America there were these mixed conversations, eavesdroppers, squawks and clickings, there were ringings that went out through the center hallways of boarding houses and two-family homes, sometimes people lifted up their phone and politely asked their neighbor to please finish talking soon, and someone else was listening behind an opaque window down the street—that was how it went. He pictured that world, and he heard those ringings; he saw the crowded banks of wires and the squads of operators who attended all the switchboards, manipulating little wired plugs on a board in front of them for all hours of the sunlit day. He saw the wires and the switches that were all so real yet of a world completely unobtainable to him; it was somehow more complex, mysterious and desirable than everything around him, but it was the past—a wistful figment that was wholly unreachable and gone.

5

PRANKS AND
FANTASIES

GREAT OGRES thundered through the forest and slept long
hours in their clammy caves. Murderers were calmly watching in the after-school hours, peering sharply from behind an
eyelet or a tiny slitted gap, and carrying long sharp knives.
In some distant time-warped world a fair and tender princess,
her flesh white as the finest April frost, was carried from her
father's castled homeland by a fire-breathing dragon. Twin
witches kept a little boy their secret prisoner behind the sooty
brick and soiled windows of a faceless Tudor, in an aged suburb
not very far removed from the great city's packed and bustling
urban core. Somewhere in some secret quarters a deranged
genius was plotting to take over the world, and the contraption he was perfecting to do it with would soon be powerful
enough to neutralize whole armies. Sharks swam hungry in
the bays—great whites thirty feet long, fat-bellied, and with
many-hundred arrowheads mounted sloppily on wet and blood-
red gums. Counterfeiters and smugglers and great networks of
organized crime thrived happily inside a nation that was under
constant threat of nuclear attack, alien invasion, and massive
retribution at the fierce and angry hand of Mother Nature in

the form of universal pestilence and plague.

Raymond lived inside a web of fantasy. It came to him in overdrive through books, television movies, the video games he knew, the legends that all children discussed in private, and the game of Dungeons and Dragons, a whole new world that had opened up to him that year and kept him fascinated and obsessed, despite all the initial difficulties—it was played by adults, the instructions were vague, there was no real game board but like a campfire story it commenced in the imaginations of the players, who in turn each played the role of a character moving about inside the action of the story. D&D had become an underground sensation, Raymond's mother bought him the twelve-dollar game box containing only dice and soft-cover manuals, and after many months of study, frustration, disinterest and return, Raymond had finally begun to figure it out. He then taught the Malvicinos, who'd been forewarned against it by Mrs. Malvicino, who told them that it came directly from the Devil; they played it enthusiastically over Raymond's house where his mother fed them lemonade and plates of cookies. Raymond liked D&D not for the castles and the monsters the game depicted, but for the experience of being immersed inside a living world—when he played it with the Malvicinos or the Kristos boys Raymond was invariably the "Dungeon Master," who never lived as a single character playing inside the world of the game but who was the storyteller, the one who made and controlled the whole fictive world. It was a role that seemed designed for him; he excelled at it and never cared to be a player.

School held all the dull hours of his life, where besides reading and the occasional craft-project that interested him, it was a place of torment and discomfort and was where his great life of fantasy was hidden: no one knew the battles that he fought; no one was aware of all his well-earned victories; they only knew him as the quiet boy, the bookworm, the loner—if they even knew of him at all. His popularity was measured at a low voltage.

Somewhere in the spring of his tenth year, while his body filled out with the awkward molts and shapings that it does in that time, Raymond learned all about the world of prank calls. It rolled out to him in a great belly-chuckling grin, and he began to make these calls himself, at first sensing the shift that was happening with this tiny step, a big wide threshold being passed. He wouldn't go back—there were greater fields ahead, lush gardens, and a long and curving river-bend. And he learned all of the other telephone legends children then acquire: the prank call where you whisper into the phone, "I know what you did! I saw you!" and you'd actually dialed up someone who'd just committed a murder, and you didn't know it, and they find out who called and then come after you; the story told around Halloween where the teen-age girl home alone gets a phone call and hears heavy breathing on the line so she hangs up, but she keeps getting this call, and then finally she stays on the line to listen and it's the police, who tell her they've been trying to reach her to let her know that a killer has escaped the prison and they traced him to her house, so she better leave because he's hiding there right now; the prank where you call up a drug store and you ask, "Do you have Prince Albert in a can?"—and when they admit they do you holler, "Well, let 'im out!"

Raymond discussed this last prank with his mother; he knew that Prince Albert was some kind of cigar, but he didn't know very many people who smoked them, besides his friendly neighbor Hal Andersen across the street who always had one clamped in his fat lips and who gave his empty cigar boxes to Raymond. To Raymond's great dismay, the boxes were never Prince Albert, but rather bore the stout, zesty, and unpronounceable long surnames of Latin America; he strongly suspected that Prince Albert was an old-fashioned and perhaps discount variety that may very well no longer be sold, but he still thought the idea was nice and wanted to play along with it.

He tried more pranks, and soon grew bold with them. In the Malvicino's wood-paneled family room that summer, when Mrs. Malvicino was in the bedroom tending to their baby brother Marty, he encouraged Joey and Toby to get out the fat telephone book from its drawer and they'd gleefully look up random names and call them. They called dozens. They'd pick a name that caught their fancy, dial up the number and ask for that person. And then, their cheeks flushed pink, their eyes compressed to tiny beads behind fresh slits, they'd hang up, choked speechless with their giggling.

A man answers the line, old and serious: "Hello."

A child's girl-voice, holding back its laughter: "Mister Reets? Mister *Reets?*"—a tangle of laughter rises in the background—"What do you like to ee-e-eets!"—a crowd of young hands press the handset back to the receiver as the family room explodes in redfaced laughter. Dozens of names published in the *Greater Clifton White Pages* won the pleasure of their sniggerings and howls that year.

He'd also learned how to "make the phone ring," which was a clever fifth-grader trick. If you dialed the digits 551, it was explained, plus the last four digits of your telephone number, you'd hear a dial tone; then you'd hang up the receiver again—and then the telephone line would ring until someone answered it. The official purpose of this was to test the ringers on your phone, presumably for housewives to know that everything was in working order—but for certain children, when they reached that age where such things were discussed, it became a great new ability, one that was especially shown off at public pay phones—and watching others pick up the phone only to find that nobody was there was altogether amusing.

The telephone would jangle for attention and whoever picked up would hear a red-ringing whine and know that it was a prank. Raymond and his friends would make the pay phone in the school lobby ring like this all the time, infuriating the teachers and all adults who fell for it. When these unknowing dupes picked it up to answer and heard the bright whine, then hang it up in confusion—for they never seemed to learn—the giggles of children across the hall sputtered out uncontrollably as they bunched and wriggled like a pack of young monkeys, their high-mounded eyes glinting over. But this always infuriated the principal and all the teachers, and the children knew that when they dared to do this they were flirting with unspeakable disaster.

It brought particular offense to his fifth grade teacher, Miss Karb, a weighty, stout-hipped woman in her early thirties whose wardrobe was heavily biased toward polyester slacks and jumpsuits. She often wore an airy brick-red scarf around her neck, and her face colored a complimentary shade of crimson when she had a fit of anger, which seemed to occur daily— and always when the hallway phone would ring. She'd been a student at Sohola's Duke State University a decade back, when shootings had happened there, and one spring morning she quietly explained this legend to the confused and horrified class. Raymond had never heard about it before, had no idea that it was such a pressing issue in the world, and yet she was so serious: she calmly explained, to the quiet terror of the children, that men in our nation's military had been ordered to shoot upon the students, and that some had even died from it—"So you should *always*," she elocuted slowly as she wrapped up the story, "*question* authority"; according to her this seemed to be the sum-total moral of it, but to Raymond it seemed like it was all a terrible mistake that everyone had somehow fallen into.

When he complained that he couldn't read the blackboard from the back of the room, he was taken out of class for an eye exam in the nurse's office, and to his surprise he was referred to an optician's office where he was quickly prescribed eyeglasses. A pair with dog-brown plastic frames and a matching vinyl pocket-case became his new accessories. His mother blamed this new necessity on his incessant reading: "That's what you get for reading in bed at night with the flashlight! I told you, that's not enough light for your eyes, I told you, so that's what you get!"—and it was true, he read books rapaciously now, but she still quietly encouraged him. Most weeks she took him to the library, and never complained about the tall stack of books that he checked out. Books, to Raymond, had become like gold. In his ambitious fervor that fifth-grade year he'd made stunted attempts during recess to read the entire classroom encyclopedia, the fat and oversized Webster's dictionary, and the school library's well-worn copy of *War and Peace*—all of which brought doubtful criticism from Miss Karb.

But she did introduce him, indirectly, to an important book. It was on a reading shelf she kept in the back of the class, above the large radiator box that ticked and snapped on winter mornings. When caught up with work you were allowed to pick a book and read quietly; Raymond tore through the collection in what seemed like weeks. He liked most of them but the one of greatest influence was called *The Mad Scientist's Club*, and described some neighborhood youths of approximately Raymond's age who formed a club around their interests in scientific experiment and hobby projects and whose role models were the mad scientists of old movies. Joey read the book next at Raymond's urging and they discussed its implications.

Joey was now like a young Muhammad Ali, with the black-eyed stare, locked jaw, hard eyebrows, the pursed nostrils, chubby lips—all of that, but white-skinned and fat. He was picked on at school and, for him as well as Raymond, the idea of a member's-only club only reinforced what had already begun. They quickly agreed to form their own Mad Scientist's Club, which became the target of much after-school energy, replacing their previous "He-Man Woman-Haters Club," whose name and purpose they'd cribbed from watching old episodes of *The Little Rascals* on UHF television. It hadn't lasted long because there seemed to be no purpose in it except to stomp up to the adults and announce the fact of your membership, an action Raymond thought would be considered "cute"; besides, he decided that he certainly didn't hate women, anyway—mysterious as they were. The Mad Scientist's Club was so much better.

The club met in the cedar-wood tool shed out in the far back of Raymond's yard, which Raymond's father had paid two muscular men to build a few years back; it was a source of great displeasure to Mrs. Malvicino, who complained constantly, even to Raymond, how the shed had ruined their back-patio view forever. The massive door was secured with a padlock whose combination Raymond learned after begging and pleading his father, and the numbers were etched into his brain: 14-47-4 sang out in a shoe-shuffling melody; he would never forget.

Inside, Raymond had commandeered a corner for their clubhouse, which now held his little cabinet of electronics scrap and robot parts, his Jaymar microscope, and—for every potentiate must bring something in order to take part—the two-dozen white plastic vials that made up the remains of Joey and Toby's chemistry set. They'd meet out there and sit on upturned crates, with the door closed, amid the tools and grassy lawn-mower, in the choking air and dim, stony light from the small window on the side; in the evenings they found illumination by a large camping flashlight that Raymond's father used on hunting trips. Once, in a pouring rainstorm, they took shelter in the clubhouse and talked about the club while taking turns holding the door shut from the muscular push of the angry storm wind and its resplendent showering of ice-cold sea-spray.

"This is what life's all about," Raymond thought, his arm soaked and dripping. "It's just like in the book!"

But he wasn't entirely convinced. It still was Roman Valley, after all, and the greater world was elsewhere—so when the door slammed hard with the pushing of the wind it was like his own soul and spirit had been banished from all the gorgeous sunlight and the day.

That languid summer had just begun when Raymond's mother took a telephone call and then, hanging up some minutes later, called out loudly for Raymond.

"What!" He came galloping down from his bedroom, where his body had been lying motionless on his bed, his mind waltzing quickly through the colorful world inside a book.

"Mark's coming to town."

Raymond wasn't sure what that would mean. They'd exchanged a letter or two after the third grade when Mark had moved away, but life had rushed forward and forgotten: once this summer ended, they'd be starting sixth grade—in another year they'd tackle all the rough hurdles of junior high.

"That was Mrs. Laynkord," his mother said again from the sink, where her hands were buried in a moony landscape of suds. "She says he's coming in two weeks. You can see him—he'll be staying with his grandparents."

In the story of his life he still thought of Mark as his best friend of all time, but that was wrapped away inside the sarcophagi of the past; Joey was probably his best friend now, and Stephen Kristos would be if they'd only get to see each other more.

His mother was still looking away, into the sink. "Aren't you excited?"

Raymond felt nervous, but he didn't tell his mother. When the day came that she drove him up the hill to spend the afternoon with Mark, Raymond's mind was a rabid cyclone of everything that had happened to him since they'd been together, of all the things he had to say—his many discoveries with the telephone, his growing fossil collection, the joy of prank calls, the game of D&D which he played incessantly, and the club; he thought that Mark could be inducted as an honorary out-of-town member, and they might carry out some sort of official correspondence. And there were the many books that Raymond knew, and the worlds they'd taken him to—he wondered idly if Mark had known any of them, too. There was so much to talk about.

And then there they were, at the top of the drive, overlooking the white house of Mark's grandparents—it didn't seem to change in the great vacancy of time since he'd been here last, it still had the concrete stoop before the front door and all the evergreen bushes mounded along the foundation, the giant oak was still in front, and even from the car Raymond recognized all the bumps and cracks in the smooth, moon-grey slabs of the walkway. He somehow regretted the time apart. There was no way to return. He regretted. But now: they were here. And so was Mark.

The car doors slammed brutally as they got out. Raymond was wearing his favorite shirt, a blue and white striped polo, and his best pair of blue jeans, and he suddenly realized that Mark had never known about his eyeglasses—and he also wore his hair differently now, parted sharply to the side. The front door was open behind the outer screen, and as his mother pressed the doorbell, chiming its two-noted song of exultation distantly within, Raymond wondered if Mark would look different from the third-grade visage that stood there at attention in his memory.

He did. He swept sidelong into the shadows of the doorway, tall and calm. His lips were parted and he looked almost like a teenager—his eyes were part hidden by a long sweep of bangs. He was bone thin.

"How you doin', dude?" he said, opening the screen door and taking Raymond's hand. He shook it, and Raymond felt shame in front of his mother. What was he doing, shaking hands—who was he for this? He was no one that Raymond knew.

Raymond's mother stepped in the house and hugged Mark in a happy greeting, and before long had gone over to Mark's grandma, who'd shuffled into the main room and was pulling at the edges of her pink flowered blouse.

"You two probably want to catch up," Raymond's mother said to the boys, "so we'll let you be."

With that, she disappeared quickly into the kitchen with Mark's grandma, whom she called by her first name.

"So ... how are you, dude?" Raymond said as soon as his mother left the room, feeling awkward, resentful and self-conscious as he did so. He'd never used "dude" before.

"Excellent," said Mark, nodding his head quickly.

"And how's it been, living in Seattle?"

"Most excellent—I brought my Atari! We'll have to play games. And I brought music!"

He turned and grabbed a stack of 45s that were resting on the couch—Raymond saw Duran Duran, the Go-Gos, and "Bette Davis Eyes." Raymond looked at them dully as Mark fanned them out; these things were for teenagers, for young adults—Raymond had no interest in the music, but also thought the way that the people were dressed in the photographs and the expressions on their faces were quite racy and not intended for his eyes.

"C'mon, man, let's play Atari," Mark said, spinning quickly around and commandeering the console stereo. He turned and grabbed one of his records and put it on the turntable. When it started, he twisted the volume high.

"You know this?" Mark shouted over the bright, upbeat cacophony. "I love this song!"

It was loud and uncomfortable to Raymond, who didn't know it. In fact, he didn't listen to music at all; music never played in the Valentine household. He was relieved when Mark's grandmother called out bitterly from the kitchen: "Mark! Mark, would you *stop* that? Please turn that down!"

Mark rolled his eyes. Anger swelled his face as he hollered: "*Yes*, grandma!" Then to Raymond: "C'mon, let's go outside—I need to get outta here!"

Mark was more outgoing, energetic, and impatient than he'd ever been—and seemed to have entirely lost that connection to the secret world that had once been the great bond between them. He'd seen a lot in his new life out west, in the public schools; he was focused now on the physicality of girls and the scraping yawl of rock music, and talked incessantly about these things—while Raymond felt intimidated and shocked by this metamorphosis, feeling as if his own life had been preserved by the stunting outlands of Sohola.

They spent a time-shaded afternoon in the back creek behind Mark's grandparents' property, under the dense minty canopy of towering pin oaks, putting small model ships they'd assembled from wood planks and garage scraps into the creek and setting them on fire, letting them burn and watching happily as they spun and bumped along the flowing current to their inevitable charred, watery demise. They were mostly quiet. When they went back inside the house—the house that smelled of maple syrup and sausage grease and sun-warmed fabric and was where his grandparents had lived out many decades of their lives—Mark spent his time again in constant motion, playing records to Raymond's quiet dread and then fussing with the Atari, leaning casually against the pearl-white of the wall as his eyes were focused on the television screen, while Raymond observed quietly and uncomfortably from the couch, staring at the cluster of picture frames resting on a doily along its top, which told the family chronicle in photographs whose eclectic blend of years were as varied as their frames; Mark was in many of the photos but his real presence here seemed foreign and out of place, unreal—like it were a brief visitation by some figment that orbited a distant center.

Raymond had wanted to fill the chasm of the intervening years, talk about the many things they'd seen and done, and hopefully even conspire together on great ideas, just like old times; but Mark was only interested in discussing girls and rock music in blatant terms and didn't even appear to be aware that the adults were over in the adjoining room, while Raymond was frozen with shame and terror at his words. Otherwise, Mark was content to play Atari, which he'd apparently set up within minutes of coming in. Video games were one of the few great passions of Mark's life. He was mesmerized, and Raymond impatiently sat and watched him play a game called Donkey Kong: Mark was a statue focused on the screen, and the warm room was death-silent but for the sounds of the game, the sharp and constant qwips and blings and doodle-e-doots, until a hornlike wail moaned out, signaling the end of the game—

"Aw!" Mark yelled, in sharp frustration, his eyes glowing with the blue brightness of the screen, "I've beat that score before—I can do better. I can reach the next level. Watch this!"

He smacked a pull switch on the Atari, barely looking down, and with a bleat and twinkle the game began again.

With the onset of summer, there was the great and whispered promise of unburdened time: the club could hold regular meetings now, even early in the day. But Raymond knew that he wanted much more than that—he wanted the living life that he'd felt from the pages of the book. It seemed so real to him, much more so than the unbroken seal of all his breathing, searching days. Books held the key to a greater world, operating somewhere on the streets of living life—and he believed that he'd find a way in it for himself, that its gateway was waiting for him somewhere up ahead.

He felt this secret rapture from the world of books, especially the older library books and hand-me-downs which he liked better than the glossy new ones from the book store at the mall; the new books only mirrored the world that was around him, while the old ones all seemed thoroughly better, and burned with forgotten legends that came alive upon the pages. He knew all the ways of the worn, wooden bureaus of the Dewey card catalogs, he felt the soft edges of the cards as he flipped through long narrow drawers of them, and like an expert he could manipulate the new microfilm machines at a high table in the library reference room, television-like boxes that offered a starry night-blue window into the entire catalog, which was rolled up inside of them in a great strip of microfilm and navigable by the pressing of two tiny silver buttons that whirred a speeding motor and spooled the microfilm forward and back in fast hustles.

He tore through the spectrum of subjects, devouring both fiction and non-fiction with equal elan. At home he'd been almost through with the entire Hardy Boys series, which were sold in a blue-covered edition from almost twenty years past and still had all the simple charms of that erstwhile era, and the library had many more such books worth exploring: he read through the whole Encyclopedia Brown series, and thick short-story compilations—all murders and monsters—bearing the important approval of Alfred Hitchcock; he devoured The Three Investigators series, thinking happily that he and Joey and Toby could fill the role in a contemporary revival; he read Elizabeth Enright's saga of the Melendy family, thinking of their citied lives as occurring somewhere near where his mother had grown up; he read the charming tales of the Edward Eager magic series; and he cherished innumerable old paperbacks that offered him their legends and their mysteries with sultry whisperings, and had names like *Secret Castle*, *A Sound of Crying*, *Mystery of the Haunted Pool*, and *Riddle of the Lonely House*.

All the good books were older. They had delightful painted covers that Raymond wanted to see in their enlarged original, with all their details and exquisite beauty as they hung framed upon the wall; their stories described events that happened sometime just before his own life had begun. That lost, unreachable world seemed to contain something essential, something that seemed better to him than the dull and haunted place where he was right now—it had more of a living glitter. He saw this, and in a desire to go inside the world of a book himself, he habitually measured out the distance from the publication date inside the cover to the year that he was born, and he wondered gloomily on the length that separated them—why here, why now? Could he ever go back? When would he ever live? An answer was coming, he was sure of it, he only had to find the right connection and the way—and everything would turn out wonderful, his whole entire life would end up like a rich and satisfying book.

BOOK TWO

THE CALL
   OF THE
NET

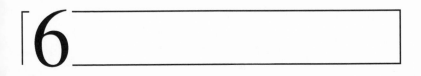

6

HOME COMPUTERS

THERE WAS a voice that began to call to him from infancy. It went back to the early dramas of childhood, to first lights, and to the dawn. It was in a set of switches and a whirling wheel; there was also an icy machine hum and an underwater glow.

What was it?

It was just a single word: computer. The computer was a concept and with all the speed and heat of silver sparkling rockets it came bolting into the life of Raymond Valentine that season. He already knew that computers were somehow behind all the bare essence of electronic power and filled the core of it; he knew about the workrooms lit by rows of ceiling lights and stuffed with hard, metal boxes that housed electric brains, their colored panels showing whirring tape reels and blinking lights and slots that would spit out reams of ticker tape in wavy ribbons. He knew that some of these vast computers took paper punch-cards and had dials and knobs to adjust and turn; that through their workings the desired calculations could be made; that there would be a cold awakening of lights, a reel would twitch and spin, an answer would be had.

He'd played with his parents' adding machine, a heavy tabletop appliance that took a tiny roll of paper, but nothing came of it—with the right presses on its pillow-soft keys he could get the numbers to spit out on the paper, while his parents could sit before it at the kitchen table for long hours of the night.

He knew the muffled rumbling of his mother's electric typewriter, that device for stamping characters on leaves of paper, and he knew that the computers now were small and something like that, where you could have them in your home. Discussions with the Malvicinos and the Kristos boys would sometimes glean these isolated bits of information—someone had a cousin who had one—and they knew that it worked like this: it was like a typewriter, but connected to your TV set just like Atari. They worked on screens. You controlled what came upon them, and the characters you typed would float in a steady shimmer that could move; the speaker blipped out the sound you wanted; advanced models had colors, and even lines and boxes could be drawn. The screens would flash like movies, and words would be written out like books. There was a dark shimmer where your typings would glow phosphorescent green inside the murk. It was exciting—as well as mysterious, effervescent and ethereal. It was quickly coming.

"It saves on disks," said Raymond, who'd just read all about it. "If you have a disk drive, you can bring back what you do at any time!"

"It's just regular tapes," said Joey.

"Nuh uh, they're disks."

"Some of them have tapes—I've seen them."

"Really?"

"Yeah! They have tape drives and you use a normal tape—a cassette."

"Cool!"

Immediately Raymond preferred the idea of having a computer that could read and save to cassettes rather than the square platters of disks he'd seen in illustration. He thought of them neatly stacked together, a long collection on the shelf, and he wondered if that might be his teenage future.

"They have 'em for sale now at K-mart, I saw 'em," Toby blurted in excitement. "I was there last week, I saw 'em, they have 'em now!"

Raymond took a slow, cautious, studious approach, with

many trips to the library for further edification and support. After some exploratory reading he formed a basic understanding, and he knew that home computers had recently evolved from the giant room-sized mainframes of the past; he began to learn which models were recommended for their sound and graphics capabilities—some were only black and white, while others had sixteen colors and the images would glow like a picture made of Lite-Brite pegs, a milky constellation of a thousand tiny pin-points on the screen. They were all different, incompatible, and had their own benefits and failings, and he learned which ones were best avoided. He still never saw one except inside the pages of a book, but he grew favorites and harbored prejudices; in his mind, certain brands were heroic while others were to be mocked and shunned.

From there he began to study the essentials of computer programming, the writing and input of instruction codes. This was clearly the way to get the power. He took out books on programming BASIC, which was the popular computer language for hobbyists, and he found a quick tutelage in the computer magazines that filled a rack at the drug store—he greedily devoured their pages while his mother shopped; sometimes, when an issue was particularly tantalizing or worth further study, he asked her if she could buy it for him. She often acceded, and he took in all the wisdom offered by the columnists: he caught up with reviews, learned about what was expected soon, took to heart all that they proclaimed, heralded, and warned about. He felt that this coming home computer world was going to be good for anyone who could only figure out all the confusing jargon of the modules, cartridges, compatibilities and "function" keys.

Then at an office-supply store he saw a heavy paperback book that contained a hundred programs you could type in and run on your home computer. They were written in BASIC and compatible with most systems—the book was just a collection of program listings. This would be a wise and careful purchase, Raymond thought; surely, with a hundred programs on his computer, he'd never need to buy commercial software, the programs that were sold on disk at high prices ... and with this as the basis of his argument, his mother bought the book. At home he studied it, with no computer to input in the listings—he just read them over carefully, stepping through them by each line of instruction as if he were the computer, and writing all the output down in a school notebook that became his "programming journal"; he filled the ruled pages with lines and lines of BASIC code, devising unique programs that would work as games; quiz the operator by asking questions; draw abstract pictures; make sounds. For months he built up his notebook with these programs, pages of carefully-constructed works that waited for an opportunity to be typed in and brought to life.

His obsession didn't pass unnoticed. Everywhere he went, he was enjoying the beginnings of a reputation now, as the "computer whiz"—and he didn't even have one. Adults would sit him down silently at a computer and let him be, and he'd be contented under its green-shadowed glare, staring intently at the tiny porthole of the screen, typing away with speed and confidence, throned at the helm of a machine whose purpose wasn't even comprehended by the adults who owned it—they just knew it was the future, and that it was coming quick. For home computers were everywhere—the land went ripe with them that season. He saw computers demonstrated at K-mart, and in department stores, and when he saw them he'd run up to them and type. There'd be computers now at birthday parties, where the boys would want to play the games, while Raymond wanted to test and explore, type commands and trace out all of the connections. Kids casually mentioned that they had computers or were getting them and it was often assumed that Raymond had one, too—and sometimes he pretended that he did.

"Oh, yeah, I just got one last month," he said once to the kids on the bus, spoken calmly while he leaned up against the massive padded seat of green sticky vinyl, his tawny glasses clamped snug upon his face, and they queried him while clustering around with peering, curious eyes. He was the expert, after all.

"What kind did you get?"

"Oh an Apple."

He felt shame forever for this casual lie.

One of the great joys of sixth grade was the Saturday Morning Enrichment program that was held at the local public high school—it was a program of extracurricular weekend classes on a diverse rainbow of topics that were offered to the students of St. Bart's, and over winter break Raymond was immediately excited about one called "Introduction to BASIC Programming." He needed no such introduction now, but he lusted at the thought of hands-on access to a machine, so he quickly enrolled, giddy with naked excitement and expectancy.

The class was held on the second floor of the high school, and walking its halls gave Raymond a glimpse of this world of the older teenagers. He wouldn't be going to a public high school and because of his schooling at St. Bart's he harbored an enormous fear of them—they were giant assemblages of atheists, of kids who fought daily, who were rough, shockingly promiscuous, and the faculty was helpless to maintain order and control. He knew that schools were different now than they'd been just a few decades back, in the worlds of the books he read—things had changed; it was no longer the time of the Hardy Boys. There'd been difficulties, and today the kids were wild and going to a public school meant subjecture to all manner of bad exposures, constant fights, unruliness, and extravagant decadence. He feared it greatly—what would it be like to endure this horror? And so the halls were strange to him, weary, faintly odorous, and distinctly like a prison: the bleary rows of lockers, curved halls of bright orange brick, cavelike stairwells that connected levels of the same.

But on the first day of class, all his fears were immediately subsided and flowed away to nought. The students were a quiet mass of unfamiliar faces all his age—there was a plump-cheeked girl in a denim jumpsuit, a fat boy, and a crowd of thin, weak-looking children he'd never seen before, from the public schools, and none of them were threatening nor even particularly interesting; in fact they had a drab, tired aura about them as if inwardly their brains were fast asleep and Raymond quickly tuned them out, focusing only on the computers that he'd soon be touching. Dulcet-drums banged out their quick expectant rhythms.

They met in one half of a long second-floor classroom with

a doorway on each end and a divider screen in the middle that was partially closed. The other half was dark and empty and the room smelt weakly of walnut; the instructor, a tall, bear-bellied man who kept a spiritual distance from the children, passed out handouts about the principles of programming in BASIC. Raymond was openly crestfallen on that first day when the man swept in and said that the students "wouldn't touch a computer" for the first two Saturdays while he brought them up to speed.

What he said was all old news to Raymond: a computer "program" told the computer what to do; it was merely a list of instructions, in some programming language that the computer could understand; BASIC was a language that was designed to be easy for beginners to use. There were drawbacks, of course, and commercial software was usually written in the more difficult languages, but BASIC could be used by anyone to make simple programs that more or less worked on many different brands of computers.

"So a BASIC program's just a series of *instructions*," the man reiterated to the blank, white eyes of the fourteen children. "Each in*struc*tion's on a line of its own, and each *line's* preceded by a *num*ber. You got that? Hmgh?"

As soon as he saw a single nod, he went on. "Yes, and the computer starts at the *lowest* number in the program, that's the first line—it starts with that and keeps going, line after line after line, *in*-cre-*ment*-ally, until the end. When it hits the end, it just stops. Usually you tell the computer to end on the last line, you say 'END'—that's one instruction, 'END,' it ends; got that? Hmgh?"

The girl's cheek twitched, her eyes screamed for aid, she shuffled in her seat and before the instructor could continue she gracefully, if timidly, raised her left hand.

He remained calm at all times. "Yes."

"But why does the program here start with line ten? Where's line one?"

The instructor bowed his head to the inquisitor, and blink-ing away all doubts his response was confident and easy: "Be-cause that's just a convention. Hmgh? A con*ven*tion? You can start it with line one if you want to, you can start it with ten, you can start it with one hundred—you can start it with a hundred *thousand* if you like, hm? Well, I dunno if it goes up that high—but you can start it with any number you like. It's just a convention, for BASIC, to go ten, twenty, thirty, forty, to do it in tens just like that."

The inquisitor nodded, which cooly satisfied him, but in a second thought he turned, bent forward, and added more: "Plus, by doing tens, if you wanna add something to your program, you can do that—like if you see that you wanna do something in between what your program does on lines twenty and thirty, you just add a twenty-five. You can do that. Hmgh? Yes, you can."

He smiled and was quite satisfied with that—he held the open smile for a moment, and then standing quite erect he explained in a serious drone how common instructions included PRINT, which printed to the screen the quoted line of text that followed it, and GOTO, which instructed the computer to break out of the chronology and immediately go to the line number specified. On the blackboard he showed the famous two-line "infinite loop" program:

```
10 PRINT "Hello, world"
20 GOTO 10
```

"First what happens here," he said, placing a long finger on "world," "is that the computer gets to this line, line *ten*. It sees the PRINT, and what it does is print the text you give it"—his finger tapped neurotically—"so in this case, it prints 'Hello, world' to the screen. You see that? Hmgh?"

His long chalky finger lifted off the blackboard and then touched down again to the empty space after the second line. "Okay *now* it gets to this line here, line *twenty*. See? That's the GOTO. And what it says here is go to line *ten*. Now that's back up *here*"—the finger bounced off the board and pressed down hard on "world" again.

"It's back *here* now, and it prints 'Hello, world' one more time, and then it goes *here*"—the finger jumps up and again lands in the empty space after the second line. His eyes were staring hard and satisfied at the blackboard. "Now it's gonna

do this *again* and *again*"—the finger moved between its two
positions on the blackboard, quickly, smearing chalk—"because
that's how the program's written. As it is, the computer's
caught in a *loop*, and it won't get out until you stop it. It won't
stop until you hit the Break key. All right, now we're gonna try
it ourselves on the machines. Infinite loop."

The class was shuffling with excitement but Raymond already knew about these loops—they were a favorite to quickly
program at places like K-mart where unattended home computers were on display in the electronics section. Of course
the messages printed on such opportune occasions were no in-
nocuous greetings, but were usually something meant to be
provocatively disturbing to adults and other hapless innocents,
simple profane blurts proffered from the mind of a naughty
eleven-year-old boy.

"Okay," the instructor said on the following Saturday. "Input statements. Today we're gonna learn *input* statements.
You already know PRINT, huh, to put a line on the screen? Now
we're gonna learn how programs can ask the *user* for input, and
print it."

Raymond knew all this. The Saturday mornings here were
just a time for him to be close to a machine; each week his
father drove him to the wide, icy curb of the high school in the
bright glare of January snowpiles, where he'd stand alone to be
picked up an hour later—but meanwhile, the programs in the
class were nothing he hadn't done before ten times on paper.

The computers were on a row against the wall to the hallway, where they looked like a bank of mainframe terminals
with their sculpted, single frames of black and tan, a square
monitor eyeing out from above the keyboard. They couldn't do
color or sound, but he liked them anyhow—he just wanted to
write BASIC programs and watch them run. This might be the
way to making monuments.

When the class had their programming time, the instructor
turned out all the lights to avert the glare. There was just
the faint walnut odor in the air and the sound of clicking, of
all these kids focusing intently on their screens and carefully,
slowly, clumsily manipulating the machines to do the work.

The instructor wandered from seat to seat, watching from

behind, showing the students how to turn the system on, explaining where to type, and answering their questions in his booming, chipper voice that always cut the relative silence of the room. When he came to Raymond he looked quietly at the screen for a moment where the program was already running in triumphant blinks of milk-blue letters on the screen. His face was frozen in the dumb shock of silence.

"You're *done* already?" he finally spurted.

Raymond nodded quietly, his face clamped in an air of solemn gravity.

The instructor peered closer at the screen to see how he had fared. Raymond had improved the program significantly: he'd gotten some lines to blink, while others glowed in inverse video, so that each character was drawn in black on a bright phosphor background square.

Bent down so that his face was close to Raymond's screen, the man held a motionless and empty gaze. "What's that?" he finally asked, in a restrained tone that masked alarm, as if the computer was broken and would have to be taken in for service.

"Inverse video," came a voice from somewhere far inside of Raymond—a casual, quiet mumble. Strangely, he felt shame: he knew that the other kids were still figuring out how to type in the lines of the program, and he was trying hard for more.

"*You* don't need this class!" the instructor bellowed in astonishment, his long body straightening up, while some of the other faces of the children looked over from their screens. In the next long, frozen instant they seemed to Raymond like mannequins set into position while he sat there trapped among them, alone and naked in the oppressive shade of the room.

7

THE WARGAMES GENERATION

RAYMOND WAS the master. He knew all the ways of the computers, he could program them, he knew their names and the feels of all their keyboards. Sometimes when he saw the seagreen phosphor on a screen he thought of touching it, of somehow scooping all the characters and letters up and holding them upon the inside of his palm, pocketing them, carrying them around with him, even lifting them into his mouth and chewing them. Computers worked their ways for him, spread open all their secrets, and he sought to penetrate them further and again.

What he'd also learned at this point was that you had to have a modem. This was a way for reaching out, it connected your computer to the telephone so that you could dial out and reach into a distant system. He wasn't exactly sure of how it worked; it was still a burly-clouded mystery to him; he just knew it was the way: you could use your home computer to get computers that were far away—even large, complex mainframes with their many rows of panels, or great expensive Cray machines that filled special air-conditioned rooms. You could somehow open into them, there would be a window to them made upon your screen and you would go.

He read a book that told him how the modem worked: it turned the output of the computer from its electric pulsings into sound, a bright silver scream that would be transmitted over the telephone line; on the other end, the remote computer's modem would convert that screaming noise back into the proper pulsing signals, and going back and forth like this the two computers could exchange their data. It was a way to reach out, to broaden your command and gain more power.

Raymond lay fascinated on his bed for hours, reading about the modem, carefully examining the many photographs and pondering the long descriptions: the book told of bulletin boards, which weren't like the corkboards for posting flyers in the lobby of the supermarket, but they were computers set up for public chat with modems. You could call it with your computer and read the messages that others left on it, and you could add messages of your own so that those who'd call it later could read and know. The suggestion was fantastic, a swirl of human faces and voices in a misty dotted fog—he wondered of the messages that would come to him and all the ones that he would leave, he imagined all the words from far-off people scrolling down upon the glowing screens, burning all their phosphors. There was an acronym to describe it, BBS, that stood for "Bulletin Board System"; they were popular in California.

The modem hovered in his conscious mind that year, inflaming it, and like all the other mysteries of adulthood it was a capability far beyond his present reach—and when school let out for summer, a motion picture came into his life that ended all the speculation and confusion. It began during a lunchtime telephone call from Joey next door, when he reported that his brother Toby had just seen something exciting on TV.

"J'you hear about *WarGames*?"

"No-o-o," Raymond sang portentously, wondering if it was a good new army game they saw at the store. "What is it?"

"It's a new movie about computers—this kid runs a computer for the government."

"Ye-e-ah?"

"Yeah, it's all about home computers!"

What did computers have to do with war? Were they that dangerous and powerful? So strange—but as a new Hollywood movie aimed at the age group just above theirs, the study and understanding of its fables and concepts were a requirement of life. So Raymond filed this information away and kept a careful watch for new developments.

They came steadily: later in the week the Malvicino brothers gathered in conference with Raymond on the evening summer lawn, and as a soft filter of dusk came on around them between the two groggy homes, Joey reported in an excited hush how he'd now seen the commercial himself.

Raymond was at once jealous and excited. "What happened? Whud'ja see?"

Joey impersonated the electronic voice of a computer, slow and stunted, each word pronounced mechanically with no stress or inflection: "The computer asks him, 'Shall—we—play—a—game?' "

"It—it *talks*?"

Raymond had read about speech synthesizers, which were expensive speakered hookups to the computer that made voice-like sounds in a monotonous plodding emulation of speech. But they were expensive and practically mythical—he'd never seen one or heard their sound.

"Yeah, his computer talks! He connects to the government computers and launches their nuclear missiles!" Joey's dark eyes were aglow.

Raymond tried to picture this. "So it's about a nuclear war?"

"Yeah," Toby interjected loudly. "Nuclear war! I think he somehow starts a nuclear war!"

A tiny bird, in bat-like silhouette, shot up in a high arc above the tool shed and then glided quickly over the stout row of fir trees along the far edge of the yard.

"It's hackers, that's what hackers are," Joey said. They both explained, fighting for control of the conversation, how there was an outline of the United States drawn graphically on a computer screen with bombs exploding on it, circular areas of bright phosphor blotting over all the major cities.

"So hackers start a nuclear war?"

The boys wondered. Would the world end in the coming season? Was this a warning of their ways? Raymond had heard about hackers and he didn't understand their connection to nuclear war—he wasn't quite sure what they went about doing, but he was certain that they had nothing to do with war. And he knew that he had more time, that distant winds were rising and there was somewhere far to go.

As soon as the film was released they all saw it at an afternoon matinee and were dazzled. They milled out of the red-carpeted theatre into the bright world of the shopping mall with great smiles and starry eyes of wonder. Yes, there'd been a hint of war when a government computer mistakenly assumed a simulation game was a real attack, but that wasn't the important core of the movie—it was all about the life of a teenage hacker, David Lightman, who used his home computer and his modem to call out to the computers of the world, to pass through screens and wires and to wander far, right from the dark and sacred lair of his upstairs bedroom. That was what a hacker was, and Raymond knew it was the way: he had to be one. He had to get a modem and computer—he'd be a hacker, call out and connect, he'd know the ways and he'd walk the winds like ghosts.

That week at the Drug Mart down the street Raymond saw the paperback novel for the movie. He greedily snatched it from the rack and presented it to his mother, who was analyzing the colorful wall of laundry detergents two aisles over.

"Can I have this?"

She looked down and absently answered in the affirmative.

"Thanks!"

He deftly placed it in the cart. Before he fell asleep that night, satisfied and drained of energy, five chapters had been read and closely studied.

What had briefly flashed by in the darkness of the theatre was now laid out for him in all the clarity and elaboration of the text: Raymond learned all the details of what it meant to be a hacker, someone who was a master at manipulating through this hidden world of wires, who knew all about telephones and computers and technology. They were the ones who could open all the doors, who traversed the secret corridors, who connected and who wandered far—which had been the very thing that Raymond had been always after.

The book elaborated on the techniques that Lightman used, like when he made a free call at a pay phone by taking a metal tab from an aluminum soda can that he'd found in the dusty rubble by the road, and by connecting it from the mouthpiece of the phone to the metal guard on the coin return he'd cause a short in the circuit and could make the call for free. This concept lingered with Raymond when he saw the Malvicinos next.

"Remember how he makes a free call at a pay phone in the movie?"

"Ye-e-ah?"

Raymond let out a fabulous, wide-eyed whisper: "We should try it!"

For an instant, the implications were silently measured by all. Then Joey brought them to reality.

"There's a pay phone by the arcade—we can try it there!"

They often rode their bikes there now, to the strip mall where the arcade was—it was a two-mile journey out of the development and down the winding bumpy sidewalks along the main road—and in their summer hours they browsed and wandered through the many stores, spending their pocket change at the candy shop to fill their hungry gullets with gobs and handfuls of the confections in their elaborate varieties, and parting through the cool, rich-smelling air of the Uncle Bill's general store, poking and fussing with the many wares that hung upon the racks. The Malvicinos liked to spend long spates of time in the dark cavern of the arcade, but Raymond didn't; the graphics and sound of the many video games intrigued him for a while, but he thought that the expense—twenty-five cents for access to a game that might only last a minute—was extravagant and far beyond the pale; rarely in his life was he ever given a quarter for the gumball machines that dispensed small shiny toys encased in domes of clear plastic, while the Malvicinos thought nothing of spending three or four dollars worth of quarters on each visit.

They journeyed out on their bikes, and found a can tab on

the sidewalk near the supermarket at the other end of the mall; over at the pay phone both Joey and Raymond tried rubbing it between the open metal clip inside the mouthpiece and the metal plate of the coin return. It had taken great effort to unscrew the mouthpiece—it seemed to have been sealed with powerful glue—and now every time they dialed the Malvicino's house, a recording asked them to deposit twenty-five cents. They had to concede defeat.

"It doesn't work! It doesn't work!" Toby exclaimed, running in circles around them. The Malvicino boys were quick to accept this harsh fact, but Raymond was shocked and dumbfounded and everything around him went hazy in the mauve tintings of afternoon shadow and light. People walked by but were not real. He held the telephone receiver in his hand but there was no connection—it didn't work.

Undeterred, he later theorized that for sake of liability the movie had to mask reality just slightly, and that the true way to make the short-circuit on the line would be through an electric jolt. So he tried to do this with a 9-volt battery and two wires—but that also failed, and again life returned its deadpan silence to all the exhibitions of his dreams.

For in that summer Raymond encased himself inside the world of *WarGames*. He read the paperback novel again and again—as if he'd find, somewhere in its pages, the instructions for how to operate. He read it on the family vacation that August, when sharing the tan-leather back of the car with little Sally on the way down to the beach at Hilton Head, in South Carolina: they drove all day and night between West Virginia mountains and over the Carolina hills, the car swaying along on the smooth curvings of the highway in another state, and in the sleepy cool of early twilight he'd look up from his book to catch the warm red taillights of cars blotting the same blue dusk, glimpsed once and singled out as friends and fellow travelers from a throng of quick freeway traffic, all sloping through foreign valleys and never seen again, the whole entire moving crowd of cars now gone and scattered too—and then he dove back down into the comfortable and moving world of the book until it became too dark to read.

Then he read it in the icy breeze of their condo rental in

between salty, sandy afternoons on the long, baking crescent-cookie of the beach, and wandering through a brisk and constant turnstile of gift shops, and engorging on thrown softballs of rum-raisin Häagen-Dazs ice cream while easing back at a wire table just beneath the fat red and beige stripes of the light-house that was the island's landmark centerpiece. Outside, the Carolina heat came prancing up with slow, sultry exhalations over the low salty plain of the sea, and its whispers flitted between the dark palms and feathery leaves of trunk-heavy trees; in his mind, whole other worlds had come forth now and risen.

Raymond loved the excitement and the freedom of the summer months, his time spent away from school, without any thought of it clouding the tender fairways of his mind; junior high was coming, and now besides the adventures with the Malvicinos and trips to the arcade, there were long hours in the air-conditioned, tomb-still luxury of the county library, where he spent whole days reading in the stacks. He'd abandoned the Childrens section, was weary of the Young Adult offerings with all their flash and shallow pomp, and spent his time almost exclusively among the tall, austere shelving of the Adult section, where all the treasure was. Thick novels contained the confessions of whole lives that fired out again through the axons and dendrites of his brain. He also enjoyed the summer days spent fishing with his father on one of the hundred little lakes spread out in the fertile woodlands and green ripened valleys of central Sohola—days of long, quiet car rides in the nacreous shadowy dawn, of passing through a creaky wooden screen-door at the bait shop, buying worms or maggots packed in a Styrofoam cup, walking on the sooty oaken floor, and then the slippery fast slam of the door behind him as he stepped outside with a bag of chips and a can of pop; of being underswept by the bright heat of summer at noon, and of passing through the great pools of shade on a dusty path to the lake, beneath a receiving line of gargantuan trees in full emerald bloom and to the tweety fanfare of a dozen high-hidden birds. Long afternoons on warm docks or thinning tufts of grass on dry banks along the gurgly shore, under the unblinking rivet of the sun and near the glass-blue hover of a dragonfly. Or out on the giant waters of Lake Catawba, which seemed borderless, seemed to flow down along the wide curve of the earth and spill around it as Raymond sat there speechless for an afternoon on an anchored boat along with several men—his father, one of his father's fishing friends, and the captain—listening groggily to the slow winding patter of their strange adult talk, the occasional brute cursings and the spitty endless chuckles; or of days on the long steel charter boats with thirty or forty other anglers who were excited and expectant over the big one they were sure to land that day; of the huge horn scream, rattling his frame, at the mouth of the rocky harbor just as the endless lake has neatly opened up in front of him; of the chugging of the power boats and the rich lingering smell of burning marine oil; of the gigantic billowing smoky clouds hanging high above them, rolling forward with a fiery outstretched power and tumbling steadily toward the far horizon; the blood-curdling shriek of sea gulls; the humid stench of bony bleach-white fish upon the docks and near all the shoreline buildings; of a dead opossum in the reeds near the berm of the road, the white of upper jaw exposed, its dozen fetal half-born babies squirming, spilling out, shouting mutely in the open mass of unspooled bowels and collected blood; the girls his own age that he spotted on the boardwalks and at the beaches, standing in their flat tube tops, with boyish ruddy faces and looking out from blank alien eyes—this was what the summer gave to Raymond when he was eleven years of age, in those last weeks before his birthday came and made him twelve.

8

CODES AND PHREAKS

ERIK DREXEL was a boy of Raymond's age whose family was
very rich. Raymond wasn't close to him, but he'd have to see
him occasionally because his mother had somehow become
friends with Erik's mother. She'd take him along when she
visited their home—a spacious colonial estate with a shady
center portico, dead dark windows on each wing, both indoor
and outdoor pools—and for those hours Raymond would have to
play with Erik. He'd be shuttled off to Erik's bedroom where in
a steely, quiet boredom Erik would show Raymond all his latest
toys, all of the biggest and most popular and coveted objects of
the season—he had them all, and he was completely bored with
them.

Raymond felt uncomfortable around Erik, who for his thin
bony frame and with his wet lips and limp, stringy hair didn't
look as strong as his bold personality asserted itself as being;
however, he did have a computer, a good one, and Raymond
wanted to see and touch it. But there in the house—which
was stuffed with shiny mahoganies, gilded paintings and cold
marble—they didn't go near it because Erik was bored with it.
It was an Apple, and it seemed to Raymond as if Erik would
mention it only to tantalize him—Raymond was desperate to
see it, and when he heard that Erik had a modem he drew their

conversation toward it.

"So do you call any bulletin boards?"

"Sure," Erik said casually with a slight shake of his head, and he told Raymond about all these places that he knew—places that went by the titillating, suggestive, sometimes racy names like Poison Chalice, Emerald Phorest, Pirate's Cove, and Forbidden Fortress—and he'd tempt Raymond with any one of these references and say, "Maybe we can set you up with an account on it tonight—or I dunno, maybe we'll want to do something else instead of the computer"; but Raymond, who yearned for this access, was fed hopeful by these comments: he saw himself coming home with a wrinkled slip of paper containing his very own username and password for a board.

Raymond tried steering the course of their evening away from the D&D game that Erik wanted and toward the computer, toward the boards, asking for more information, trying to get a demonstration of one being called. Erik finally yielded with a tiny glimpse into that world by admitting that he used a special, advanced method to call a board in California without there being a long-distance charge.

Raymond wanted to know how—he remembered the pop-top trick from the movie. "Is it free because it's a computer call?"

"No," Erik laughed evilly, his dark eyes contracting. "No, everybody has to pay. But if you know certain hacker techniques, you can get around it." He said this in an aloof manner, almost haughtily. He said that he was friends with the hackers who were on the California board, and that only they knew these secret methods.

"Can we go on there tonight?"

Erik looked doubtful. "Maybe," he finally said. "They won't like you, though. They'll probably call you a rodent, because you don't have an Apple."

Raymond didn't care. "Can we see?"

"Eh, let's go outside now."

They wandered out in the hilled front grounds and the broad, leafy yard of the colonnaded white estate, overlooking the blacktop pancake of the cul-de-sac and the deserted lane beyond it. They trudged over the brown crusts of wilted leaves in piles along the side of the property where all was quiet in the cool early autumn except for the crunch of the rolled-up husks crumbling under their feet. Eventually they migrated to the deep wooded backyard toward Erik's tree house—Raymond was excited to see it, but Erik wanted to go back inside as soon as he pointed it out; he didn't even let Raymond go in it. Then in a second thought, Erik climbed up inside to demonstrate. A moment later his head looked down at Raymond through the trap door, saying, "Let's go inside and play with the computer"—and after his descent Raymond trailed him back to the house, to Erik's bedroom where the computer was.

"So you don't know about codes?" Erik asked mysteriously, with an evil smile, after turning on the computer and then having sat down in the plush chair in front of it.

Raymond was standing behind him—there wasn't another chair—and he didn't know what Erik was talking about. Codes—Raymond knew and liked making codes and ciphers, but Erik chuckled; that wasn't it. Programming codes, computer codes, Raymond had no idea so he finally answered, "No."

It looked like Erik was going to show Raymond something with the computer, with the modem—he was getting the Apple set up to call a board; green characters on the screen were flashing.

"Well, I'll call a hacker board here in town," he finally said. Then he explained how in this online world, you had to have a handle; Raymond immediately thought of the handlebars of a bicycle, but Erik explained that it was like a code name that you went under. He said that it became your identity in the underground world.

"You never *ever* want to give out your real name," he warned severely. "*Everybody* goes by handles in the hacker world."

He stressed that since some of the things that hackers did were illegal, you could never reveal your real name; you risked getting caught. You had to cloak your identity well. Erik told him now that his own handle was Agent Orange—"But don't tell anybody at your school!"

He tried to connect, typing in a number on the keyboard, but it didn't seem to work, and finally he announced that the board must've been "down."

"I'm gonna call the sy-sop," he cooly announced, as if he

were talking to himself; his gaze was still locked on the monitor. Raymond knew the word "sysop" was short for system operator, which was the owner of the board and the one who ran it—except in his head he'd been pronouncing it "sis-op"; he thought Erik's way was less literate and somehow sloppy.

Erik swiveled his chair to the side of his desk, reached over for a small pocket address book, flipped through it and then quickly dialed a number on his shell-white phone.

"Hello, is Terry there?" There was a minute pause. "This is Erik," he said quickly, dark eyes focused sharply at a lower drawer of his bedroom set. He nodded his head. "Yes, I'm a friend of his."

There was another pause. "Okay. Oh, okay. Thanks. Goodbye."

He hung up the phone and then turned to report his findings to Raymond. "He's out at summer camp for a week. I guess he had to take the board down while he was gone."

"Oh."

"I can't believe you don't know codes," Erik suddenly said.

"No—no, what are they?"

"Well," Erik said ponderously, and with a touch of scorn. "Never mind."

But Raymond wanted to know—it had an air of mystery about it. "Really, what *are* they, what can they do?"

Erik's face was still wrinkled up in scorn. "Codes are powerful," he finally said.

"Yeah?"

"Yeah—if you know how to use them. You can do all kinds of powerful things."

"Yeah, like what?"

"Well, you can call all over the world and nobody will know—and it'll *never* show up on the phone bill."

"Wow! Really?"

"Yes," Erik said, matter-of-factly, his eyes narrow and serious. Then he brusquely took out a scrap of white notebook paper from his night-stand drawer, a paper with all kinds of numbers scrawled on it in blue ink. He was hesitant, but at this point Raymond knew that he was going to show it.

"Do you know what a phreak is?" He spelled out the word.

It sounded vaguely dirty. "No."

"You don't know *phreaking*?" Erik looked aghast. "Phreaks?"

"No." Raymond felt like he was being taunted. He wondered with horror whether it had something to do with drugs or naked people—was Erik about to show him something that the adults in his life wouldn't approve of?

Erik sighed heavily, rolled his eyes, and then reached for his modular phone. It was the kind whose curved handset had the keypad in it, and he held it in his hand as if he were gauging its weight while he looked furtively toward the doorway and said dryly, "Close the door."

Raymond stood and did it in a timeless swipe without breath or sound.

"If my mom comes in here just pretend we're doing something else."

Raymond nodded, watching carefully. The boys were silent. There were dark blinks.

Erik then dialed a number that he got off the piece of paper, and he listened tightly to the receiver.

"This is called Metrotel," he said in a low voice. "It's a local access number to their service. When I connect I give them a code"—he looked down at the paper and punched in a six-digit number—"and now I can give it a long distance number and dial it."

Erik punched in the number to a board in California.

"For free?"

Erik's eyes were bulging when he answered. "Yeah—for free!"

"So a phreak is like a hacker but with the phones?"

"Yeah."

Raymond understood. These numbers were access codes for Metrotel that businessmen used when they made their long-distance calls; phreaks would get ahold of these private codes and use them for themselves. The businessmen would be billed for the calls.

"After all," Erik added a moment later, when his modem had connected and characters from the long-distance board were stomping on the forehead of his Apple monitor, "the telephone network is the largest and most powerful computer in the world."

There was a quiet moment, and then this awesome statement was mounted high in the lobby of Raymond's mind, where he would see it often and repeat it: and in a slow panoramic sweep he glimpsed all of those wires spooled taut around the globe, all the cablings and the twisted ligaments, the many arms of switching networks, the woven matrix of ten million keypads, dials, relays, repeaters, ringers, bridges, clips and circuits that connected powerfully and were somehow brought together into one. They made a global net that had been laid out upon them over the long reach of time, and every day it moved and shifted all its billion little nodes and ends—and the world he needed was out there just beyond them, in the far breezes by the forgotten banks. That was the final destination, the land he had to reach.

Raymond prepared mentally for his ascendance to the throne of hackerdom, and he actively debated with himself about what his handle should be. The matter required careful thought, sharp consideration, and a detached neutrality. He'd seen the handles that were on the boards that Erik called, and he went through all the possibilities and arguments, contemplating the many variations and the themes: should it have the technological sleekness of outer space, or like the animations imported from Japan should it be an exotic mixture of biotic life and mechanical regimentation? Should it be picked from one of the revered, timeless, classic themes—a monster, pirate, brigand, burglar, or gangster name? The name of a popular character, or an ironic twist on some common phrase, finding a clever rhyme with some computer term? Or would it simply be a person's name, such as Alex Jones, a secret-agent undercover identity that would provide a cloak but, seeming "real," never arouse the faintest whiff of suspicion?

He needed something traditional, yet reflecting magnificently of all his life and interests. This problem puzzled him and occupied many passing moments, and the answer finally came to him in a surprised rush on a chilly night just before Thanksgiving, when he'd been brought with a group of schoolmates through the inky tunnel of the evening streets to a Chuck E. Cheese's video arcade and pizza parlor for the celebration of a twelfth birthday.

Jim Alpes, an elfin boy in his class whom he'd begun speaking with owing to their familiarity through the Boy Scouts, had invited him to his party in what was a significant social advance for Raymond. Although he wasn't familiar with many of the boys, he eagerly accepted the invitation; after a quiet car ride where Raymond was swimming through his nervous energies, his father dropped him off at the Alpes house in the neighborhood just up the steep hill from their development, near where Mark's grandparents lived.

The boys were packed into the huge Alpes van and brought over to the arcade, where after a comforting dinner of flat, bendy pizza lifted off nicked round platters, and tall plastic glasses of cola they refilled endlessly from full pitchers chinking with ice, they were set loose in the huge summer carnival of the arcade, exchanging their moist handfuls of quarters for game tokens.

The boys quickly dispersed and manned the many games—Raymond alone wandered the bright maze of rooms and aisles and at this moment, in the blink of the corn-yellow circus lights, he knew what handle would be his, could only be his. It came to him as he stood alone among the flashing, chirping arcade games, each one mounted by a boy who for a quarter mined its prospect—and spotting a lucky charm machine that cost a single quarter token to use, he turned the metal arm to make a charm that spelled out his secret handle. He fed his token to the machine, yanked the long lever and heard the crunching stamp as the charm was pressed into existence. Then with a tinkle the lucky charm spat out of the mouth of the machine and was ready for him in the shade of a little tray. It was a flat disc of green-painted metal, embossed with a lucky Irish clover on one side; the other had been branded with the name: DAVID LIGHTMAN.

He thought that this charm would guide him and be with him wherever he would go in life, as executive or airborne pilot, or traveling over seas at the helm of some shining bone-white yacht; he'd always have it with him, this charm that was his good fortune to obtain, and it would aid him in his travels, tucked safely away inside his pocket. He'd stare Luck in the eye and tell her that he had her in his strong possession, that she was under the firm grip of his control. His life was magic and he knew it: it was a feeling that haunted him, and that told him something big would come whispering to him in the wind. He was twelve; he'd lived and seen, and had known all the joys of childhood. Soon he'd be reborn a teenager. Yes, great things were coming.

9

THE PCJR

IT SEEMED that everyone had a computer, or was getting one—they were inescapable now. Raymond had to have one, and after much inner deliberation he settled on a new offering by IBM, the PCjr, a "family" model designed specifically for home use. They cost over a thousand dollars and he knew what his parents would be thinking: why not a Commodore for just a hundred, like everybody else? Wasn't it just as good? Here's a VIC-20, what's wrong with that? It's only forty dollars—and Timex has one that's even cheaper!

But Raymond's choice was the result of a studied decision, made only after elaborate research of the magazine advertisements and department-store circulars. He'd put up all available home computers for consideration, tried to be honest with himself, and now he pleaded his case to his parents. The choices went like this:

1. The Apple. It was supposed to be the best computer for "education," and Raymond knew that most hackers advocated it, but it was simply too expensive when you considered all the extras that were necessary to do it right: the plug-in card to give it color; the color monitor; the card to give you smaller characters on the screen; the dual disk drives for storage; extra memory chips to make the more advanced programs run.

All this equipment came from Apple, and was sold at a premium—so when everything was bought, the system would cost at least two thousand dollars, an unquestionable amount. It was consigned for the rich "academic" types, and best avoided. As the most expensive option, he very consciously brought it up first.

2. The Commodore 64. This was a toy, a cheap, vulgar machine for playing games, so you might as well just stay with your Atari. Hackers called it the Commode. It could be bought at K-mart—that was no place to purchase a computer! Raymond needed something powerful and serious, something formidable and strong. Commodes only had BASIC and their disk drives were famously slow.

3. The VIC-20. This was simply a less capable Commode. It had no disk drive, but stored its programs on cassettes—which he knew were even slower. It was outdated and entirely out of the question.

4. The Timex Sinclair. The Sinclair was the joke of the computer world, and worthless—there was no expandability and it didn't even have a real keyboard. Raymond told his parents when they asked that it was clearly a waste of money, at any price.

5. The TRS-80. Radio Shack's flagship home computer, the "Trash-80," wasn't even in color. It seemed vaguely shoddy, and the "computerized" font of its logo was distasteful to Raymond, preventing further investigation.

6. The IBM PC. This was the businessman's choice, and a solid, conservative option; he instinctively felt that out of all of them, the PC would last the longest—it'd be the wisest long-term investment. You could expand on it by plugging new cards into its chassis, therefore opening it up to new features as they became available, there was room inside to grow and explore. But the trouble was that it was simply boring: it could only draw with three pale colors, and its sound came from a tinny twenty-five cent speaker that beeped at varied frequencies. Although he disparaged video games, he was still dazzled by the sights and sounds of computer capability, and these limitations of the PC were irreconcilable with his expectations.

7. The IBM PCjr. Based on the PC, this new model was

meant for home users; to fill this task, IBM had given it a graphics mode with sixteen colors and an audio capability of playing up to three notes simultaneously, which they called "three-voice sound." This was about as good as home computers got, the magazines spoke well of it, and in the excitement of these promised capabilities any warnings or trade-offs didn't seem so bad: it had a slow microprocessor that wasn't exactly identical to the PC's. This deficiency seemed negligible to Raymond, since the PCjr was said to run "just about all" of the software available for the PC; besides, it came with double the amount of memory than a standard PC, or even an Apple.

All options clearly pointed to the PCjr. He stopped debating; the matter was settled in his mind. Raymond felt that he was being reasonable and wise: by this choice he'd save his parents from both having to take the most expensive option and from frittering their money on toys. It was from a reputable company—yes, it seemed to be the best choice. So could they please get it for him?

"We'll see," his mother said to him one afternoon in a passing confession that really meant, "Yes, but wait." When he persisted at this line, she'd only add, "Ask your father."

"No, *you* ask him," Raymond pleaded. He wasn't one to approach his father unnecessarily, particularly if it concerned matters of money. In the Valentine house, father and son were distant—it was his father's temper, that came out in bursts of violent cursing, that had initially frightened Raymond, but that emotion was now slowly turning over into the tides of resentment and loathing. With his sunken eyes, creased forehead, wan rounded head and the unhappy moustache he now wore, Raymond's father seemed to vaguely resemble Edgar Allan Poe in street clothes—but when his temper rose his wild eyes would glare with wordless animal rage.

"If you want it, you should ask him."

"Oh please, Mom, why can't you?"

Mother and son went round and round in dry circles of pleading and retort until finally the subject was broached with his father, who remained silent on the matter. Unearthly weeks stretched past where Raymond felt all of life moving beyond him. He pictured Erik on the boards, imagined some of his classmates even going online, saw them all conversing happily and didn't think that he'd ever be a part of it himself—the computer age was passing him by, the PCjr wasn't forthcoming, and even Christmas came and went away that year with a bundle of toys and books in its wake and the disappointment of no computer.

Yet it seemed like they were all getting computers—everybody had one now. Joey and Toby next door had gotten a Coleco ADAM late in December, as their parents' way to compensate for all the other children who were getting Christmas presents. The ADAM was a new, affordable system that the computer magazines had all viciously denigrated, and Raymond didn't know why—the excellent graphics on the Buck Rogers game it came with were colorful and three dimensional, and it had great sound; it even came with a printer that spat out your typings from a daisy-wheel cartridge in a steady rain of loud iron stampings, just like an electric typewriter. There were built-in joysticks. It connected to your television, so you didn't need to buy a special monitor.

But the Malvicinos were rough with theirs and the printer broke in days. The ADAM itself lasted barely another two weeks before it too had broken, and then was unceremoniously thrown into a dank corner of the basement, a heaping pile of plastic and wires laid to rest beyond the pantry full of canning jars.

Meanwhile, the PCjr grew in Raymond's mind.   He remained adamant. He continued to present his reasoned case to his parents and held firm to it. The PCjr was a part of his life—it *was* him. In the theatre of his mind, he already owned it.

The Valentines, as a family, grazed the aisles of Best Products in the dark-brick building outside the mall. It was their great After-Christmas Sale, and what products remained on the shelves all bore red tags with high markdowns. It drove Raymond's parents into a frenzy—they descended hard upon every object in the store with eagle-eyes, while Raymond broke away to look at all the offerings in the home computer and electronics section. It took him less than a minute to find a modem in an open bin on a bottom shelf. The box said it was fully "PC compatible," so he assumed it would work with the PCjr. It was a battery-powered grey plastic box that fit between the computer and the telephone line; you dialed the number of a board with your phone and then slid a switch on the modem to go online. Raymond brought it over to his parents.

"This is a modem for the PCjr," he quickly informed them. "You can use it to get much more power out of the computer. Everybody has one. This is the cheapest model. Can I have it?"

They bought it for him without comment—only a dark, resentful glare flashing out from his father—and at home Raymond carefully studied the booklets that it came with. The instructions, he thought, were alarmingly sparse. He didn't completely understand the process so he put it away, thinking that he'd just have to try it out whenever his computer came ... which happened unexpectedly, on the cold Sunday of New Year's Day, when his dreamy longings were finally matched by the pageantic doings of life: his father had ordered a PCjr from a computer store across town, and when they took it out of the box and wrappings in the living room, a room they weren't normally allowed to even enter, there was the acrid smell of the white IBM hardware; ripping open the protective plastic bag around the keyboard, Raymond's nose stung with the strong fumes, chemical yet clean. He figured that he'd be online within an hour, once he'd connected the modem and gotten his parents out of the way. It would be a year of twinkling things.

As they set it up in the living room to test it out, his mother raised the question, with some concern in her voice, of where in the house the computer would go—but Raymond already had plans that were non-negotiable: the core of his bedroom.

"Your *bed*room?" his mother balked in alarm, her face contorted at the thought. "*Oh,* no!"

Raymond wasn't expecting her sudden trepidation. "But Mom, where *else* can we have it? Besides, it's for me, anyway!"

Right now his father was just anxious to get it going, and had been pulling out wires and plugging them in without even looking at the "Quick Setup" guide that had come in the box; Raymond, on the other hand, wanted to take the careful route, and wasn't happy with his father's impatient assemblings: while the thousand-dollar system was being plugged together in a fast chaotic rush, Raymond was sitting in the background, calmly unfolding the instruction sheet and trying to concentrate on what it said. He had his modem out and was comparing the cable that it came with to a chart of the outlets in the back of the PCjr, and he couldn't find a match—the modem cable didn't seem to fit.

"Are you going to connect that thing to your computer?" his mother asked, looking over at him.

Raymond didn't answer. Reality was bumping into all of his fast dreamings: why couldn't he have a life that worked right? According to the manual, the PCjr had its own type of connector, which he didn't have—so there'd be no way to connect this modem to it. He was stuck here—he wouldn't be able to go online.

His father already had the monitor out on top of the buffet table, plugged into an outlet. It was a special display that could also be used as a television, and while the antenna was still inside its wrappings, his father had flicked it to life. A college football game came in fuzzy display, the burly players in helmets and white football pants running over the white-lined field, an outdoor game played under bright sunshine. His father played with the volume slide and there was the shrill sound of a referee whistle, the drone of a sports commentator chattering in his heated frenzy and the fuzzy grey noise of a crowded stadium in the background, of all those people and their motions, yells, and callings.

But it was bitter January, and in Roman Valley there were no leaves.

The bedroom was his sanctuary. The pine-doored bedroom, the walls of clear-sky blue, the wood trim that raced around the door and closet, the window overlooking all the ranches across the street, the second-storey bedroom in the front and middle of the house, it was his home; it held his heart. And despite his mother's protest, the PCjr was carried up there within hours.

After an impatient week of operating it on the tiny desk of his bedroom set, Raymond's father bought and installed a

wood-grain computer hutch and he gave Raymond an ergonomic chair that rolled on casters. Raymond had wanted it—this
was just like David Lightman in the movie—although his mother had warned him: "If you're gonna want a chair with wheels
like that, you can't have carpet. We'll have to take out the
carpet if you want that."

Raymond liked the flat red carpet whose ridged sections
made him think of brains and continents and pebbles, but he
decided to let it fall back into his childhood—it was torn right
out, and Raymond used the chair to glide quickly over the bare
hardwood floors. And there he spent all his time in front of the
new computer. He lived inside its world, in the land beyond
the windowed glass. Right away, he learned the magic of disks:
how they could hold much information and recall it perfectly
again at any time.

"This disk here," he said to Sally, waving the charcoal-
colored square in his hand, "can hold a *thousand* pages of a
book!" With air-blue eyes beneath her black bangs, Sally was
his enraptured five-year-old audience, and she quickly
agreed—who would ever need any more than that? Perhaps
in rare occurrences, yes, he conceded to reason that one may
need a second disk and switch between the two, but that was
for only the very largest references; for daily living, all one ever
needed was a single disk: a disk for living, a disk for life—an
incredible, economical, and wonderful disk!

Programs took more space on the disks than pages of text,
however, and as opportunities to copy software from friends
and contacts now came rushing in he had an acute need for
them. His father would drive him across town to a Comput-
erland store on the east side of Clifton to buy them, where for
twenty dollars they'd get a boxed, sealed pack of ten, and Raymond would label them carefully as he filled each one of them
up with programs. He neatly filed them, kept them stored away
in tidy boxes that were labeled on the edge. In his leisure he
developed a system of color-coding with a set of magic markers
that seemed to have floated up into his life only for that express
purpose.

He came to know the living pulse of the machine, which
threaded together to him over the course of many screen-dark

moments: the sharp blip when he flicked the switch to turn
it on, the low engine hum, the red blink of disk light and the
breathless pause before the disks would churn and grind, and
then the flash of screen in dainty flicker. He knew just how
long it took to warm the system up and get it going, he saw
it a hundred times, he knew exactly what it had to do. He
learned the grumbles of the disk drive, the revving sputter that
it made and then the steady clanking clack as it'd heave data to
the disk in massive plops; there was the red all-knowing eye of
the disk light when it was on and glowing warmly, the healthy
mumbling whir of the fans that was always present when the
machine was on, and the last fizzy plip that came when the
power was cut by flicking the black switch in the back corner of
the box, and then with a last long blady moan of airless fan the
machine went cold and quiet until he came back to it again.

He learned to recognize the error messages it gave whenever the drive door was left open, or when disks were unfor-
matted or had become corrupt; there was a mad rhythm to it:
the motor sounds, the red shines of the disk light, the pause
before a system prompt came back. He learned these rhythms
and came to know them well, to mimic them in his mind. The
error messages came as sing-songs when he read them on the
screen—in the choir of his mind he sang them out in somber
Gregorian chant: "Non-sys-tem disk or di-i-isk er-ror / Strike
an-eee key when reh-dee"—and then there was the quick curse
of those three words that spun out in his mind over and over
again, in an awful witch's cant, that message that would ask
forever, "Abort, retry, fail?—Abort, retry, fail?—Abort, retry,
fail?"

It came with two large manuals, hundreds of pages long,
on loose paper that was three-hole punched and tucked neatly
into slipcase boxes. He studied them. They retained the sharp,
clean smell of their manufacture, and Raymond loved this
paper-money odor; they made him feel studious, vaguely like
a smart, wealthy executive. One was for BASIC, and the other
was for the system utilities that controlled the floppy disks, the
"Disk Operating System," DOS. Raymond pronounced it "dee
oh ess" and thought that somehow there was hidden power
there, that by patiently mastering the secrets of this manual

he'd eventually harness the system. These manuals were serious, clearly for adult executives who sat in leather chairs at shiny desks. There was also an air of studied difficulty about them—he thought that one could spend a fruitful lifetime with them.

The PCjr came with a demonstration game, the manuals said, a special typing program that you could access by pressing a certain combination of keys. It made noises and there were graphics: a friendly little man dressed like a vaudeville character fell happily from the sky. You could make him move and he clicked his feet; he was always shouldered to the side. Raymond played with this for Sally, who carefully took the cheerful actions from that world behind the computer screen, watching it from the floor beside his chair with glee and laughter and brilliant fascination. She loved the antics of the little man.

He learned how to write programs to disk, and how to read them later. He typed in programs from *Compute!* magazine and he worked diligently every night at the expense of his homework, filling all the pages of his notebook; it brought his life a quiet joy.

Joey and Toby were excited about the new computer and they'd often come over, obediently leaving their tennis shoes in the foyer just inside the door to the garage, then rushing upstairs in their tube socks to observe Raymond's latest programs. Soon their parents got them a PCjr, too, and they'd trade programs—Raymond went over their house with his box of disks to show his latest work, and he'd see what they'd learned and done as well.

On one such night of playing at the PCjr in the Malvicino's basement, after they'd been bored by the games, the boys decided to enrich their knowledge of the system by going through the technical manuals that it came with. Raymond noticed that even here in the musty, malodorous basement of the Malvicino house these manuals had their smell. But unlike the neat copies Raymond had at home, theirs were already scuffed and soiled, blotted with stains and crumbs, and whole sections had been folded over. Some pages of the BASIC manual had already been ripped out of the binder.

They flipped through the DOS manual, which listed all the

commands that you could type to do things on the PCjr. Raymond already knew some of them: COPY would duplicate a file and the TYPE command would spew its contents to the screen; CLS would clear the screen of everything. They stopped at the entry for EDLIN, which said it was a line editor.

"What's a line editor?" Joey asked in pure, if friendly, bewilderment.

"I don't know."

"Lemme try," Raymond said, adventuresome. He took the helm of the machine, typing EDLIN at the command prompt; the system quickly and diligently loaded the program off the DOS disk with a slow flash of red light and a clinking whir. In a few moments a new and different type of prompt came up: EDLIN was waiting for their command. They scoured the manual for clues.

"Well, it says here that you can insert lines and write them to a file," Raymond said, and after some experimenting had entered a line of typing, and they saved it to another disk with a name of EDLIN.HAK.

The disk drive's red light lit up again, a slow-winking port light in a harbor. Raymond typed Q to quit out of EDLIN and back at the DOS prompt he typed DIR to list out a directory of files that were on the disk—and EDLIN.HAK was there. He spilled its contents to the screen, a single line of text:

```
WE ARE INSIDE EDLIN. WE ARE HACKING INTO A LINE
EDITOR!
```

"That's it, that's what you typed!"

All the boys smiled and the room rang out with the excited cheers of adolescence.

"So EDLIN's a way to type and save it to a disk!" Joey exclaimed.

"Yes!"

"Awesome!"

That was how their nights went. Each advance spurned another, as confidence and interest grew; they got better with EDLIN and the DOS tools. They learned how to use DEBUG to peer at the inner code of programs, and they figured out how to use it to change the text of the messages these programs displayed. Raymond changed the COMMAND.COM file on his boot disk so that instead of greeting him as "The IBM Personal Computer DOS," it'd now proclaim that it was "David Lightman's Homemade DOS"; this appeared every time he turned the computer on. There it was, it was a name, and it was him—this feat pleased him to no end. He was living like in books! A bold emotion rose high. Rivers surged and flooded warmly into deltas. Heavy breezes whipped against the willow trees. He sailed strongly over turgid seas.

When Raymond ventured out on neighborhood expeditions with the Malvicino boys they were now accompanied by the Malvicino's youngest brother Marty, a tiny side-stepping boy with yellow curls of close-cropped hair who took to tilting the oblong egg of his head as if it were top-heavy. The four boys would often spend all day together, and Raymond would some-times request permission to go on long bike trips across town, coming home when the rest of the Valentine family were al-ready seated down at dinner.

"Where's he been?" his mother snapped angrily.

"With Malveenos," his father flatly answered in a weary exhale of great effort. It irked Raymond when his father mis-pronounced their surname as the vulgar "Mall-*veen*-o"; Ray-mond tirelessly corrected him. Whenever Raymond heard their name, his mind sang out the melody it held, "Mal-vih-*cheen*-o."

The boys often went "exploring," a favorite game in which they'd venture out on bike in wide probes of the neighborhood. They'd patrol the side-streets and cul-de-sacs, along all the trim lawns and smooth curbs, and discuss the pressing matters of the day, steered by the mythos that falls into every childhood: who lived at that house, and at that—and what went on over there? They theorized, postulated, and expounded upon the "mean man," the "nice dog," the "bald guy," the "crazy lady."

Sometimes their presence in far, foreign outskirts would be detected, and they'd be chased by hostile kids who banded in packs and always had a sentry on duty, ready to round up the others. There'd be a distant holler and with the rude bellow of a Viking horn the enemy would descend quickly, in a vicious swarm. Raymond and the Malvicinos didn't know the names of any of these other kids, but they knew them all as mean, enemy soldiers. If they strayed too far into their territory, these rough, merciless faces would come bounding out of nowhere and go running after them. One of the boys would see them coming, and with a warning shout the group of them would quickly escape.

That summer they grew bold and spent hours venturing into this hostile territory, exploring the distant streets of the neighborhood, advancing slowly, carefully, noting every house and curb and curve along the way, and finally probing out toward the furthest street of the development—a long bent stretch where all the houses were the same familiar styles but somehow never with people out, like it was an abandoned model of suburbia, and which led across a concrete bridge over the highway to an area where an agglomeration of new office buildings now existed on one side of the road. On the other side was a barren area of dirt and scrub, a wasteland of several acres that eventually gave to the small dark forest that separated this open land from the highway. It was of great interest; there were a series of deep ditches running across the middle like long clawings in the barren earth, and here they happily simulated the battlefield trenches of World War I. Raymond somehow took to this land, considered it his own, and soon he gave the land a name: "The Ruts," named after this most prominent geologic feature of the many trenches that scarred its face. The name stuck and soon even the parents knew what it was:

"Where are you boys going?" Raymond's mother would ask, calling out from behind the open wedge of the front door, her voice strained with concern, as the band of the young explorers prepared to launch from the slope of their driveway in a squadron on their bikes.

"We're just going out to The Ruts."

"Be careful!"

"I will."

But the other side of the road held their interest, too. If The Ruts was their last bridge to a childhood playland, this other side was a new, wide-open vista into the adult world that they knew they'd eventually be part of. There were a series of modern office buildings here; the one closest to the road was an eight-story cube of green mirrored glass that seemed to tarnish like a set of antique silver spoons in the strong afternoon light, and other complexes existed further down an access road behind it—long, low structures like adobes of white clay, with thin slits of black-tinted windows, vaguely sinister. What went on there? What companies made this their home, and what did they do? Raymond pictured small laboratories for independent experimentation; he imagined new inventions, advances in industrial technology, being tested and developed; whatever happened there, it was part of an adult world he couldn't fully grasp. The front building had a sign identifying it as Williams Electric, which he knew as a company that manufactured appliances they had in all the stores—was this just the business office, or could this actually be the home to all their research, the place where these ubiquitous appliances were born? It seemed unlikely that Roman Valley hosted such an important part of the world. Why here? They speculated, driving their bikes in long round loops and circles through the parking lots on purple weekday evenings.

What marked their paths? What felt their visits? Who remembered, where saw, and when recorded? Why, and when would it be gone? There, the dry stretch of a bike skid—a long curved comet-smear to prove the path of a slow careen, a single moment left in time. Left for nothing but the laving rush of time. For what is time? Time throws away its loss, and here the rains would beat this mark away, no one else would live to know it, even the voyage long-forgotten by the voyagers who were gone to conquer other worlds. Why worlds? Where wends the final voyage? And what is time? No footprints and no paths, all of this will be unknown to all the outer world, and even all this outer world will sigh away in the scrimp and shake of deadened, weary and unfolded time. For that is time: a low, long whisper in the wind. Reaching out like the flailing arms of long-dead spectres comes this call of time, and here the heavy doleful rain will weep and fall, and there begins the washings of another year. The worlds of summer and of autumn were only tiny breaths away—and yet all of it was gone. The deepest worlds of winter now were gone, and in hot oozing thaws the green will come, in pokes and prods and the minutest finger-push, in breathing clouds and fulgent spires, there the crocus points and hidden wood-calls and the flash of speckled hides, with wet tires and thick muds will come the green, constantly the green, and with Pan-pipes tripping in the glade will come great the green and down will drop upon the earth a milky silken net in the heavy nascent faery-rush of spring. Through the seasons they will cycle and the winds will always call, the moons will shrink and grow, molting things will coarsen and bitter brittle things will fall away and finally die. New things will have been brought to earth, greatly then the green will grow, and without even this tiny memory of old time there will be a shift and cycle of the seasons' spin. Where goes? Who knows? What will ever mark it—or remember thus, suppose?

Winds howled in April with the purple soaking rains. Summer burned; there was a sclerose and scrimp of autumn and the winter was a dead and bony ghost. They were alone, the seasons haunted them, and something up there saw it all with soundless, blinkless eye.

A new fascinating hobby opened to them now as they pried into the adult world. On weekend afternoons out to The Ruts they began to gravitate toward the back dumpsters in the parking-lots of the offices across the road to excavate the week's discard of the businessmen: they pried open the iron side-hatch of a dumpster, reached for the many charcoal-colored plastic trash bags and piercing deep into their bulging sides they'd pull and rip them open, picking through their contents, checking out what rare and priceless treasures this company had so carelessly and freely thrown away.

They were still, even at their age, electrified by the quest for "robot parts," for finding the useful adult discards that would help them build vast mechanical wonders of technology, and its fever came to them again: they wondered if good, useful things could be found in the bags of this giant iron bin. Raymond hoped to find an adaptor for his modem. They ripped and dug, and in a moment Joey pulled out a collection of three-ring binders with hard vinyl-coated covers—with rosy apple-cheeks he proudly declared he'd use them in school next year. There were metal-scraps, screws and bolts, large plastic spools nearly empty of their thin wire, bags of office papers. They held these up one by one, like game-show prizes, and their faces were painted in the bulging roundness of an overwhelming glee. Raymond thought that it was somehow "advanced" to be doing this, to be making use of the throwaway remnants of the office world. He considered it a hobby.

And in a moment they hit gold: in a plastic garbage bag of office papers that Joey had torn open and was madly sifting through, pushing aside layers of paper stacks in waves, was now revealed the mother lode—a collection of computer disks! They spilled out of the bag, a happy cavalcade of flat coal-grey squares, and the boys grabbed madly. They also found a few of the very large disks for use on industrial computers, squares almost as big as placemats, which they also kept to have as "conversation pieces" in their bedrooms—they'd hang them on the walls and tell others of their exotic travels. There were nearly a dozen of the regular-sized floppy disks, and Joey passed them out to Raymond and Toby while Marty stood behind them, watching in his quiet, tilted way.

Raymond was fascinated by the promise. "I wonder what's on them!"

"Let's go see!"

Immediately they returned to the Malvicino house, dreaming of passwords and secret files, and once in the basement they inserted the disks into the PCjr one by one for examination. They did a DIR on each, to list the files that they held, to search through all the secrets.

Some of the disks didn't respond: they might've been corrupted, or formatted for a different system, or were simply blank. But on others there were gems of interest: program files, documents, files they couldn't make sense of—listings of raw data, tables to decipher—and on three of the disks were copies of the WordStar program.

"Hey, this is a word processor!" Raymond exclaimed, realizing what they'd found. He recognized the name. He'd read about it in the magazines.

None of the boys had any need for a word processor. None

of them had ever seen one before, and in fact they didn't know just exactly what such things were even used for—Raymond thought it vaguely had something to do with secretaries and dictation—but by their excitement, one would think it'd been the height of Christmas and they'd gotten all the toys they'd ever dreamed of. So they tried running WordStar from one of the disks, and saw the main screen blink into place with all its unfamiliar symbols and line of rules. They pressed the menu buttons and saw how to adjust margins and enter text.

"Wow, this could be pretty useful," Raymond quickly declared. WordStar was a big-name program, famous, something from the adult world and that which adults paid great sums of money for; and they the voyagers had gone into the dangers of the uncertain wild, had found it there and captured it—for free. It was a trophy, a sign they'd gone after life and conquered it and conscientious of this fact he now was gleeful; the raw emotion bubbled out and spilled. "It must be worth at least two hundred dollars!"

"Trashing" now became a favored pastime in their lives. Further expeditions out to see what treasures might be found in the office dumpsters were quickly arranged, they promised to make it a weekly routine, they thought the habit should be cultivated, perfected and applied to every place of business that they went to, dreams were made public—but difficulties soon arose. As the summer drew close the enemy kids were out in greater numbers, they had scouts who found them and brought on the full wrath of the pack; there was always the chance that they'd chase them back toward the long bridge over the highway, out to The Ruts and the office buildings, sealing them off from the only way home. And then it seemed like there was always a man in the front building now, even on the weekends. This made trashing impossible, for it meant the threat of police and the terrifying menace of the law.

The fast accumulation of these new threats, especially the man who came outside the door and yelled, marked the final end of their voyages into this foreign vista, the moment when it was washed away by the laving rush of time. On the cloudy Sunday when the boys made their final approach, they discovered that a chain and padlock had been secured around the dumpster door—and even the very moment they finished inspecting it and had decided to leave, the man saw them, appearing suddenly in the doorway again and shouting out the hard, wordless sputterings of a menacing adult.

Marty turned and shouted "Book!"—and with that cue all four of them jumped on their bicycles and with pedals spun at wild speed they careened out toward the bridge and over road and sidewalk and all those empty, indifferent lands to the ease and comfort and the safe harbor of home.

10

THE ONLINE KINGDOM

THROUGH THESE shady, luminescent days of Raymond's life, a hot desire had been raging—he had to get online. He needed to go there, to see that world, to connect to the computers that were out there.

He had a computer now, and a modem, but they didn't work together and for a time he secretly thought they'd never work, that his only hope was to convince his parents to buy him another, more expensive modem—but when paging through a computer catalog he learned that an adaptor was available to connect his modem cable to the PCjr. It wasn't cheap: at fifty dollars, it cost as much as the modem itself, and Raymond knew that for this added price he could've gotten a better modem to begin with.

At the kitchen table he explained this to his father while his mother was in the far reaches, clanking pans over the sink. "We need to get a part to connect my modem to the computer," he said, as calmly and quietly as he could, uttering his words in a meek and careful measured tone. His cheeks were full and smooth; his eyes, dark and sorrowful. He then humbly pushed the open catalog forward across the table, saying, "This is the one, this is the cheapest place to get it."

His father responded to this indirect request with a characteristic sputtered growl; he cursed beneath his breath, his dark eyes gleamed angrily, and any discussion that Raymond hoped for had been preempted. Raymond's father didn't know what his son was doing, nor did he care. Neither did his mother, who called out with half-interest from her perch across the room.

"What does he want now?"

His father snapped bitterly. "He says he needs a part for the computer!"

"Oh, doesn't he have enough already?"

His father sighed loudly and muttered out a faint cuss beneath his breath, and then everything in the room was whittled down to the steady sound of scrubbing that was coming from the sink. His parents didn't know what the modem was for, they had no idea about the boards, and for this Raymond was very glad.

Shouted, strident arguments between his parents were common now; they seemed to've always been part of the household air and the happy days of his early childhood were buried far beneath them, under many Phrygian moons. Raymond hated living there in that big and empty house in Roman Valley—he couldn't wait to connect out to the world, to extend his reach, to use the systems that were out there on the phone lines—to go far from his bedroom to some other secret place beyond.

But despite all his father's anger and hostilities, an order for the adaptor was quietly placed, and it was three fretful weeks before it arrived, appearing silently for Raymond on the kitchen table one day after his father had checked the mail. Raymond took it upstairs to his bedroom in a quick, bounding gallop and he connected it in an expert fervor.

He'd already connected the modem to the telephone that was now in his bedroom, and he'd also overcome other great hurdles: to go online, you had to run a modem program, a heartbreaking fact that Raymond had learned from study. He had none. He'd checked and re-checked his references, flipped through the manuals and when he saw a one-page listing for a simple modem program in his IBM BASIC manual, he'd typed it out and saved it to a disk. It had no options, no features, but it simply made the screen a window to what was out there on the line.

He'd also needed the number to a board, and only through a strike of brilliance did he think to try the phone book—which was where he'd gotten the number to the Clifton Connection.

Now Raymond ran his modem program and the screen went blank. He picked up the telephone and dialed the number of the board. After an easy, casual ring the distant modem answered the line. There was a second of silence and then came the screeching silver peal of the distant modem; he flicked the switch on his own modem and the telephone receiver was drained of life and the room was silent as the modems presumably screeched out their pealing cries together over the line.

He tapped ENTER on his keyboard a few times, as the BASIC manual suggested. His heart shimmered high with excitement, he waited several breathless seconds while the screen was completely blank except for the sleepy cursor in the upper-left corner—and he thought, "Will it even work? What happens now?"

He waited, and then he saw: the cursor awakened in a jerk and there was text being written across his screen, text from the distant board—it was scrolling in from far away and spilling right into his bedroom, and he read it in spurts of comprehension, words: "welcome," "to," "the"—he could almost hear it, a faint, light scraping as the cursor marched across the screen and left a track of pearl-white lettering behind it. The message from the remote system was drawn in slow wide sweeps of the cursor, line by line:

```
WELCOME TO THE CLIFTON CONNECTION
---------------------------------


NEW USERS TYPE "GUEST"

USERNAME:_
```

Raymond typed "GUEST." He went through a registration process and identified himself as DAVID LIGHTMAN, eager to see what lay beyond the doors.

"THIS IS DAVID LIGHTMAN," he eventually typed into a new message that he posted on the main forum, "AND I AM A HACKER!"

When he saw the message stream back upon his screen, he smiled in a secret glee. He was advancing outward, into the expanse of the wired world—and he called the number back immediately just to try it out: when he connected again, he proudly logged in with his brand-new username, and as the door swung open for him once again he was awestruck. He quickly disconnected, smiling uncontrollably with vainglorious pride at what he'd just accomplished.

"Wow, I really am a hacker now!" he thought, sitting in the ergonomic chair that he was rocking side-by-side upon his hardwood bedroom floor. "I have an account on a board as David Lightman—I'm a hacker!"

He knew that the Clifton Connection wasn't a hacker board, and when he called it up the next day there was a single response to his message, which was already being forgotten amid all the busy clatter and shuffle of the board. The words were brief and his heart cringed hard with embarrassment in that moment when he read it:

"You lamer! You must be thirteen!"

But no, that person was quite wrong: he was only twelve. And knowing this, his heart swelled outward with accomplishment and pride.

That summer Raymond spent most of his days on the telephone, in his room, at the computer. The boards of Clifton opened up to him, and it began a new set of days for Raymond, the BBS days—the days of calling other computers on the telephone and watching their data scroll across his screen, of reading the typings of others and then nervously sending his own words out to be judged by a hundred nameless sets of eyes; of staying up until long after midnight on a Saturday, calling systems; and of spending his evenings engaged in dialogue with people he only knew as names on his bedroom screen. But in their typings and their words he saw so many real and living faces, and he heard a thousand voices; it was a new land and they were joyful days of secret, soundless travel into these unknown cities.

He grew used to the sound of so many modem screams, and almost heard meaning from the pathetic cries of a computer's blind tongue as it came, predictably, that instant after he'd dialed and the line connected; he cruised the wide networks and roamed the dark abyss of all the gnarled, unspooled wires; he wandered on his way upon the circuits—and the world was like a dream.

His first friendly outpost was RailWorld, a local board for railroad enthusiasts. Unlike most boards, access was granted quickly; a new user could sign up and be able to post immediately. But not much ever happened there, it was an older crowd and the discussions were technical and quiet, and solely about the model railroad hobby: the trading of statistics, part numbers, catalogs, repair shops, lists and tables. But he came to know that board like a friend, and he memorized its number and would call it at all hours, and was strangely comforted by traversing its halls and pathways, knowing that he was reaching out and winding through the tunneled mazes of a computer in some distant room.

There were many other boards: Med-Line, an Apple board run by a medical student from a rented house somewhere on the edge of the Clifton Rock campus, and was geared toward the exchange of information concerning the practice of medicine, but Raymond somehow felt it too was a familiar place and he liked the fact that through his PCjr he could run commands on an Apple; the Highland Hide-a-Way, a musty board that was assembled on an IBM PC in an east-side basement and whose many discussions were lively and updated frequently; Clifton Network, run by a college professor, a board whose message bases seemed dull and quiet, smelling stuffily of leather-bound editions, dirty pipes, and waxed mahogany. He wrote his logins and passwords for these boards on a scrap sheet of paper that he kept carefully hidden in the drawer of his computer hutch.

Here on these Clifton outposts he pored over messages that others left, imagining the living personalities that made them; rarely he replied to them. Here on these boards he made his first postings; he fumbled and he turned red from embarrassment, was mocked and chided—but the thrill of exploration, of reaching out and extending through this window of the screen, bolstered his pride and pushed him onward.

There was the surprise and bolt of fear when he saw the name of Erik Drexel attributed as author of a post on Clifton Connection; Raymond had registered again under his own real name but now he was afraid to post, and he'd pause at the keyboard with sweaty palms, afraid of some kind of humiliation in front of Erik. His first predilection now, when calling a board, was to see if Erik was on it.

And he learned that all boards could be classified as a "type": there were software boards, dreary loading docks that were used for the steady trade of programs, and Raymond imagined all their sysops as dullards, as buck-toothed men who lived in the basements of their mothers' homes and who went around at midday in white short-sleeved shirts, bulky spectacles, and clunky dress shoes; there were hobbyist boards that were meant as forums and resource centers for advancing a particular hobby or endeavor; there were chat boards, where the purpose was discussion between the callers, who were usually older and made Raymond distinctly uncomfortable with all their adult gestures, jokings and concerns; and then there were the hacker boards—where codes were traded, tips and techniques were shared, everyone had handles, and the purpose was to spread the secret knowledge and the way. These were the type of boards that Raymond was interested in.

But the hacker boards were much more difficult to find, and they weren't as friendly as the other boards. He was intimidated—these were teen-agers, and if pushed they might get his home number and harass him, or even harass his parents. There were legends of coordinated gang attacks; one boy in Rockport had been assaulted by a group who tackled him and tied him to a telephone pole outside his school, and Raymond didn't want that. Even the numbers of these hacker boards were hard to come by, since they weren't usually listed on the respectable boards, but he knew that they were out there. After keeping a strong watch for them he found the number to Lucifer's Lair, an important hacker board he knew that Erik had been on and whose name he thought was awful and wrong. He attempted to log in as David Lightman but had to hang up on the system while filling out the new user registration form because it asked for either three references or "a deposit of useful info"; he had neither.

In excitement he began to mention all his travels through this world to Joey, and he showed him on a languid moment of a summer's day.

"What do you do on the boards, play games?"

"No, you can talk to people from all over!"

"Oh. Well can I see?"

Raymond gave a demonstration, connecting to RailWorld and then to the Med-Line. He explained what was happening on the screen while Joey patiently watched and nodded. He showed Joey how messages were posted, and how they remained visible on the board for any other caller to read.

"See, look at that," Raymond said energetically, and pointed to the screen where a line of text was written. "I did that," he blurted wildly, "that's me!"

Buy Joey didn't care to sift through all the words and postings—there was a hard barrier. Raymond knew that he couldn't tell him everything about hacking, phreaks, and codes—and that something in their friendship would always remain locked inside of the smaller corridors and candied valleys of childhood.

As they headed outside, Raymond's mother called out to him from the kitchen. "What are you doing on the computer all day long," she queried, in a tone of curiosity and worn complaint, "with the door closed?"

He walked past her, but didn't answer. The boys ran out to the blinding summer lawn.

11

RODENT

IT DIDN'T take long before Raymond tired of the boards that were within his easy reach—he'd had enough of listening in on the chit-chat of model train collectors and medical students. He wanted to go further, to find the hidden coves of all the hacker boards and take the position where he instinctively felt he rightly belonged: at the captain's table with the brigands, discussing all the secrets of the systems. And he realized that there was a great distant world out there of boards, the many hundred long-distance boards of all the nation. He'd found and recorded the names and numbers of these long-distance hack boards, and their allure, flirtatious and strong, obsessed him—they were waiting for him to call, so what he needed was a code. And a code would give him the "useful info" he needed to join Lucifer's Lair.

The hacker boards required special validation, and without any connections it was tough to get past that front door, with its iron bolts and guards; references were always required. So Raymond turned to Erik. He had no choice, and through his mother—who was delighted by the sudden request—he arranged for a Saturday afternoon meeting at Erik's house.

But Erik didn't want to use the computer then—he wanted to go swimming. Raymond didn't bring his trunks, so he watched in a chair at the edge of the pool while Erik and his older sister Emily—an athletic bone-legged girl whose eyes and hair were the exact caramel shade of a Tootsie roll—paddled a few leisurely laps in the shady cavern of their indoor swimming pool. It never seemed to end; they splashed and shouted with their plastic water-goggles on as Raymond breathed air that was suffused with chlorine. The water shimmered flittering reflections along the cedar walls and distant tiled ceiling, like silver fish scales or vast billowy netting, and then when they came out and Erik had finally changed into shorts, Raymond mentioned his PCjr and told Erik about its important features. "And I have a modem, too!"

"I know," said Erik casually, his hair still wet and in a glossy clamp upon his forehead, "I saw you post on Clifton Connection."

"Oh"—Raymond was scandalized to hear this observation about his life so casually revealed. As soon as he could, he brought up the subject of codes; Erik didn't seem to want to talk about it. Finally, Raymond asked outright: "Do you have any extra codes?"

"What do you mean?"

Erik looked perplexed, his dark eyebrows malposed like rearing serpents.

"I mean—I'm looking for codes," Raymond heard himself saying. "I was wondering if you had any extra ones."

"You mean you want me to give you a code?" Erik looked shocked that Raymond could ever suggest such a thing. A faint drib of water had fallen downward from his temple to the nob of his ear, leaving a shiny slug-trail in its wake.

"Yes."

"Hm," he said stiffly. "Well, I don't know if I should."

But he did. The code, a six-digit number, was for Metrotel. Erik gave him the local Metrotel access number, and explained how it worked: "Dial the access number, and when it answers you'll hear a humming sound. Enter the code, and then enter the area code and number you want to call. And *don't* give it out to anyone else!"

Carefully Raymond used the code that night, late, after his parents fell asleep in the cavernous darkness of their large bedroom down the hall. He'd dwelled on it all evening, planning it out, dreaming on it, waiting anxiously for the moment. Working stealthily he pulled open his drawer with the minutest tug, unfolded the paper, lifted the receiver with a stony careful rigidness, and then with precise but nervous pecks he dialed the number. It rang, something picked up with a careful click, and then there was the hum, a bright throaty greeting that was an open mouth waiting for him to feed it a code. He did—as soon as he pressed the first digit the humming stopped—and then he dialed the number of a board in Miami that he'd saved for this moment.

There was a silence, and then a windy rush came upon the wires, the sound of a great distance opening up—and then a distant ringing, positive but faint—he heard it answer with a slow mechanical click, like all the other boards, and then there was the modem scream on the line. Quietly he flicked his modem on and carefully tapped ENTER on the keyboard several times. Then with mouth agape and stellar eyes he watched the characters drawn slowly across the screen, an intricate banner welcoming him to Miami's famous Pyramid South: this was Florida that he was seeing on the screen! The banner, the login, this was coming from the white-hot sands of faraway Miami, and it was streaming into his bedroom right now, and it was free! Free! All of it was free! He was gleeful: he'd made a long-distance connection, on his own, with a code, untraced, in his bedroom, and he'd reached out to Miami in the night.

He registered as David Lightman and spent the evening browsing upon the screens and pages that he found. He called other boards across the land, hacker boards, picking them only for their name and location, relishing in the great new freedom that he had—he was reaching out all over! The boards, the innumerable boards he came to know, sang out at him in name and number, they were all within his grasp and there was so much excitement in all this delirious reaching-out and far-connecting—he now had a new freedom, the freedom to call any number in the nation that he liked. He'd call any board in the whole entire land. There was no fear of cost; it was all reachable to him; his travels were limited only by the mind. To where, to who? In his mind it came out like a floral ballad and it sang with sudden softness in his dreams. He made long-distance calls for pleasure, he ran around the world, he dialed randomly and listened.

Downstairs he'd commandeered the phone books and he kept them up inside his bedroom now, to the anger and annoyance of his parents; he ripped out the page that had a map of the United States showing all area codes, and he taped it to his computer hutch—he memorized the codes for major cities and was well on his way to learning them all, to dialing numbers in every one of them.

He tried to take the Valentines' new cordless phone, too, and was flatly denied; it was a novelty, working with a metal antenna that you extended from the top of the handset, like a walkie-talkie—this was a phone, but there was no cord! You could freely walk around most of the house with it; it seemed the future had arrived. There was mystery in it, too—a warning in the instruction manual about how the loud ringer could cause hearing loss if handled improperly made his mother immediately forbid the children to even use it, although eventually he finagled his way. But he didn't understand the warning, and thought it was just the horror of technology's stretch—that some sacrifice would have to be made to go there, to live without a cord.

He called Lucifer's Lair as David Lightman, and this time he completed the new user registration, providing the code as his "tribute of useful info."

When he called back in a day he saw that the sysop, Dr. Dialtone, had granted him access to the board's general message base, where he read Dr. Dialtone's brash and sometimes cruel comments toward all the local, lesser hackers—whose names he learned as they all came forward in a flurry of messages: Captain Chip, Pirate X, Micro Master, Linebreaker, Phone Wizzard. Some were named after the boyish interests of the age and time, plucked from Dungeons and Dragons or *The Hobbit* or *Star Trek*, from medieval themes to popular rock music references, punk and heavy metal, to the cult of science-fiction that so many hackers loved: the books of Heinlein, John Brunner's *The Shockwave Rider*, the movie *Silent Running*. The flavor of the time was reflected in the crowd of names: Lord Chumley,

Deth Knight, Space*Ace, The Programer [sic], Astro Man, The Stranger, Stam Bentley, Sir Mordan. Mental visions of the faces that lived behind these names rose up and were painted vividly in the theatre of his mind, it was an exciting all-star cast—and he was now a part of it.

Raymond spent days in the spell of the code. It took him far away from his quiet bedroom in the white colonial perched upon the corner of Barset Place and Sussex Drive in Roman Valley. Even with the door closed he saw the stifling atmosphere, the brand-new hutch, the dusty quiet of his shiny walnut bedroom set with its two sets of drawers and shelving connected by a desk, the little blue wastebasket beneath, the dresser near the door and, behind him, his little bed whose headboard had the matching walnut bars. The silent walls and the wood molding that lined along their bases, the open closet teeming with the detritus of his younger days—none of it had promise. He was stuck there and he had to leave. This is what the code brought.

Merrily he called out-of-state boards, announcing to any who would listen that he was hailing from Sohola. This usually granted him instant access, without having to give info or provide references at all—hacker boards loved having long-distance callers, and treated them as visiting dignitaries from afar. They'd quickly shuffle him to the back room and latch the outer door. There, he'd see all their secrets, be privy to their plans. He passed a weekend talking about the local climate with sysops from east and west and all around, from northern desolation on the plains to the humid plantations of the south. He ran in giant circles on the map, dialing numbers.

Sometimes he even dialed random distant numbers just to feel the reach, and he called all the places he could think of. One muggy, quiet Monday, on a gleeful whim, he telephoned IBM's headquarters in Boca Raton, Florida, where a friendly woman answered immediately: "Good afternoon, IBM, may I help you?"

"Yes," Raymond announced, in the most adult and business-like manner he could muster—his voice was on its way to changing, and prone to uncontrollable swings in timbre; he spoke slowly, from the back of his throat, to pry out the deepest, maturest tone his instrument was capable of making. "Uh, do you have a catalog I can send away for?"

The chirpy query of a faceless receptionist and switchboard operator quickly replied, "For what item, sir?"

"Uh, computer," he answered with a pause, thinking quickly, "software—"

"Is there a particular item of software?" helped the lady.

"Uh, no ... just ... *entertainment* software." Then he quickly added, "Made by IBM."

"Entertainment software?" she repeated this nicely, masking any sign of her emotions.

"Yes," Raymond answered stolidly, again in his most firm and businesslike manner, as if he were calling from his desk, in his luxurious office, a man of import, a man of many deals and official manners. He tapped the rich mahogany as he waited for the operator's answer.

It came preceded by a moment of silent contemplation. "All right," she said suggestively, "would this be for the Engineering and Scientific catalog?"

"Uh, yeah!" A squeak in his voice escaped in this happy affirmation.

"Would you like to purchase the Engineering and Scientific catalog for $10.95?"

Suddenly he felt troubled—he was getting himself into something big. Such expense, for merely a *catalog*—why, it would require a credit card!

"Uh," he stalled again, "I'll call back in a little bit." His finger jumped down on the hook of the receiver, disconnecting them forever.

But even with such stumblings, it was joyful; he knew the voice of the lady on the telephone error messages, and he learned all of the things she ever said; he called numbers to hear the sound of distant faceless voices, he called out of curiosity, and with vibrant imagination—he pretended to be radio station and TV program hosts with congratulatory calls to contest winners; he pretended to be a businessman looking for important "contacts" to partner with; he called for interviews, and made rambling senseless pranks, and sometimes he honestly admitted to the strange voices that he was only reaching out, madly, desperately, that he just wanted to be friends, to know them, to reach and connect and find.

"You have the wrong number," curtly came a voice, with a living personality but completely disembodied and detached from the physical place that Raymond now was sitting at. This answer, said in such a manner, would always come to him in response to some meaningless inquiry he made: "Well, then, is James there?"

"No, wrong number."

"Jane?"

"Wrong number."

"Okay, is Josie there?"

"No."

"Jeffrey?"

"No."

"George?"

"*No!*"

"Is *anybody* there?"

"Wrong number!" the male voice yelped, desperately, irate and exasperated, and the connection snapped away with a click. In thirty seconds he pulled up another voice, from another section of the North American continent—this time a lively woman of indeterminate but fairly middle age.

"Hello there!"

It startled her. "Hello?"

He was smiling brightly. "Who's this?"

"Jackie."

"Oh, *hi!*"—Raymond spoke heavily, with a welcome warm relief, as if he knew and spoke with Jackie all the time.

"Who's this?"

"Your frie-e-end," he answered cheerily and drawn out in a long whine. He wanted to talk, wanted to reach out, to know her. Could he ever be friends with Jackie forever?

"*Who!*" This was a demand.

"Guess." Raymond couldn't elaborate—he realized that he didn't know the answer himself.

"I can't hear, there's too much static."

"Well, *guess!*" This plead is almost a desperate cry, spoken in the voice of a young boy—one who was connecting out, reaching now with fingers many miles long and stretching out to satellites, and extending down upon the spinning globe, seeking for an answer in the whispered wind, a tiny voice that was calling out and wanting to be heard.

All through the following week Raymond kept inside his bedroom, with the door closed, enjoying his reach, calling hacker boards and distant numbers with the code. Then the next weekend came and he called again, and abruptly on Monday afternoon there was a roadblock in his progress: he tried to dial Pyramid South, hoping to catch up with any new discussions there, and he received an error signal, a fast-busy; he tried again, and the same thing happened. It then happened with other numbers. His confused shock melted past when the realization lowered, like when witnessing an evening shade being drawn for the night, and the far amber light was gone: the code had gone bad.

Until he could get more codes, he was stuck right there in Clifton, with all the local boards, all of which he'd long grown bored with. He now called them all in rapid succession, reading the few new postings that'd been made since earlier in the week. But when he logged into Clifton Connection, a notice said he had a private message; he checked and saw that it was from Erik: "I see you gave my code to Lucifer's Lair! Nice going. I knew I shouldn't have given it to you. Everyone is calling David Lightman a rodent!"

Raymond was mortified; his hands fluttered in a quick tremble. He didn't reply to Erik but instead with his cold, heavy-shaking hand he typed Q to exit the message reader and then X to log off the board. It asked him to confirm and with a sick, sinking feeling now somewhere in the dark chambers of his middle he found himself stabbing the Y key.

He hung up the modem and then quickly telephoned Lucifer's Lair—busy—and the feeling of dread in him subsided, slightly, while he bided his time with quick visits to Med-Line and RailWorld ... but when he tried Lucifer's Lair a half hour later and connected, the feeling returned and dizzily intensified when he tried to log in as David Lightman and received an "ACCESS DENIED" message shouting back at him, and then the distant modem dropped the line—Dr. Dialtone had banned him, completely thrown him off the board!

His face flushed, fingers trembling hard against his will, he flicked the modem off, and with the press of two more keys he exited the modem program so that the PCjr now drew the crystal emptiness of a blank screen. Quietly and soundlessly he stood up, pulled the green-metal charm from his right pocket, took it in his hand and tossed it carefully into the little blue wastebasket.

12

THE WANDERER

RAYMOND SPENT the next days in a miserable gloom. He couldn't fight back; he'd have to disappear. And then? He wasn't done with this world—he couldn't keep away from it. But what to do? David Lightman's reputation was destroyed.

He'd have to find a new persona, that was it. He'd go forth again and nobody would know that it was him. He wouldn't tell anyone about it, and any reputation that he might gain would be one that he would earn.

Yes, he'd start again: the thought was palatable because there was hope in it, and he realized that David Lightman didn't represent him, anyway—in frank dialogues with himself he could admit with blunt, blue honesty that he was tiring of it. After all, *everybody* was David Lightman—he saw that there was one in almost every area code. It was a beginner's handle, and in fact he'd been ridiculed for it more than once in his long month on the boards. "Oh, another twelve-year-old who just saw *WarGames*!" had come the cries.

Besides, he told himself, it was a name of some other character, and not unique to him: no more should he use the name of someone else, but he needed something that would fully represent him and honestly depict him for who he was—a name that had the inimitable stamp of his own being. What would it be?

This question consumed his thoughts through all his waking hours—he thought about it during dinner, and while laying in his bed in the night, and in the early shadows of the morning; it was inconsumable. It'd have to be something good.

In his bedroom with the door closed he sifted through a hundred ideas, some that made him laugh aloud while others were stillborn or distant and remote.

And he'd also need a code. Determined to hunt for one himself, he removed his notebook from the drawer and he wrote down a random six-digit number: 658300. He lifted the handset of his telephone and carefully dialed Metrotel and used that number as a code. Quickly then he dialed the number to a distant board, and when the fast-busy error tone came to tell him that the code was no good, he flashed the receiver to disconnect the line. At the dial tone he quickly dialed Metrotel again, and this time he tried 658301 and then the same number of the board—and when that too brought an error, he hung up and quickly tried the next code, and then the next.

As his fingers mechanically dialed, his mind was occupied in an airy space, gliding in a happy frenetic emotion that he was living like a secret agent in a new adventuresome lifestyle. The danger of being caught was great, so no one could ever know.

Once many minutes of his dialing had gone by and almost fifty codes had been tried, his ecstatic mood began to wane and deep fears clouded his composure; he was turning gray with doubt, wondering whether he was dialing it correctly and whether he'd even had the proper number of digits for the code. What if the number for this board was somehow wrong, and no working code would ever get to it? Doubts glided smoothly over the placid surface of his temperament, a swarm of dark, ugly forms that he could neither avoid nor control—meanwhile he continued to try the many codes.

Not long after he'd gone through over a hundred of them, when a tiresome hour's worth of work had passed and his fingers were sore and bitter-numb, there was a pause of breathless silence after he'd dialed the board's number—and then with a quick wink of satellite and a rain of static coming somewhere beyond Sohola he heard the loud ringing of the number, and a victorious horn-note flooded over him, shouted yes; he heard a second ring and then a click as the line picked up and the distant modem was wanging in his ear—he'd gotten there, he'd found a working code!

He carefully wrote the code down in his notebook. He could stop there but the victory had renewed his stores of patience so he continued at it, and in two hours' time he'd philosophized that code hunting was something like fishing, and that there were good spots as well as bad spots in the wild mass of numbers, and that if you were unlucky enough to start near the beginning of a bad spot you'd be needlessly dialing for a long time before ever getting a code, but that a good spot would yield several clustered together in a close tight space. It just took persistence and careful dialing. In this time he found three codes that he neatly recorded in a column. He didn't label them; should his notebook ever be discovered, he reasoned, he'd dumbly shrug them off—they were just numbers.

He still needed a new handle. He thought of all the different "worlds" he knew and how he flittered quickly through them, always looking, always watching, waiting, reaching, never really staying to be a part of them. But he had to see and know them; that was his way. He had a fever to reach out and to know—that was what what his world was all about. But what would be the handle?

He admonished himself: "Think! Think!"

He thought. Yes, and he'd chased through the circuits, wandered all the wires; he'd looked and sought, and in far lonely places he had seen.

Long and hard he thought that day on his swivel chair at the computer hutch, while he scanned through blocks of random numbers in faraway and distant area codes. He made a chart in his notebook for the numbers and took notes on all his findings.

Suddenly he turned, looking out the window to the street below and the roofs on all the boxy ranches that were like little caps of brown and gray, the homes themselves were shrunken heads laid out on the fine sloped greenery of their lawns, and he thought of his life there in that place he wished to leave. He wished to go—somewhere, but he knew not where. There was a whisper far away along a twisted river-bend.

"What am I doing?" he said aloud, sitting with the telephone handset in his ear and the base of the phone in his lap. He put an index finger on the release and let it go; with the new, fresh dial tone he quickly dialed the local access number, and when that answered he dialed the code that he'd already memorized, and then another number in a long-distance sequence he was scanning—to who knows where he would go. "I'm only wandering," he answered dreamily to himself.

Wandering! But wasn't there a way in wandering? He freely wandered, consigned to no one group; he walked upon the many wires, he was out among but never *with* the others, always an observer, trying to get the feel of it, trying to grasp it all, to see as they saw and think as they thought and experience all areas and aspects of the wild greater world—and he was like this with *everything* in life, he knew inside his heart of hearts that he was so, that it was a base component of his character, this feeling of having to take it all in, to see and experience everything in the world and cruise over every inch of it, live it all out to the utter fullest—that unspoken fever of wanting and needing to know all that could be known, and of remembering the shapeless, weightless, immeasurable moments and holding them as the most treasured possessions of the waking soul: no downloads interested him as much as connecting to the thousand modem carriers, to making a million connections, and to finding what was on the other side.

He cared more about reaching out and seeing, pushing through the dark abyss of time, reaching out among the wires and the airwaves, speeding through the night over the highways and the sleeping farm-fields, peeking through all the windows of every suburb, and exploring every hall and tunnel of the city. He saw how in his life he was really after a much greater hack, not merely access on these boards but a connection that was well above all these brief contacts, and this wandering was a part of it.

"*Wan*dering," he said aloud, in half-whispers to the blue-walled room. "That's what I'm doing here, I'm *wan*dering!"

And then the name that he would take sang out to him: it came suddenly and called, and with sudden shock it hit him with all the rectitude and power of its truth and inevitability, the idea flowed its sparks through all his veins and he became it: he would be The Wanderer!

He spoke the name aloud as if in awe: "The Wander-er ... The *Wan*derer! That's who I am, I'm the Wanderer!"

He began dialing the long-distance boards that he knew and liked, and on each one he registered again with his new handle. He carefully set up a new page in his notebook to keep his passwords. When he was required to leave a "deposit of info," he gave one of the codes, one that he'd carefully marked in his notebook as a "giveaway"—he decided that he wouldn't ever use that one for himself. He was careful and he was learning and there was somewhere far to go. He had to wander now and know the wide expanses—they'd take him to the far and final end.

13

THIRTEEN

IT WAS THE summer of the Olympics, and for Raymond it was a time of joyful calling, of haunting all the boards and learning. When school let out he'd begun to spend long days indoors at his computer, soaking in the bliss of the screen, living on all the nation's boards: there were the local boards he called each day and was overly familiar with, and hacker boards with all their hushed discussions and secret tradings, and the excitement of distant boards, operating from far across the nation—come July, before the first clumsy rattles of the tree-bound cicadas, he could identify the names of all the callers and would associate the patterns of their talk with the geographic location of the boards they posted on, feeling that he'd gained something, some concrete knowledge of the outer world.

Soon even August had passed beyond its sweltered middle and Raymond's thirteenth birthday came. This meant a visit from the Kristos family—Stephen and Teddy and their parents—and together the two families celebrated in the backyard summer night; after the cook-out dinner and the Dairy Queen ice cream cake the clear evening came upon them, which was always a surprise that harbored a far and heavy sadness: the day was done, darkness had folded over, and then when it could be constrained no further his mother made the night official with the audible flicking-on of the back light—and with the fluttering moths they sat out on the Valentines' open patio beneath a wrinkled tapestry of faint and distant pearls. In this hour it seemed to Raymond that all of life was one vast treasure cache—and that like those stars it was out there in plain sight, so that if only he'd be able to reach and scoop it up, he'd be holding all the heavens for just one instant.

Raymond's parents had bought him a boom box in what he knew was a gigantic stride towards becoming a teenager. It'd been a welcome surprise that morning, waiting for him out on the wooden game table in the family room, unwrapped; it seemed to impress his little sister, but he also felt an embarrassment and shame to acknowledge that he was gaining interest in such teenage pastimes as listening to pop music—it meant that he was leaving childhood behind.

The Kristos family had given him a night-blue Izod polo, still smelling like the mall, one of those short-sleeved shirts with the little red-mouthed alligator sewn at the left breast, its tail curled happily; and now he was uncovering a small, hard thing—when he pulled away the blue and teal "Happy Birthday!" wrapping paper and saw the fat red lettering on the spine, he knew it was a cassette tape. It was *Born in the USA*, the Bruce Springsteen album. Raymond already knew the title song—it played on every radio, and blared in short spurts from the television, and was this year's anthem of a happy America—and the album cover where Springsteen in his denim was facing off to the American flag appeared everywhere you looked; it seemed to be printed on everything. But never were such things in Raymond's possession; until now rock and roll, the teenage culture of the land, was only something he glanced at privately, or took in with fast, furtive gulps while wearing a studied mask of disinterest. So having to acknowledge this interest in rock bands and popular music in front of his parents and other adults now for the first time gave him feelings of terror and dread and distant loss—it came with a kind of sadness that he was already aware of in life. Couldn't he just advance to adulthood instantly, and without these thousand little clumsy pains? Or couldn't they just slow it down somehow, postpone it? Did he have to become a teenager right this instant, and did they have to give him this right here, in the oily light of the back patio, so far below the cool glade of stars? His ears burned while he gave an embarrassed thank you, manufacturing an eager spark of excitement while masking his true shame and sorrow, and he set the tape down upon the picnic table as quickly as he could.

They sat for a while longer amid the scattered wrappings and cups and empty plates, where the tape stuck out to Raymond like a spotlight had been pointing at it, while their shadows twisted and mingled and occasionally were zapped by sharp beams from the porch light. The boys were holding a conversation of their own that was being conducted adjacent to the talk of the adults. Suddenly the boys' topic shifted to music and Raymond tensed, listening with painful strain for it to end, as the Kristos boys loudly informed him about the radio stations that they now listened to, the bands they liked.

"Don't you want to play your tape?" Raymond's mother cut in with what was nearly a sloppy holler, to his great irritation—for surely she realized this was a first, but around the others she acted as if it all were nothing. Raymond knew he'd come into this life alone.

He sat quiet, his chest stiff and iron-tense. He knew that they were changing now, him and the Kristos boys; he knew that it wasn't like last year, that it was somehow different, that even the sky and the ground had changed. At Raymond's instigation the boys rose to wander the yard, away from the harsh pointings of the back light. Out on the lawn with the stars thickly spread above them, the adult world seemed far off and small. The long bladed grass, black in the dark, poked at the sides of their tennis shoes like the spindly hide of some big creature. They huddled together in a group to discuss and formulate a plan for the rest of the evening—they still had a few hours before the Kristos family would be leaving. And then suddenly the oldest, Stephen, blurted out happily, "Let's go listen to the tape while we use the computer!"

So they broke from the huddle and in a fast stampede they bounded to the house, through the sliding patio door, past the dazed wide eyes of Raymond's little sister, and up to his bedroom where that afternoon he'd placed his new boom box on the top shelf of his computer hutch. On the way up Raymond had quickly grabbed the tape, and now they listened to it while Raymond gave them a tour of the boards. With the bedroom door closed and the space of the room overbrimming with the burbling and wailing of "Dancing in the Dark," Raymond introduced the online world he wandered. He showed them the boards and all the messages and communications that were happening out there, and he explained the whole mythology of it to them, telling them how what hackers did went on in secret, like this, over the wires.

They were awed by it all—they were even impressed with the dull silence of RailWorld, the local board where model train collectors gathered; they'd never seen the modem world before. Raymond showed them the Med-Line next—the board run on an Apple by a med student at an east-side university—and as Raymond commentated, they read the threads of messages it contained, the words of other people's posts tacked together in long scrolls, and they saw revealed to them the debates and conversations of adults in their twenties that were now unfolding for them from this hidden world.

Minutes later, filled with carefree excitement, Raymond showed them how he accessed the long-distance hacker boards. He called one with a serene casualness and logged in as The Wanderer.

"Wanderer?"   Stephen asked, in a tone that Raymond couldn't tell was confusion or disapproval. The Kristos boys didn't know about handles. Raymond didn't answer, but coyly smiled and with emboldened fingers he continued to type, sitting in the master's chair before the screen. "You don't reveal your true identity in the hacker world," he finally said, slyly hinting at all the intrigue to be found there.

Then he added in an informative voice that was muttered low, as if it'd been tempered first with some kind of primeval shame, "This is my new handle—I just picked it the other day. For a long time I used to be known as David Lightman, that's the name of the main character in *WarGames*."

"The movie about the kid who's a computer hacker," Teddy brightly answered in a speedy, energetic mouthful. His voice was changing now, and to Raymond it seemed like his child's voice of last year had been toasted a reedy umber. "It's where he breaks into the Pentagon."

Raymond turned sharply over toward him. "Yeah."

He couldn't resist showing them his inner secrets—but somehow he couldn't look them in their eyes when he did. He pointed at all the handles on the screen with gleeful familiarity and explained to them who all these characters were.

"That guy's a famous hacker—he's known all over the country!" he said at one, bright happiness painted on his face. "Wow, I can't believe he posted here tonight, right here on a board I'm on! This is really something!"

And so he went on. In a fever to impart everything, Raymond showed them board after board, telling them where each one was, geographically—this was on the Hudson Valley in New York state, here were elite outposts in Las Vegas, Nevada and Sacramento, California, this secret hollow was just beyond the waterfall at Pigeon Falls, Minnesota, and of course here was a classic hacker board, one of the most famous in the nation, and it rose from the grand swelter of Miami.

It was a hidden world, the boys were awed by it—and after the Bruce Springsteen tape ran out on both sides and the title track had been replayed a second time, they tried the radio dial, and traded knowledge about the stations that they were familiar with, and attempted to find "hidden" stations, which could only be picked up if the antenna was held a certain way. They hoped for something, a mystery station—for this too was a place of lost worlds—and in scanning they found college stations, and public stations, and they tried the flat antiquity of the AM band, and all of it sounded good to them because they were young, the night was new, and they were exploring.

The Kristos family had been around forever in Raymond's life, but it seemed like in recent years the boys had seen each other less, and Raymond had been conscious of the wide months that spaced their visits. He wanted to share all of his online world with them, he wanted to keep reaching out with them, and as they were all growing up and getting close to the days of high school he wished he knew them better and saw them much more often; he fantasized hopefully that if the boys got a modem they might chat together after school on it, and form tighter bonds over the hard distance that stretched between their homes. Then they could call the boards, and Raymond would show them the way. But the fantasy would abruptly shatter when he realized that he had different personalities on each board, and they'd have to see that: he suddenly wasn't sure if he wanted the Kristos boys to see what he was like among these other crowds—they might not mix cleanly with the rougher teens who were on some of the boards, the troublesome deviants, streetwise hoodlums, and those who cussed and were crude. For Raymond, the boards were a place where he went to experience the great range of life that was out there, and to experiment among it all, to shift and change and cast the personality and character most fitting for the realities of the crowd that was around him at some moment, to seek a way and find a home of his own belonging; the Kristos boys, on the other hand, didn't need to seek or find—they were the same everywhere they went. They were solid and unchanging, like firm rocks, and they'd undoubtedly project that self-same image onto all the boards they called. He couldn't see them thriving there, in the modem land; they wouldn't survive.

This growing fissure between their lives was plainly demonstrated in a week's time when his mother confronted him about that birthday evening: "I just got off the phone with Mrs. Kristos," she said quickly, and with what Raymond thought was a strange neutrality, "and she told me about how you talk to people on your computer."

There was a shrill lash on Raymond's heart and he shrunk away in cold, tongueless horror. They'd told their mother! They told her everything, informing her about the entire incident: "Raymond calls up bulletin boards with his modem and uses a fake name to talk to other people!"—"Raymond makes long-distance calls, he calls California with the computer and doesn't have to pay for it!"—"Raymond talks to hackers on his computer, they're older teenagers, and they talk about breaking into computer systems!"

Sadly, Raymond knew that as the childhood bond between himself and the Kristos boys stretched into adolescence, it was beginning to snap apart. He felt a sharp twinge of shameful regret that later returned, as if on cue, whenever a stray thought of them came bounding onto the stage of his mind.

In their school and hometown the Kristos boys were involved in clubs and activities, they were part of church groups, they played soccer, and maintained a set of regular chores—their lives were full of regimented duty. Raymond had none of that, and wistfully he admired them and wished he had a life like them—it was like a life from books.

The Kristos boys' soccer team took them well past Roman Valley to the other suburbs that ringed the downtown, and this past spring it'd taken them on a ten-day trip to Europe. When it was first announced that they were going, the idea had seemed like a scary ordeal to Raymond, to go that far away and be gone for a bulk of time. He knew they were different from him in fundamental ways; they'd approached it gleefully, and when they came back they told him about the experience in ecstatic sputters: Stephen recounted how they'd been up in the flowered meadows of the Swiss Alps, where the land was richly green, and yet the bulky, ragged mountains of rock grazed dreamily all around them. There were deep cool valleys, and people lived in quaint chalets with chafed timbering and scalloped bargeboard, gazing out amid the balustraded walks and those curling streets that were all cobbled nubs of rounded stone. It was a land of well-swept paths and bright flowers, of beer and pungent cheeses, and there was always song; men in felt green caps would yodel, and their voices would be carried down the hills, over flowered valleys, and then would greet them shinily again from the cold hard face of distant, stony mountains. Stephen related gleefully, and with a sanguine warmth in his face, about how this one man had given them a demonstration of a long wooden pipe that made a low flutey note: it was mounted on the grass, and extended for yards down a stiff green slope above a meadow, and they stood at the top with him while he blew a sharp lungful into it and they heard it echo out among all the cracks and dunks of the land. It was carried up to the silk-strung clouds, where it was enveloped and finally stopped and everything was quiet. Breathlessly they watched the slow-drifting clouds leave their cold shadowed touch upon far-strung slopes, and they saw the windswept flow of fields with little flowers pecking out like weeds, the man smiled broadly, they breathed—and then a moment later, coming down the blank face of the mountains, was the distant woody echo of the pipe-note he had played.

Raymond was thirteen years old—and not allowed to go on such trips. They were not familiar shapes in the hard-woven patterns of his life. They emblemized a kind of life that he knew he wouldn't have, and because of it he felt that the Kristoses' present destiny was more experienced and full and stable than his could ever be; where he stretched and tilted, they kept a wholesome balance. He wished he could be like them, that he could live in an older house like theirs, set in an established neighborhood where he might walk to his school in the long orange light of morning, just as they did every day. There was something old-fashioned, all-American, and somehow very right about the life that they were living, and it was entirely out of Raymond's reach. Roman Valley wasn't like their hometown of Dover at all: here it was all much newer, and the houses were bigger, but he knew it was somehow dingier, emptier, less connected to the past—and with less to give the future. Even on family visits here the Kristos boys looked like temporary insertions, starkly out of place. He wished he could live by them, grow up closer together with them, have a life like theirs, but none of that was to be—he just couldn't, he didn't have a world like theirs to live in. He had to make his own world. And although he'd tried, now he knew that he couldn't share this hidden, manufactured world with the Kristos boys—he couldn't share it with anyone. It was his own world, part of his inner life, and it had to be his own unspoken secret—there was no one he could ever tell.

And so thirteen years old, he played alone: he dove into crystalline and soundless waters of his own making; he jumped and vaulted determinedly, with the hope of eternal pyrrhic victories; and as the last great ledge of eighth grade approached his adolescent life that autumn he sprinted far, in the world he'd come to haunt, alone, on the computer.

14

GROUPS AND BOXES

WHEN EIGHTH grade began it seemed that every competent child whose family was of able means now had a home computer, or was said to be getting one—even the athletes. Raymond figured that most of these new owners were negligent operators, but at least their parents knew that it was important equipment for them to have.

There was a popular Irish girl in his class whom he never really spoke to, but when he discovered that she had a PCjr it gave them reason to chat—she sat in front of Raymond and would turn sideways with a delicate arm on the back of her chair, and while he was helplessly captivated by the lucid, living waters of her eyes she'd tell him about their cartridges and equipment—"My dad bought the extra disk drive and memory add-on," she muttered once with wild-cherry breath—and they'd exchange this information in passionate whispers, developing a slow correspondence between classes.

Raymond discovered that to his surprise and bewilderment he had the ability and effect of a top-caliber salesman; everyone around him seemed to take his strong advice concerning home computers, especially the adults. It seemed that he'd become the unquestionable authority, and the adults banked on his view; whenever the topic of computers came up, they consulted him. He knew that he'd taken on the role of guru. One night his mother even put him on the telephone to talk to Mr. Kristos about it—and Raymond lay awake in bed that night in a gleeful incredulity, thinking to himself, "Ah, but what if I'm all wrong?"

On Raymond's word alone Jim Alpes had gotten a PCjr, and at Christmas a new PCjr came for the Kristos boys as a result of his telephone consultation. Mr. Malvicino brought home a modem for his kids that week. Joey and Toby registered on Clifton Connection right away but after a few calls and brief exchanges on the public boards where they'd used sentence fragments typed in all upper-case letters, their modem was relegated solely to calling up the library's computer system to request books and records out of the new electronic catalog. Joey also had a fantasy that he obsessed over: "Maybe in high school we can turn in our homework over it!"

The modem was becoming an everyday concept. Now all kinds of people were beginning to utter the word and even hold an idea of what it meant—even Jim Alpes got one for his PCjr, a fast new Hayes. "Yes," Raymond thought when he'd heard the news, "there's still time for Jim to get caught up, the history of the online world hasn't been entirely written yet, there's surely time for one more, yes"—and to his strange delight, he saw that Erik wasn't calling any of the boards.

Jim Alpes knew that Raymond was The Wanderer. He was one of the only ones who knew. They were close friends at school and spent much time together now; Jim filled most of the compartments in Raymond's life—together they could talk about almost any subject that graced his mind, and with mutual passions for all the boyish outdoor pastimes of camping and fishing and biking they found many activities to pass their days together; the only negative zone in their friendship was around the topic of literature—Jim didn't read books and they didn't discuss the unseen land that Raymond was reaching after. But together they'd travel the streets of their neighborhoods on their ten-speeds, they explored all the strip malls of Roman Valley and the neighboring Alva with its vast suburban grid, and they often passed long hours at Alvatown Mall—like on the first bright Saturday early that spring when Jim's mother had dropped them off by the entrance to the food court with its curved row of illuminated signs glaring from the inside. Once they passed the double sets of glass doors, the air smelled heavily of sourdough and caramel.

"Maybe we can get lunch here at Athens Gyro," Jim suggested right as they came into the bustling, long-shadowed cavern of the mall.

The gyro stand had become a favorite of theirs. "Sounds good to me!"

Jim smiled. "You know, whenever I tell the Greek guy I want a 'gye-ro,' he says 'yih-ro.' But whenever I pronounce it 'yih-ro,' he calls it a 'gye-ro'!"

They laughed happily.

When Jim was younger he'd looked remarkably elfin, a short boy with cheeks feathered in a rosiness that never faded, and he'd had a cowlick; but now in the culminating heights of junior high his inner clock had gonged pubescence loudly: his body spurted upward against the low drag of gravity, the cowlick was almost gone, and his face looked carved of wood, with grim long cheeks and calm, steely eyes of blue. His birdy voice had warmed and came like brass.

The boys took a carefree, happy stroll through the mall, which was already clogging with its weekend bustle. They looked with brief interest at the blues and pinks of the tropical fish in the back room of the pet shop, and then they headed toward Radio Shack where everything was blinking and new and plastic, while the organist at the adjacent Lowrey organ store played "The Girl From Ipanema"—and the notes and chords shimmered and sleeted through the tiled cavern of the mall like a flotilla of colorful balloons that poured forth, floating freely, before congregating somewhere high up near the skylights; and in the distance was the cool refreshing whisk of water fountains in full foamy jet.

"You don't know about boxes, do you?"

Jim looked at Raymond cockeyed.

"Boxes?" It was as if Raymond had said "pencils" or "horses."

"Yeah, *boxes*—they're these special electronic things that phreaks use on the phone lines."

One of Jim's eyes twitched quickly, and then he smiled. "Oh really?"

"Yeah. Phreaks use 'em all the time. You can get plans to build 'em on the hacker boards—it's all just parts you'd find here at Radio Shack. There's all kinds of 'em. They're usually named by color—like there's the blue box and the red box and the black box—and each one does something different. The best phreaks have a whole arsenal of 'em."

As the two of them touched and fingered the rows of electronic parts, Raymond happily went through a rundown of the boxes that he knew, showing off the knowledge he'd gleaned from weeks of study on the nation's best hacker boards.

"The black box lets you get incoming collect calls for free. The red box lets you call for free at any pay phone; the green box lets you trace a call, and then there's the cheese box, which automatically forwards all incoming calls to another location."

Jim was looking at Raymond as if he were caught trying to pass a ridiculous lie. "*Cheese* box?"

Raymond smiled. "Yeah, really! That one got its name because the first one was discovered tucked inside an empty cream cheese container. It was used by some mobsters or something—when the cops raided the place that's what they found! And the most powerful of all is the blue box—it's a keypad with a couple extra buttons that give you all the power of the operator. It makes a little 'wink' sound, a telephone control signal, at the exact frequency of twenty-six hundred Hertz, which is the most important tone in phreaking. I think there's a sound of it on that Pink Floyd album your sister has. If you know how to use it you can connect to anywhere—you can make links between different phone lines, assemble huge chains of 'em. A blue box is basically a console that makes you an operator. It's pretty much the king of boxes."

"So all these boxes give you different powers on the phone lines?"

"Exactly."

Jim smiled. "It's almost like casting spells or something."

"Yeah, it really is, it's pretty magical!"

But it was old and dusty magic—Raymond knew that while phreaks used the blue box in the 1960s and '70s, its time was quickly ending; the new computerized, electronic switching systems that telephone companies were deploying now no longer made it possible to use a blue box. If you'd even try, the telephone company would trace it. You could probably still box from somewhere out in the country where the rural telephone systems were yet to be updated, but for reaching out over long distance from here in the city, codes were now the best and safest way.

"And what also happens is that most of the big hackers are members of groups," Raymond said as they were examining a tape deck display. "There's a lot of real powerful national groups, and actually one of the best is based right here in Clifton, the Fourth Band. They're known all over the country as one of the best. That's what Lucifer's Lair's a part of—Dr. Dialtone's a member."

"Do any opposing groups call it?"

"Not really, but a lot of individual hackers do. I'm sure there's spies. Sometimes groups have pretty big wars with each other."

Jim smiled at the thought. "Do they use their boxes to fight?"

"Yeah, actually they do—they battle on the phone lines and attack each other's boards and stuff like that. Sometimes they'll disconnect someone's phone line and stuff."

"Ugh," Jim muttered, and then he laughed.

"Yeah, that would suck. But the big thing is they try to get each other's stats—if a hacker ever posts your real name and number and all your private information, you're finished."

"Now that would *really* suck!"

"Sure would. But the whole idea of being in a group is to gain knowledge."

They'd wandered out of the Radio Shack and were heading towards the bookstore. "You're not in a group, are you?" Jim suddenly asked.

"No," Raymond answered in a morose exhale. "No, but I'd *like* to be. Realistically, I know I'm not ready for the Fourth Band—those guys are all like eighteen, and they know a whole lot about hacking. But I'd love to be in it someday. I think there's a big need in Clifton for another good group. I was thinking that this area code could use another good underground hack syndicate to get things going. Hey, why don't we start one!" he added brightly, looking over at Jim hopefully.

Jim smiled a deep, inward smile, his blue eyes hiding great cliffs and ranges as they passed into the front of the bookstore, where a dozen tiny amber spotlights glared at the prismatic colors of the books filling all the shelves and open tables.

"Who knows," Raymond added, "we might be able to get enough phreaks to combine powers and trade boxes."

They quietly flipped through the military and the computer magazines in the front racks and finally Jim said, "Underground Hack Syndicate—I can see it now!"

"Hey, yeah, that'd be a great name!"

They spent the rest of the afternoon meandering through the wide, open corridors of the mall and daydreaming about the group and what it would be about—it was the common theme of the day and back at Jim's house they went into the family room and turned on the PCjr; after an hour of doodling with the keyboard and drinking Pepsis from tall wide-mouthed glasses they came up with a trademark signature for the group: "–uHs–" would be the signature that members would place beneath their names after every post.

"But there's only two of us," Jim suddenly remarked.

"Yeah, we really need a few more people. You know, I wonder if anyone at school would be cool enough to be in it—"

"There's Dean Amato, he's on the boards."

"Yeah," Raymond whined slowly, "but he's not much of a hacker. Actually, I really don't think we've got any other hackers at St. Bart's at all. But I do know a couple local guys on the boards who might want to be part of it."

"Yeah?"

"Yeah, remember Mr. Bond, the guy I told you who sent me a letter once on FBI stationery?"

"Yeah?"

"Well I'm sure he'd want to be in it. And maybe he knows someone else, too—I'll contact him."

Raymond called Lucifer's Lair that night and sent his acquaintance Mr. Bond a private message. Bond was all for it, and gave the name of other locals from his school who'd also want to join: The Game Doctor, Captain Chaos, and Chaos' friend Lt. Magnus. Raymond had seen them all on the boards.

"Great," Raymond wrote back to him the next day. "Tell them they can start signing '–uHs–' to their posts and people will start talking about us."

There was no other plan for the group; it was assumed that there'd eventually be some sort of telephone conference and discussion, and Raymond thought that it'd be useful if they shared codes—it'd make it less of an effort for having to find new codes every few weeks.

Bond's friends immediately announced their affiliation with the group. Then Mr. Bond made a post on the general base of Lucifer's Lair and put "uHs" beneath his signature. Raymond thought this was the beginning now, that people would soon be talking—and when he saw the post that followed Bond's, he saw that they already were.

It was the sysop, Dr. Dialtone: "Uh, uHs, what's that mean? Oh, I know: Game Doctor, Captain Chaos, now Mr. Bond—you guys are a bunch of 13-year-old rodents! uHs is lame. Haha-haha!"

Raymond read this in shock, thankful only that he hadn't gone public with his new affiliation, and now he knew that he never would—while Jim laughed it off as if he expected it to happen, Raymond was disappointed and crestfallen. But he still hoped to advance his powers, and he collected the plans for building many boxes. They usually involved complex electronic circuitry, but a few of the simplest boxes weren't difficult and he focused on them. The black box was the easiest—it was just a particular type of resistor that was placed across the two incoming wires of the telephone line. Theoretically, you could make a fancy contraption for it by mounting it inside a little black box that plugged into the line and had a push-button switch to turn it on and off, but Raymond just laid the resistor over the bare wires in the open wall plate of the phone line, and once it was in place he had Jim call him up. He sounded dim and in a windstorm.

"Can you hear me?"

"—eah, we're connected! Woo weer eee?"

"What?"

"Do you hear *me*?"

"Yeah!"

"So if you *call* me coll*ect* from somewhere," Raymond was hollering, "*I* can pick up the *phone* and we can *talk* like this, and there would be no charge!"

"No what?"

"No *charge*!"

Next came the beige box, which was simply a telephone handset with an alligator clip on each of the two wires of its plug. Telephone company workers tested the phone lines by clipping them onto the connecting bolts or open wires; wherever there was access you could tap in. Raymond built his own out of a handset telephone that had come as part of an AM/FM alarm clock radio his mother had gotten as a free gift for opening a bank account. He'd recently taken it over, and he was openly proud of the fact that the handset was appropriately beige in color. He brought it over to Jim's house in his backpack as soon as he built it.

"Does it work?" Jim asked with a smile.

"I dunno, I think so, but I haven't really tested it."

"Let's try it on our line."

They snuck down to Jim's basement where Jim carefully clipped the ends onto the two bolts where the open telephone wires came into the house; with the phone's mute button depressed, they could silently eavesdrop on the line—and while Jim grinned nearby, the whites of his eyes glowing fishy in the dim, Raymond eagerly listened in on one of Jim's older sisters communicating with a girlfriend in a series of staccato bursts, sharp squawks, low groaning mutters surprisingly boyish, and piercing squeals that came without warning; there was also, counted several times each, the loud uncontrolled exclamations of "Nu uh!" "No way!" and "For real?"

Jim and Raymond were quietly becoming best friends, and together in the months of that school year they observed the trends and fashions of the world, and were acutely aware of the differences presented by the opposing sex, and the bitter struggle they were about to face in all their coming high-school years; they pieced together the knowledge they'd gleaned from all of the major Hollywood films that had been released within the past decade; they shared a good, boyish pleasure in wandering the Army-Navy store that smelled of unused canvas and rubber boots, and they collected the telephone numbers of pay phones wherever they went, reading their incoming number off the dial plate and believing this information would advance them in life. Back at home Raymond called these numbers constantly, and when someone answered he would listen, thinking that somehow, by hearing this, a part of him was really there.

15

CHILDHOOD'S END

MAY THAT year was giving way to summer in its cheerful chipper way, with soft white blooms and bees that shot in quickspun arcs, there was the rumble of distant mowers and the heavy redolence of sun-warmed grass and all across the land there was a kind, warm brightness and a blossom. In these hot, shimmery yellow days Raymond was finally leaving St. Bartholomew's for good. A part of his history lay locked inside its halls, it was a nameless cipher that was unheld by any other, and now he felt himself floating away from all of it. The place itself was like a stoic figure, steady as a rock, and he knew that it would be there long after he'd deserted it—he'd only tunneled through its maze of time. He gazed deeply down the halls, looked through open doorways, and felt his footsteps tracing through the rooms; these places where he'd walked would always bear witness to the sure stampings of his ghost. But for him, the breathing figure, it was much less—all of this would soon be lost to him forever, and those tiny first-grade children who'd seen him in the halls today would only know him as a dim shadow cast somewhere in the lost and tired kingdoms of their dawn—he'd be far away and gone.

This eighth grade year was also the first time that Raymond had a yearbook. In the past his mother had never wanted to buy him one, and he'd been rather nonchalant about it, too—he was never featured in it, anyway, besides the mandatory class photo—but it suddenly achieved a great swelling importance and so with some insistent begging he was allowed to get one. It came in the last week of school and so right with the rest of the kids he fervently passed his book around, collecting the signatures of his peers, those hasty marks and promises and ink-scrawls that would entrap the flavor of a time and stage of growth forever. Raymond was leaving victorious, as attested by the signatures: Jim Alpes proclaimed, beneath his autograph, that "I.B.M. rules," and Dean Amato called him "an awesome hacker"; others with whom he'd barely ever spoken in all his elementary school years, male and female alike, many who'd never once acknowledged him and some who'd even greatly taunted him, suddenly had something big to say. They now gave Raymond their home telephone numbers so that he might "keep in touch" during the unknown blank expanse that was about to hit them and that threatened to divide them—a gesture which even then he thought seemed a little ridiculous but calmly figured that yes, should this coming time get so harsh and tough as to be unbearable that he could always call on them, and together they would find a way; still others wished him well in all his future years, and those who knew that he was to attend Monsignor Darcy High School made mention of the name. A freckle-nosed girl named Michelle spelled out the sum-total effect of his life on her in a mathematical equation:

```
  2 good
+ 2 be
  ---------
  4 gotten
```

There was the class nerd, a stocky, red-faced boy named O'Henry who wore sharp-pleated slacks, got straight As, and liked science—it was assumed by all that he'd go into NASA after his years of schooling and help build the rockets that would explore and populate space—and he signed Raymond's book hinting at the prosperous future that was to be found by the both of them in years to come. Even the bad kids cor-

dially signed his book, the kids he'd never dared to speak to before—tall Jim Jensen, a pimply basketball player with a large
clownish mouth and a scraggly swab of fudge-brown hair, a
kid who excelled in gym class but for whom the "D" grade was
standard, and who'd done his share of taunting Raymond over
all the years, even he took up a pen to cheerfully inscribe Raymond's yearbook. With the passing of the yearbooks came a
kind of unspoken admonition: they all seemed to know this was
the end now, that their class as banded together had functioned
as a unit and that it was breaking up, they were at the gates
and it was time to give a last goodbye: and that there was no
hate forever.

In the final hours of the last day even the principal came
into the room, asking the teacher to please step out for just
a moment, and then he shut the door and in a rare intimate
moment he told the room of watchful eyes that he usually didn't
like to get personal with the leaving class but that he had to
admit with serious candor that, in the final assessment, there
was something special about them now.

"You kids were quite a group," he said in a low, frank utter,
and his eyes penetrated the seated class with a wide, discern-
ing sweep. He was seated on the front of the teacher's desk,
arms out along his sides, knuckles white, his torso leaning
forward. He was a dark-haired Italian, stoutly built and with
jet-black liquidic eyes, a man whose folded flabs of cheek were
shaded dark with stubble every day and whose stringy hairs
rode starkly over the bulgy lump of his head. The children
always knew him as the distant leader of the school, someone
to vaguely fear.

"You kids, I want you to know that I'm not ever gonna forget
you. This class was special. You don't see something like this
often," he admitted quietly and with a slow shake of his head.
"You were quite a group."

Somewhere in the class there came the soft slip of a tearful
sob.

So the summer had come, all bright and languid with its
thousand warm delights, and it was now the last of something—he'd lived many years at St. Bartholomew's and would

never enter the refuge of its halls again; there was the ominous heavy note of high school right in front of him, where some of his classmates—particularly the middle group, the ones who were average at everything and whose stars would not rise higher than in these days of school—would be reunited in the fall and continue on with him at Darcy's, but not all of them would be there. The class had been scattered to the winds. This was a fundamental shift, a sweeping change, and in the breezy rush Raymond had the distinct feeling that life was commencing out upon a stage, somewhere down below. A wind had whispered far among the willows; boughs were shaking like a long and weepy sigh and there was somewhere very far to go. He'd even known a world that almost none of his classmates had ever seen, and he would go much further yet. The years ahead were long and far.

On the Sunday before school began, Raymond went out to take a walk with Joey Malvicino around the neighborhood to wear off some of their nervous excitement and discuss the coming prospects of their futures. They slipped under a hole in a back fence and went down a well-worn trail through the middle of a small copse and then a low field that led out to a park, built at the foot of another neighborhood. It was like a hole away from the world they knew, where they could emerge in the wide, wheaty fields of an alien land. This was one of their many secrets, the site of childhood fables and adventures, but today in the dry, golden end of August the path was taken without comment, only with this heavy unspoken knowledge: come tomorrow morning, they'd both be high school students. Raymond was attending Monsignor Darcy, a Catholic and recently co-ed school some five miles away in Alva, and Joey would attend John F. Kennedy Memorial High School, the local public school that'd been built around the time of the first Roman Valley developments. The whole world around them now was breathless—there was no breeze at all.

"So you'll be out at three-thirty, and I'll be home at two-thirty," Raymond said for the third time.

"Yeah, and I'll have to get the bus at seven forty-five. School starts at eight-fifteen." Joey had already said this, too. Both boys were anxious and tense and nervous, and in quiet waves their voices kept revealing it. They were trudging through a field, following the winding path that eventually ended along a fence behind a park at the foot of another neighborhood. Sometimes they saw the creased and wrinkled, rain-stained shards of pornographic magazines here, by the swing sets and underneath the baseball diamond bleachers.

School would start for Raymond at eight-thirty; Joey's day was longer but he had a longer lunch period. Darcy's had no recess, and their lunch period was brief, so more was packed into a shorter day. Raymond liked this arrangement so much better.

"But we'll probably be so busy with homework at night that we'll only get to see each other on the weekends," Joey said glumly.

Raymond considered that fact with nervous expectancy. "Or maybe only during vacation periods." What hard work lay soon ahead, what toils and unexpected ordeals were on their way, he didn't know. Even the name of it hinted of advance and of the roughness reaching upper heights that was sure to hit them: *high* school!

"How about report cards?" Raymond asked suddenly. "Do you know how often they'll come?"

"No, but Kennedy has the old grading system"—the public junior high that Joey had attended gave a different grading level, A through E without plus or minuses. Now he'd have the traditional system of A through D and F, with plus and minuses, just like Darcy's had. This made Joey gleeful. "Now we can finally compare each other's grades!"

Raymond felt a nervous shock with that—he wasn't competitive, and no longer excelled in school as he had during his earliest years. He followed his own interests now, principally computers and reading, and he'd been steadily slipping downward in everything else. He was excited to compare progress with his friend, but felt that in any direct grade comparison Joey would certainly emerge as victor. Raymond was more interested in the access that high school might bring them.

"I can't wait to see what kind of computers they have."

"Maybe they'll have mainframes!"

The thought of combining the computer knowledge and access of two high schools excited them both, and as they weaved back through the field and toward the gate that led to home they let out a flurry of gleeful shouts in approval of their plan to compare facilities. They meandered back to the neighborhood sidewalks—the familiar ones they'd always known. Each house along the way, every crack and bump and shape in the concrete, all the landscaping, existed above all this in abstract symbol, as something greater than their presence here. And the tremendous pattern of shape and color that they made would live on, Raymond thought, was forever latched to him in memory. In the lull of quiet as they walked, something calmly ratified this idea, and he knew that it was a solemn truth of life.

They ambled back to their homes and then walked toward the edge of the property line between their yards—that thin, mounded strip of grass on the Malvicino's side yard, now piled with fresh mounds of dirt. From behind the toolshed, over near Joey's flat slab patio, came the sound of the patio door sliding open in a cold, low rumble.

"Joey!" called his mother sharply, with venom in her throat. "*Come* here!"

The boys knew immediately that something big had happened. "Uh oh," Joey muttered nervously. "Hold on."

He ran over to her and went to face the matter. Raymond heard Joey respond to his mother with a sharp, unhappy call: "What!"

She spoke quickly and harshly to him in a burst of hushed angry tones. In a moment he was at the corner, turning to look at Raymond, his face washed with sadness; he could only call out weakly, "Raymond, I have to go in now."

"Okay," Raymond said to his friend in a tone of equal glumness, but also mixed with confusion: what was wrong? He didn't wish him well for the next day because he thought they'd talk later in the evening. He wandered to the front of his house, figuring he'd learn the mystery of Joey's wrongdoing later. But when he went inside he learned immediately what had happened from his angry parents, who were glaring at each other in the kitchen: Raymond's father, arguing with the Malvicino family about the property line between their yards, had called them up and swore bitterly at them. Raymond's father never liked the Malvicino family, and after Mr. Malvicino converted his backyard into a huge gated garden complex with all its makeshift fencing and boards and ropes, the relations between them had crumbled. On those rare times when the men did interact it was brief and tense with short, dark mutters and each man being curt and rude to the other. Now, Joey's father had been piling up dirt on his lawn, and it formed a slope to the back of the Valentines' yard, and during rains the water collected there in the brown circles beneath the fir trees—so Raymond's father called up Mr. Malvicino on the phone.

"You're killing our trees!" he'd shouted into the kitchen telephone, and then in a fit of rage he swore and yelled and with his brutal guttural vulgarity he said that he never wanted to see or speak to them again.

"So *that's* why Joey had to go!" Raymond now cried out, suddenly realizing that he could never see his friend again.

As dark anger returned to Raymond's mother, tinting freshly in the unripe almonds of her eyes, she turned quickly toward his father and snapped at him again: "Why did you do that? That's his *friend*!"

With wide, moon-shot eyes Raymond stared at them, and then he turned and stormed mightily toward his room, both angry and mournful—and as he mounted the stairs he heard his mother cuss and swear at his father again, call him names and shout, "That was his friend! Tell me, why did you do that? That was his *friend*, you jerk, that was his friend!"

BOOK THREE

THE NET
AND THE
YOUTH

16

FROSH

HIGH SCHOOL began for Raymond as it does—with unwavered excitement and with dread. There was a shallow sleepless night, an early rush, cold and fearful walks and waiting, rooms of huddled faces all like his, calm and welcome speeches from adults that dragged on through all the drowsy hours, and orientation meetings held in cold, alien classrooms that came and then let out like strange morning tides.

First was Orientation Day, just for the freshmen, which took up all the best and freshest hours of the day in the final summer moments despite all his earnest hopes for otherwise; and then the Monday came when there was a forced immersion into this new pattern, and each day was over in a tousled, intense relief. There was a whole new set of teachers and the hard promises of work to come.

There'd been some fellow classmates from St. Bart's in the crowd, but they all looked different here in these new surroundings and Raymond knew that they all were lost together. Some banded in little cliques; Raymond stuck by Jim Alpes but was otherwise alone. He'd seen all the new faces packed in this unfamiliar building—all the striped shirts and knit ties, the pale colored blouses and the deep brown skirts, the feathered hair and silver-metal spectacles, the girls and boys of every shape and variety—some gangly, others pudgy round balls, some sweetcurved girls he liked to look at, and the thick, muscled blocks of imposing wild beast-men. The tall quiet ones with beady blinking eyes, and the dark, runty cronies who stuck close to their honchos. Yes, and all the faces. He'd anxiously scanned the large hall that was filled with all these new and unknown faces and he'd thought to himself, "These are my peers, my fellow classmates. I will know them now, right here, inside these years."

His mother had made a trip to the Darcy bookstore a week before, bringing home a brown canvas duffel bag he didn't like. He'd stared aghast at it, with its Darcy logo on the side, deciding that it must be what only the most awful rejects of the school would use. Then came all of the freshness of his supplies: uncracked, unmarked notebooks; a box of cheap blue pens whose ink was held inside their hollow centers in thin plastic stalks; a package of notebook paper ruled in watery blue with a vertical red stripe along the left margin, three holes punched down the side. There were new hard binders for organizing your papers called Trapper Keepers, with a variety of cover stylings to choose from, their patterns made by the unseen votaries of the season's current state of fashion; the front flaps opened with a ripping tug of Velcro to reveal a plastic three-ring binder and a set of glossy cardboard folders, one printed thoughtlessly with units of mensuration and a few inches of a ruler band. Raymond had gotten a generic vinyl off-brand colored in deep azure that was blank on the cover and the insides; he thought it was an improvement over the "official" name-brand ones whose design and typefaces looked suspiciously tawdry to him.

Right away the grim responsibilities made themselves known. Yes, it'd be much tougher than St. Bart's: on the first day his duffel bag was loaded up and inflated tight with books—he had to struggle to close the zipper, and it was bent across the top, the bag was hard to lug. "If only Joey could see this," he thought wryly. But Joey was probably going through his own struggles now.

By long-standing Darcy tradition, the freshmen were derogated as the "frosh," and for the first few weeks it was con-

sidered fair game by the upperclassmen to taunt and yell out
at any unsuspecting first-year student. The call of "Frosh!"
came hurtling down the hall at odd moments, was shouted
quickly through open doors, and was sometimes followed with
a nasty shove or even the pushing out of books from a silent
boy's panicked clutch. Those first few days seemed to hold
most of the freshmen in a grip of terror. It was a Darcy rite
of passage—the frightened little fawns didn't know it yet but
in the blink of a few tiny years they'd be the ones to pass it on
again.

Now Raymond was thrown in with the crowds. It was a
new world and he grew accustomed to the unguinous reek of
teen-age bodies cramped together in the stifling humidity of a
sealed-up classroom, and the sweet, winey sweat-smell of the
boy's locker room; the unsettling fumy stench of the lavatory
with its open stalls and where the flushing urinals would rattle
with water that seemed to cascade down from pipes high up in
the ceiling; in the halls where there were intimidating huddles
and pockets of girls in dark makeup and with sculpted, elaborate heads of hair, who'd sometimes turn and stare and passing
them he'd be enclouded in their purple-raspberry sweetness;
the hot beefy odors of the cafeteria that would rise and linger
torpidly in the late morning hours when the students filled long
tables to eat their lunches, still bleary-eyed and tired—and
always when coming into these places with their scents and
odors there was a cold fear hardening icily in the heart of him:
what would emerge from the chaos of this new world? Who
would ever know him and to what lands were they now going?
In quick time the first social circles began to form among the
frosh, and Raymond accepted his role with the outcasts, in the
bottom dregs, hovering close to the hoodlum element of the
school. There seemed no other way for him: the few computer
kids were impossible nerds and he didn't associate with them
at all; the thin stratum of dignified, well-bred types avoided
him by default; he wasn't a jock and so the athletes had no use
for him. He was quiet and he liked to read and he observed
the rushing crowds from his lone position at the bottom, to the
side.

Raymond was bitter about his lot, he wished for better ways, but no solution would avail itself; by all projections he was stuck there, at Darcy, among the unwanted outcasts, and would have to struggle through it for the next four toilsome years. He missed the Kristos boys whose way of life was so much more salubrious than the routine he was being subjected to right now—he kept thinking that his life was off its proper tracks, that he was stumbling through bad choices. He'd had a chance to get into St. Regis, the city's top prep school; unlike Darcy it was in the city of Clifton proper, and not guarded deep in the remote hills of the suburbs, so going there would mean using the public transportation system—and taking the bus would be an entirely new experience for Raymond. It'd also mean learning the way of the inner city, the rotting urban core of it, and that was something that Raymond couldn't do—he'd walked down the hard steps of St. Regis' after a tour the previous spring, the Monsignor in his dark cassock ghosting behind his parents with hands cupped portentously together and hoping in audible mutters how the boy would attend there in the fall, and Raymond thought to himself that this cracked and weathered building, much like a castle with its creeping ivy and its little center courtyard and sharp-spired chapel with tall speckled slits of dark-stained glass, this venerable time-encrusted campus might be where he'd come to haunt through all his high school days. He'd taken a test on a Saturday morning and had been accepted, with in fact the highest rankings and great enthusiasm from the priest who'd handled their admissions—yet after the tour he'd decided coldly against it. It was an all-boys school and he was afraid of any future he'd make for himself there—his mind played on horrors, there were faint whispers that said he'd grow to be deficient and never talk to girls, that he'd fail socially in life, and find dangers traveling to the city, that in the long tedious ride to and from school each day he'd be continually harassed, tortured, and always miserable. These terrible fears filled his body, and told him no, told him to hide in the safety of his childhood shelter, and so without any discussion or advice he chose Darcy so that he could stay there in the outer suburbs near his home.

Plenty of kids in Raymond's class had computers, but as far

as he could tell they only played video games—nobody else was a hacker, no one wandered out upon the wires.

But it turned out that a kid in homeroom had a modem—he'd mentioned it loudly in a discussion on computers one sleepy golden morning and Raymond immediately turned to look; to the confused eyes of the other kids they called out to each other across the room and traded quick notes about "the boards," so that Raymond suddenly felt like a big shot, noticing the dazed look of the girls around him. And Raymond had already made a friend in homeroom, whose name was Rick, and now Rick quietly watched this exchange happen, mouth agape in a funny confused smile as Raymond and the boy who had a modem loudly spoke of all the boards that they were on and who across town they knew.

A second after the exchange was over, a finger prodded Raymond's right shoulder in a shelling of little pokes and Raymond turned around. It was the kid who sat behind him—he too was one of the class rejects, a half-Filipino boy from the inner city. He wore plain metal glasses, a brown knit tie, and a plaid oxford with thin bright lines that made Raymond think of the discount stores they had in bad neighborhoods. His name was Ron.

"Yoo a phreak? Yoo do phreakin', man?"

Raymond didn't know what to think. But he wanted friends. He told the truth. "Yeah."

In a quick excited burst, Ron informed him that he was "in a gang," and that he liked codes and used them constantly. "Yoo know Metrotel?"

"Oh, yeah," Raymond said, opening up to him now, politely contributing to the exchange of cultures. "Yeah, I used to use them a lot. I use Sprint and MCI—and I've used nine-fifties, but they're harder to come by these days." These were the long-distance services in the 950 telephone prefix that'd been popular in the preceding spring.

Ron didn't know much about boxing, but he knew codes; he explained how it was useful for him and the members of his gang to make free calls from pay phones, and to make free calls to long-distance boards. He asked Raymond for codes.

"I need da codez ta get da warez!"

"What?"

"*Warez*," he mouthed eagerly, craning his head forward as he spoke. "Da new warez, good warez," he blurted quickly, and then squealed, "Ya know, da *gaimes*!"

"Oh, on LD boards?"

He flared his nose emphatically. "Yee-e-eah!"

"You mean like downloading wares?"

Ron chuckled. "Yee-eah, da warez boardz!"

Raymond understood: Ron used the codes to call boards that had pirated software—"wares"—available for trade and download. Ron was someone who played the many games.

So in homeroom Ron cautiously took codes from Raymond, and in return he'd tell Raymond about the gang life: they had to wear certain colors in their clothing, and had to avoid others altogether; they hung out by the trainyard not far from Ron's house in Clifton, and they rode the rapid taking it from their neighborhood station to downtown, and then out its other spoked routes to all the lands in the metropolitan area; they marked their territory with graffiti, and Ron told him how one had to do it in "gang writing," a certain stylized way to make the letters of the alphabet where the figures were very boxy and square and difficult for outsiders to decipher. The whole thing seemed crude and stupid to Raymond, who couldn't imagine the appeal.

Ron would write out the letters on the top margin of his open notebook, patting Raymond on the back and showing him how to do it: "See dis is how yo' gotta write when yo' in a gang," he said, and carefully wrote out a series of letters.

"Dis is how yo' make an 'A,' and dis is a 'B'," he said happily, showing Raymond each letter.

"So you can't write them normally?"

"No! Dis is how yo' gotta do it! See, dis is 'C,' and dis is 'D.' Da'ss how iz *dun*!"

Raymond tried to draw them on his notebook, in the manner prescribed, and then he showed his markings to Ron who looked them over studiously, with the serious gaze of the correcting teacher, tittering and humming while he evaluated Raymond's work.

"Dat's a little mezzed up, an' dat one's okay," he said with a quiet chuckle, pointing at Raymond's letters with a rough finger. "Naw, *yoo* doan got it," he said, and then offered hopefully, "but if yo' practice, yo' might get it down."

Raymond didn't practice. It seemed ugly and he felt bad that he was being exposed to such things now. But Ron was devoted to it; his notebooks were full of the scrawl.

"Dis iz how dey do graffiti," he explained. "Yo' *gotta* do it diz way."

Then a moment later when Raymond's head turned back again, Ron said, "Whass yo' naime, Raymon'? Raymon'? Dis iz how yo' write yo' naime."

With speed and agility and pride he wrote out Raymond's name in gang writing, and then held it up for him to behold. "See diss! Dis iz Raymon'!"

Raymond tried to repeat it in his own notebook and when he was done Ron peeked over and then slowly shook his head. "Na, dat ain' right."

Raymond had no interest in it; he thought Ron was a bad influence, a youth whose future seemed to be already written, stamped and sealed; he was completely doomed. Yet in homeroom and in study hall Raymond always turned and craned his neck to talk to him; Ron at least knew about codes, so he was someone to talk to about the unseen world that Raymond lived in. He'd tell Ron about a new long-distance service that he used, maybe one with five- or six-digit codes that were easy to hack, and Ron would titter and nod and listen. "Whassat? Whassat numba now?" he'd say, eager to write it down, his pen ready in hand—but he'd never give a code to Raymond or compare techniques.

School hadn't been on for two weeks, one long rush of tensions and releases as the world of his new surroundings overtook him when he made an attempt to call Joey, wondering what had happened in his friend's life. They hadn't spoken or even seen each other in this time and Raymond felt that they should still find a way to communicate, even with that parental division now wedged between them which would never let it be the same. Raymond felt that they should try and patch their friendship, that they should try to talk, at least to say goodbye and end the history of their years together with a note of kindness and a final peace. It was a warm afternoon when school was out and backyard leaves were reddening at their edges and all the trees were full and heavy when Raymond decided to give his old friend a call.

"Joey?"

His childhood friend answered with confused expectancy, the soft chubby voice of someone still a boy. "Yeah?"

"Guess who *this* is."

"I don't know, who?"

Had he already forgotten—was it even possible? "It's Raymond."

"Nu uh," Joey said doubtfully. "Is this Erik? This is Erik!" They'd met once when Erik had come over Raymond's house.

"No, no!" Raymond pleaded helplessly. "It's Raymond!"

"It's *Er*ik," he insisted.

Didn't he know, didn't Joey remember the sound of his voice? Or didn't he trust him? Raymond was grieved to know that his friend would think he'd get someone to tease him in this way.

"No, Joey, this is Raymond!" he implored. "It's Raymond, I swear! Look, I'll prove it to you—look out the window!"

Raymond was in the kitchen by the table. The phone cord didn't stretch to the patio door in the family room, which offered a clear view, so Raymond stood by the window in the kitchen. He could still see the family room window of Joey's house from here—it was over past the long sloping lawn of the Valentine's backyard and the neat line of fir trees at the edge.

"I'm over by our kitchen window," Raymond said. "Just look—look over there."

"Where, I don't see you!"

Raymond knew that he was there. Yes, there was a healthy maple still in bloom—it partially cloaked the view with its thousand open palms of bright apple green, but there was enough clear space for anyone to see. He could see across to Joey's window, which was dark.

"I'm right here, Joey, by the kitchen window! Just look!"

The plea was desperate, but Raymond couldn't see Joey, either—Joey was tucked away somewhere inside the darkness of the window. The leaves stirred noiselessly outside as a single group with a passing brush of wind and then when Joey, ill at ease, said in a nervous voice that he had to go, Raymond knew that their friendship and all their time together had ended. It'd been pulled away by something, just like the frigid wind that shook the leaves. He could never go back, there'd be no furtive friendship between them, and now he couldn't even give a last goodbye. The men we knew so many years ago as boys are far and gone—and something that had always been has drained away. With a hand we wave to nothing but the wind, our cries have been deserted by the deaf, the blind will never see; a lion sleeps in gloom and there is a wounded whale plunging far below the ocean depths.

The phone call was useless. It was all gone.

17

MANOR HOUSE

FROM THE day of the fight Raymond's parents had spoke of moving, and they began to look for a new home. They drove out on the early autumn weekends to open houses in brand-new neighborhoods that were out close to where Erik lived, and they began to see what "the builders" were constructing in their new developments, picking up brochures and discussing what they'd seen during the dismal rolling car rides home. These were joyless places, separated from reality, sealed off from the vitality of life and from the familiar scent and scenery of America that Raymond longed for; all were heartless enclosures that stood far away from any city or town center, cleared out from the deep tall greenery of trees, defiant and desolate, locked prisons that lay on fresh-made plains under the blind heat of a glass sun. Raymond felt that he was lost, that he'd always been lost, and that he was somehow missing out on the life he should've known and had. His options and choices depressed him. Why was he going to Darcy, afraid to've gone to St. Regis? Why was he living here in Roman Valley? Why was it now, in this place and time? It made him wonder and it left him depressed, without an answer. He turned to the networks and the wires, waiting for their whisperings to come—he went into the secret online world that his classmates didn't even know was out there, the world that stretched out somewhere far beyond them all.

This is how it was for Raymond in the autumn months of freshman year, when he always held his books tightly in the hall and was getting used to being shouted at as a new and lowly frosh. He had much more homework than he'd ever known at St. Bart's, but he attended to it joylessly; and there was no access to computers until the new term in January after the long Christmas break, and then he had a computer class in the school's second-floor Apple lab—a long, carpeted room with walnut-grain tables all around the perimeter holding the machines. He'd been instructed to buy a floppy disk and he'd carefully untuck it from the steel-silver cardboard pouch it came in, the label carefully affixed to the top, where in his hand he'd written out his name. The other kids were learning to write INPUT statements and process arithmetic to plot lines and draw crude circles on the screen, big blocky drawings, while Raymond was ahead of all that and bored: there were no modems in the school, no way to reach out beyond the walls.

The most interesting board that Raymond called that year didn't require codes to reach it, wasn't a hacker board at all, and handles weren't even allowed. It was a local board called The Clifton Manor, which ran the special board software for the IBM PC called Manor House that was unlike any he'd ever seen: the fantasy of the board was that it was a giant mansion, consisting of many connected "rooms" you could explore; after logging in at the Gate, you wandered through the manor, reaching down through hallways that connected rooms on various topics. Each room's discussion was a long scroll of text you read by pressing R. It spilled out to you a screenful at a time, advanced by the constant banging of the spacebar. You contributed to the unravelling discussion by pressing C, and then the lines you typed were added to the bottom, offset with your name.

The callers here were older, and he learned from them. His education in music increased tremendously through discussions in a room called Lizard Lounge, where a man named Marty Robins posted frequently; Raymond came to understand that he played saxophone in a local blues band. Marty Robins had known the music scene in Clifton back at least a decade past, the time of glam rock and new wave where men in dark lipstick wore suits with stuffed shoulder pads, a time of spiked hair and electric synthesizers, of those long-haired men whose distorted Les Paul guitars formed the naked genesis of heavy metal, and of the twangy blends of country and reggae that had marked new trends and fashions in that time. That era seemed entirely romantic to Raymond—it'd just happened, he saw it documented in photographs and films, but all of it was already gone forever—and as he asked to hear more, with a great long moan Marty would lean back to begin and then he'd happily tell Raymond all about it, giving a great exhale and then filling the entire room with stories of the famous concerts, local clubs, and hidden legends of the time.

Raymond avoided The Rec Room, where the conversation was a dreary barrage of current sports scores and prognostications, holding a power and interest over the older males in a way that Raymond couldn't fathom, but he eagerly participated in The Never-Ending Story room, where callers would append a line to continue the tale:

```
RAYMOND: his Trash-80 computer was such junk
         that he could barely do anything. So he
         decided to ...
MOE:     have another look at the TRS-80, where
         he ...
HOWARD:  learned that Raymond was right, it
         really was junk, so he tossed it out
         the window and ...
JEFF:    it hit an old lady right on the head,
         so then he jumped up and ...
TOM:     made a run for the restroom, where
         he ...
DAVE:    saw Marty working as an attendant.
         Marty explained that he needed the
         money and this was what he was best
         qualified for doing. So then he ...
MOE:     fell back in surprise and accidentally
         flushed himself down the toilet where
```

```
             he ended up ...
DAVE:        in the bowels of the greater Clifton
             regional sewer system where he was
             eventually flushed out to Lake Catawba
             where ...
HOWARD:      he decided that a TRS-80 really was a
             bad choice after all.
```

Here on the Manor House he heard stories of the drunken college parties that took place all summer long at an island on Lake Catawba called Pass-A-Way, and he heard of camping trips that some young people did with their friends as part of the freedoms of being in college, and how these collegiates were nourished by the music of Pink Floyd, which was rife with deep layers of meaning, a fact that was quickly corroborated by one of Jim Alpes' older sisters; he chatted with a teen named Dave Rogers who tinkered on his hot-rod car, parked in his parents' driveway; he learned the hangouts for the metalheads and for the old people who liked jazz, overheard opinions on what were the "cool" bars in town, and learned candidly about all the experiences of Douglas's dates; he got the local university gossip, learned of the roadside construction projects across town and how they were grossly inconvenient and wrong, and read detailed reviews of the latest R-rated films.

In all of this he was privy to a world that his classmates at Darcy never dreamed of: this was what the boards opened up to him. Without them, one had no real way of knowing other kids outside the neighborhood and the halls of school; you might meet a few from summer camp, perhaps—or if you played a sport, you'd play against them, and come to recognize their gazes, but never socialize with them, not in the way you did on the boards each night: you knew people from all over the area code, kids spread all throughout the county, from the twelve-year-old rodents who were just starting out to kids who were almost done with high school, and even adults, those board addicts who were already well into their twenties. You'd learn of local groups and gangs, end up chatting one night with a man and his wife who ran a board out of their basement in Wellington Park, befriend a couple of teens who liked the same music that you did but lived out in the east-side headlands, come to know that there were kids in Dover who felt the same way you did or who listened to the exact same music. Raymond's reach had gone well beyond the halls of Darcy. Raymond knew that the boards were giving him access to an experience and knowledge untasted by his fellow classmates, and this knowledge gave him confidence, in all his daily waking hours: he was part of this world, among many worldly others. It was a kind of double life: he had a crowd at school, and he knew them, and he had a crowd on the computer, and he knew them; he followed the trials and tribulations of both worlds, and they didn't intersect. This bolstered his constitution when he pondered it: he had access to a world outside his peers, he heard other voices in the city and from the outer banks of Clifton and even far beyond—there was a web of hackers that spun around the nation and he was in it. He was taking in exposures that were well beyond his years.

What he saw online was a broader panorama of the world: he knew the story of local legends; he learned of many kids from far across the iron grid of Clifton, and with codes he spoke to others all throughout the nation; he conversed with people many years his senior who were stationed in much higher positions in the world: high school seniors, college students, teachers and technicians, even adults who worked. He felt proudly that this was his secret edge, and he was conscious of its advantages as he carried out his days at Darcy—his joyless lunchtime meals unwrapped and ingested quietly alone in the high rumble of the cafeteria, the long dreadful intervals of classes, the swift rushes made through crowded thronging halls amid all the other lost and lonely faces.

Not everything in Manor House was public. It had secret passageways that led to hidden rooms. Their doorways weren't shown in the hallways of the board, so to get to one you had to know what keys to press. There was a secret room for hacking—and after Raymond alluded to his knowledge in this area, Doug told him how to get to it. It was called Joshua's Den, and maybe half the regular callers of the board knew that it was there.

"Here, this is a neat find," wrote Dave Rogers amid the long scroll of the room's discussion, "a chat system on a mainframe computer at Dartmouth University. It's a lot like Manor House with virtual rooms, but there's a bank of modem lines so like a dozen users can connect at once and chat. You don't need to register or anything, just give it a handle when you first connect."

Raymond called it and was hooked. Unlike a BBS, it wasn't a messaging system—instead of posting messages, your typings went out live to all the others. When you typed a line, it was written to the screens of all the other callers who were in the room with you, prefaced by your handle. This happened fast, which amazed Raymond: you'd type a line and hit the ENTER key and suddenly just that second it went out to Dartmouth and from there was sent out to all the other callers, no matter where they were—people in computer labs at Dartmouth, dark basements in small Rhode Island towns, a screened-in porch in Georgia—they'd all get it, see it on their screen in just a second. Raymond thought of the significance and he was stunned: this was a new way for groups of humans to communicate at once, together, anywhere around the world. Nothing like this had ever been before; it was radical and new; much more was coming. Here, he talked to the other hackers of the night, but he always tried to be careful and not reveal too much.

> **Anyone here from Sohola?**

```
The ninja:       No is that where your calling
                 from?
--> Jim Morrison walks into the room.
```

> **Yeah**

```
The ninja:       Isn't that expensive or are you
                 phreaking?
--> The Killer walks into the room.
Jim Morrison:    Phreaking? What's that?
The ninja:       isn't this costing you alot?
```

> **Yes.**

```
The ninja:        why are you doing it?
```

> Because my mom's paying for it!

```
--> Riff Raff walks into the room.
The ninja:        oh wish my mom would pay for my
                  long distance calls
--> Riff Raff leaves the system.
The ninja:        i would save a lot
```

> I know, it's expensive.

```
The Killer:       Hiya dudes
```

> Hello Killer

```
--> The Instructor walks into the room.
--> lord leto ][ walks into the room.
The Instructor: Ninja?
The ninja:        what
The Instructor: You the same ninja from about a
                  year ago?
The ninja:        no i dont think so why
The Instructor: Ok, just curious
--> FELICIA walks into the room.
The ninja:        why did he do something bad?
The Instructor: Yes. Hi Felicia
FELICIA:          HIGUYS
```

> Hi, Felicia!

```
The Killer:       Hi Felicia
SID VICIOUS:      Hi Felicia!!
FELICIA:          HI
The Killer:       Felicia, how old are you???
FELICIA:          18
The Killer:       I see
FELICIA:          ILL BE 19 IN A COUPLE DAYS!
FELICIA:          WHY DID U WANT TO KNOW?
The ninja:        you out of school
FELICIA:          IN COLLEGE
The ninja:        what college?
```

The Killer: what college?
FELICIA: DARTMOUTH
lord leto][:   what major
FELICIA: NURSING
lord leto][:   why dont you become a doctor???
FELICIA: TO MUCH TIME
The ninja: got passwords to the computers
                   there?
lord leto][:   i had some for a student account
                   on the vax but thats down
SID VICIOUS!:   anybody want a password for
                   dartmouth??
The ninja: yes!!!

> Yes!

The Killer: yes
FELICIA: NO

> Post it!

Jim Morrison: i know this place inside and out
Jim Morrison: you guys better learn fortran
                   before you go in here, or your
                   going to be lost, believe me. is
                   dartmouth new for you guys?
lord leto][:   what can be done? nothing?
SID VICIOUS!:   you can do alot if you know what
                   to do
Jim Morrison: Learn fortran then you will know
                   what to do. the vax is for
                   people to do their computer
                   homework!!! i know, my brother
                   goes there!
The ninja: sid what do you put in when it
                   asks for terminal type?
Jim Morrison: if you guys want somewhere real
                   to hack into, do BOCES, all your
                   grades go here, if you are in
                   high school in the southern new

	hampshire area.
SID VICIOUS!:	anybody know how to tap grades out of boces?
Jim Morrison:	Learn fortran, then you will know what to do
lord leto][:	if you change your grades they'll know. i just want to change the comments
Jim Morrison:	I am telling you, FORTRAN is the key to Dartmouth. I haven't figured out boces yet.
Jim Morrison:	Leto, it is untraceable!!
SID VICIOUS!:	If you change your grades before they send them to your school, nobody will ever know.
lord leto][:	instead of "works well in class" do "is a real jerk" for someone you hate
lord leto][:	sid, teachers check the grades after they are sent
SID VICIOUS!:	wouldn't my parents like a comment like that, "your son is stupid"
lord leto][:	at my school the teachers are stupid

> My SCHOOL is stupid.

SID VICIOUS!:	dartmouth called me back last time i accessed it and said to quit tampering with there computer or they would prosecute me
The ninja:	i heard they had a tracing device
Jim Morrison:	you guys make me sick. you think that you are going to get caught at everything you do. you can't get caught on dartmouth because it is legal as hell!

```
lord leto ][:     you can't get caught. even so,
                  who cares
FELICIA:          YOU GUYS ARE GONNA GET IN
                  TROUBLE!!!
The ninja:        sid, how far did you get in?
lord leto ][:     look, they catch you, you get a
                  warning. you're not eighteen
                  yet. stop for awhile or
                  something
SID VICIOUS!:     yeah thats what i did. come back
                  in a month when you know its ok.
```

Raymond visited Dartmouth often. Sometimes he spotted Dave Rogers on there and they'd talk, two wires from their homes stretching out to make a circuit through black mazes, tunnels, underground cablings and to that mainframe computer where their words were received in milliseconds and passed on to one another over six states. They were in an enormous room and their names were small rectangular placards that prefaced the snow-white frosted words on their displays.

It was a secret place. Raymond spent long weekends socializing on it, and he met other hackers who'd come there from afar, just as he did. He chatted with them through the night, typing at his keys and seeing their own words pressing on his screen, beckoning for his interaction and response; the hackers of the night would wander in this great online chat system from room to room, and sometimes two would conference there in private, and they'd feverishly exchange all their many codes and logins. When he couldn't stay awake he logged off knowing he'd be back—he'd return to this Dartmouth system in the black New Hampshire valleys, to this great castle in the night.

He returned often. He thought of it in school, where he was still an unknown freshman: "I'm reaching out to distant colleges already! What monumental worlds I've known and penetrated—I speak to older people in the night, even girls—I know so much more than these halls here—I've reached out, I really have, I've seen!"

18

LONG-DISTANCE HIGH SCHOOL

RAYMOND NOW scanned vast blocks of distant numbers. He recorded all his findings in special charts he made on the pages of his notebooks. The art of long-distance scanning required a calcic, stonyheaded patience; each number could only be reached by first dialing a long-distance service, feeding it a code and then punching in the area code and number—each call would require twenty seconds of key-punchings to connect. But the rewards sang graciously and urged his fingers, and so he scanned the nation, filling up his notebook as an after-school pastime. He learned the area codes and came to know many of them by heart: 414 was old Milwaukee, city of horse clops and polka, and 206 brought him to Seattle, where the white rib of the space needle stood erect and Mark was walking somewhere in its shadow; 312 held strong as Chicago, that big city hunkered in the nation's middle, pressing hard upon an inland sea—just as 213 and 212 were the great metropoles balanced mightily at the opposite coastal edges, Los Angeles and New York. And he knew the prefixes of many cities and could tell you which ones in 213 were for Beverly Hills and which dozen were for Hollywood; he figured that by senior year he'd be able to locate, on a map, the main prefixes of every major city in the nation.

Then he began finding techniques for international calling, using certain codes and services that permitted such calls, so that he could try the boards of the outer world beyond the nation. Most of these connections weren't successful; the noise on the line was so great that his screen would be peppered heavily with junk characters—and aside from a few London boards he couldn't make sense of them, anyway: the boards he called in West Germany, France, Brazil and Nigeria were all written in foreign tongues. The noise over the phone line was always too much when dialing the Australian boards and they'd disconnect from him immediately. But the attempt sparked an interest in calling other countries and scanning prefixes and exchanges in these far-off lands; their systems were very different from the American ones he knew, and the noises they made were strange, exhilarating, and unfamiliar; he loved the funny sounds of international ring and busy signals, the unfamiliar chirpings and the moaning buzzes and the desperate chattering operators.

He dialed blocks of numbers in Australia just to listen to the noises, and he scanned what he thought were prefixes in Hogarth, England; he dialed numbers in Frankfurt, Berlin, Warsaw, Bath; he listened to the sounds of life in Iceland, Finland, Belgium, Holland. He called Japan, and mainland China, and Vietnam. In all this travel there was always the sound of the human voice, speaking in unintelligible sweet gurgles—and he knew that it was a life, right now, somewhere far away. He called Cuba and Brazil and an underground military base in Antarctica where the talk in its dearth was slow and serious, and very quiet. And he found the number to a hotline in the Vatican and called the Pope, in what was a shuffling of various voices on the line while it sounded like they were conversing on the tiny shore of an ocean full of static; after a few brief words in response to questions in a foreign tongue he then hung up, humorously elated, ending the overseas billing on the account of an unknown stranger.

Raymond indulged in this. He knew that by using codes he was leading a life of crime, and that at eighteen one could be prosecuted for it, sent off to jail while one's family had to dole out hefty fines; but now at fourteen he'd be fine. This was the time for him to dare. He'd be safe for now—and he had less than four years to reach his apex and to make his mark inside this world. The clock was ticking. He had to find his way here; he was one of a thousand hackers who were out there. For there were a thousand hackers in the night: a hole had opened up and was big enough to enter with their torchlight, and they were willing explorers in this new uncharted territory—for the thousand hackers in the night it was their duty and they began to map it out. They were finding sights unseen in a world unknown to all their ancestors—unknown even to their fathers. Their parents didn't know and no one who'd raised them would ever understand—they were lost and scratching through the wilderness alone. They were charting it out, the thousand hackers of the night, thinking it through, testing, looking, staking, moving. Some day it'd become a great city on the plain, but for now it was only wild land mottled with these tiny little outposts they had made.

He saw in visions the swirls of many people, their faces, he heard voices that called like ghosts—there were a hundred thousand conversations happening online at any instant, and there was so much in the world, and he was a part of it; he wanted more. He wanted to see and know it all, to ride the channels and raise the heights. He filled up great phreak notebooks, packing them with information that he'd gleaned, and if you could see them you'd feel the passion and the unquenched fervor: his findings of UNIX dialups, of PBX lines, bridging heads, Decservers, a number that instantly "drops trunk," a "Rolm CBX," a whole page of AE lines, a block of numbers on a far-off exchange that was only labelled "strange"; he'd found a Dataphone 800 and noted that it used "7 or 8 digits," in the pages of his notebook could now be found listings for OSUNY, Centrex logins, an answering machine operated by the Protestant televangelists of the 700 Club, whole bundles of numbers drawn together in a pen-loop and labeled "weird," "strange," or "text lines"; the St. Thomas College outdial number, with former passwords crossed out heavily in inks both blue and black; a list of names once seen—somewhere—and scrawled down diagonally, desperately, on the paper, and quickly forgotten; numeric passwords and telephone numbers written in a chaotic blizzard, words and numbers writ in black, blue, and red ink, sometimes pencil, even purple magic marker, whatever had been near the computer at the time; whole pages with old passwords written down and then crossed off, the only living trace of one long night of hacking, hours of toil; numbers that gave "Compu. Controlled operator" or "N.W. Bell voice"; on other pages, phrases jumped out from the scribbled mix: "Bank of North America's password is DIRECTOR"; there were names like *Liquid Sky* and *Videodrone*, cult-film recommendations that he'd gleaned in passing from the boards—all his notes and tracings from his distant travels were recorded here.

His journals swelled with all the codes and notes and numbers—there was so much to learn, so many things to connect to: a phone number in New York City that led to a direct audio feed for ABC television; a "games" account on Portland University's VM/370 computer system; a 1-800 Dowphone login where you "hit 7 and then a company ID to get news about that company or subject"; the Congressional Computer, where he could obtain electronic copies of documents currently being passed through the austere tomb of the United States Congress. He called the Chicago Board of Education's computer and could list student grades by social security number, and he connected at night to a computer inside a resort hotel at Disney World in Orlando where he could dim and raise the hallway lights and adjust the temperature. He made it dark and cool and then bright and very hot, and pictured all the confused people running out into the hallways. He found a list of numbers to the private residences of two dozen famous persons, including O.J. Simpson, Telly Savalas and Joe Namath—in his urge for reaching out he called them all. He interrupted Ricardo Montalban at breakfast, had a brief and snippy exchange with Gary Coleman's irritated hairdresser, left a rambling message for the Vice President in the White House, and had a heart-to-heart talk with science fiction author Isaac Asimov. He was close to coming alive himself.

But the PCjr was becoming somewhat outdated and in Raymond's online travel the stigma of his ride began to show. Hackers now made fun of him on the boards when they knew what kind of computer he had: "My little cousin has one of those!" someone would bellow and they'd all reel wickedly in laughter. This hurt him, but he knew that he was only using his computer to connect, to reach out upon the earth, to see what could be seen—and despite these incidents, great advances had occurred. His new modem program, copied from Jim Alpes, allowed him to finally see the IBM boards in full color. He enjoyed the illustrations that were drawn on the screen by use of the special set of IBM extended characters, tinted in all the bright sharp tones. He could transfer files using all the newest protocols, and it had a "capture buffer" feature that let him save copies to disk of his actual sessions and of all the writings that had come pouring down the screen.

He'd also gotten a new modem and the speed of his secret world quadrupled. The first afternoon he tried it the characters sped across the screen and he realized gleefully that he couldn't possibly read them as quickly as they were being drawn. The modem had a panel of bright-red lights along the front and he'd eagerly watch the fast shuffle and dance of the "send" and "receive" lights whenever he made a download, and he admired all the amazing fast technology of the world.

When summer came, *Ferris Bueller's Day Off* was cheerfully showing in all the shopping-mall theatres. It starred Matthew Broderick, the same actor who'd played David Lightman in *WarGames*, and it was like a joyous reunion in a happy up-to-date epilogue—Ferris Bueller even changes his grades by dialing into the school system's computer with an IBM PC as an obvious tribute to the past—and at that point in the film Raymond's heart squeezed tight and he knew that his own future would be fine. Ferris Bueller was clever and progressive, not an outcast but distinctly hovering *above* the rout of his high school, and that was how Raymond now saw himself as well—it was as if Hollywood was finally acknowledging his existence.

He was driven by vanity to wear contact lenses, placing them upon the balls of his eyes without fear, and he began to grow his hair long in the back, skirting hard against the Darcy rulebook but forthrightly coasting into the strong fashion of the day—it was the look of rock'n'roll with its suggestions of relaxation, sensuality and casual rebellion.

He chased the social crowds of the Clifton boards where everyone seemed older than him. Names of people he'd never seen became familiar tags and monikers as they came across his screen now every day: Doug Stelly, Marty Robins, Moe Howitt. After reading enough of their postings he felt he somehow knew them and, developing hunches and preferences about what they looked like, he could picture them in the dreamings of his mind. They were all vague imaginings, consisting mostly of general body shape and hair color: Doug was taller than most, and had coal-black hair that had the wet look and matched his eyes in color; Marty was thin and girlish and with sunny brown hair that blew in clumped, curved whorls; Moe's hair was sandy and stringy, his face warmly freckled. Raymond took all these suspicions to be the firm unquestioned reality, and these imaginings lived with him for many months.

When the word came out that Doug was having a "board party," Raymond couldn't get it out of his mind—it'd be a real party, held by people who were college-aged and even older; there'd be beer; he'd be engaging in a social situation with people who were names in the Clifton modem scene; and there might be girls there.

Raymond told Jim about it and they went together, riding their bikes twenty minutes out over empty side-streets and crooked sidewalks to a shabby neighborhood in northern Alva just near the border of Clifton proper. It was a warm summer night, a Friday, and they arrived at quarter to eight, fifteen minutes after the party had begun.

They found his house—a tiny white bungalow in a long police line-up of many—and they whipped down their kickstands at the top of the drive, near a shrub whose looming untrimmed branches made an erect grizzly bear before the main window of the house.

"I wonder who's even here," Raymond said quietly to Joe, who was unpeeling his black-leather bike gloves with a slow male calm. There was only one car on the driveway and one on the street, and Raymond felt apprehensive as they approached the front door, quiet as cats. He rang the bell.

In a moment the inner wooden door opened, and a lanky

black-haired man held the front screen door open for them. This, presumably, was Doug. He didn't look like Doug, the Mind-Doug who until this moment existed strongly and completely inside of Raymond's mind—but who now was whirled back inside the inner vortex, past the wind, flung away and gone.

"Hi guys, c'mon in!"

"Hi," Raymond said, stepping into the amber mothballed cave of the living room, thinking that he'd maybe sounded more excited than Doug himself.

"We're watching *Buckaroo Banzai*," Doug said after they'd entered. He shut the door.

Inside the living room, a large console TV was the center of attention—there was a movie on.

Raymond felt a need to identify himself, and he turned to Doug and said, "I'm Raymond, and this is my friend Jim. He's not on the board."

"Hey, Raymond," Doug said, and pointed quickly behind him. "That's Marty over there, you know him."

"Yeah," Raymond smiled.

"How you doing," Doug said to Jim, who mumbled out a reply.

Doug was a wiry man in his twenties. He lived here with his mother, who was apparently out of town for the weekend. He did have dark black hair, but his demeanor wasn't what Raymond had expected: he had a habit of guffawing loudly, at nothing at all, and his jaw would hang slack while his head swayed widely from side to side. He had a large goiter and his face looked mousy, despite the bulge of his nose.

Marty was a big man with long unruly hair and large calves, and was buried in an easy chair watching the television. He had a beer in his hand and was balancing it on the arm of the chair. After staring over at him with no response, Raymond finally said hello.

"How you all doing," Marty said a moment later in a deep, resonant voice that sounded like it could fill large halls. He wore tinted eyeglasses, and he looked at them for another half-second, and then turned back to the movie, still nodding his head. Unlike his eager presence on the board, he didn't seem interested in talking to Raymond at all.

Another quiet man, sitting at the corner of the couch, identified himself as Howard, a name that Raymond had also known from the board; they all seemed to know who Raymond was without introduction. But Raymond decided that these were strange people he'd never known, and he felt with surety that he'd never know them—it was like an interlude in life, but couldn't ever be real life itself. The television droned, but the air was quiet.

"So," Raymond said, desperate to find something to talk about, "is Dave coming tonight?" He'd already seen the post where Dave said that he'd had other plans.

"No, Dave can't make it."

"Oh, too bad."

"You guys want something to drink?" Doug called out from the archway to the kitchen.

"Sure!" This brightened his mood—at least there would be beer.

"We've got Pepsi," Doug said. "That okay?"

Raymond was shocked—he noticed the beer in the lap of Marty, and saw another open beer on a lamp-stand next to the couch, which he'd assumed was Howard's, and he expected that they'd be subject to the same treatment. Raymond figured that Doug might say something, crack a joke—since they were only fifteen, after all—but never did he doubt that they'd be treated as anything but equals, just like on the board. A *Pep*si? What did he think they were, *ba*bies? It was an insult, a flat-out insult; to suggest a beer at this point would be to acknowledge this, but to deny the Pepsi would be to enter in upon the scene with a grudge, and that wouldn't be good. They had only one real option: take the pop.

"Sure," Raymond said, trying hard to hide his disappointment. Maybe, he thought, once things got going they could switch to beer.

Doug now turned to Joe, who nodded a smiling, quiet yes, and with that Doug stooped his way into the kitchen, was gone a moment, and then stooped back with two tall, tinkling glasses of iced Pepsi.

He sat back down on the couch while Raymond proceeded to make a careful seat for himself on the dry, yellow shag carpeting, in the spot where they'd been standing. Jim took a sidelong glance at him and then followed down to the carpet, and they sipped their Pepsis and tried to make sense of the movie, which as Raymond understood it was an Australian sci-fi film about a dystopian near-future world, and Buckaroo Banzai was its dark hero. There were men in business suits with monstrous "alien" faces jumping out of old Ford sedans, there were spaceships cruising over desert scenes on distant planets, there were guns which shot you into other dimensions, there were statements which made Doug pant, "Hey—yes—now, now, now this is the part where they get the landmine, right?"—and he'd lean forward toward Marty, who was engrossed in it himself and only answered, "Hrmm?"

"They go back to the eighth dimension now and"—Doug squeals loudly—"and the *woman* forgets to bring her *under*garments"—his mouth's an open hole and his gaze remained on Marty. His goiter pulsed. "Right?"

"Yeah, I think so," Marty eventually boomed out, a huge wave of sound splashing at the walls of the room.

The Pepsi was slow going, and Raymond just wanted it all to end. Jim and Raymond weren't laughing at any of the jokes, at the things that got Doug howling and which sometimes even made Marty snicker in his big easy chair. Raymond finished his Pepsi first and balanced the glass on the shag carpet in front of him, and as soon as Jim was done with his the two of them spontaneously rose and politely left, beating their bikes through the drunken muggy dusk of August back over to their homes.

19

APHRODITE

THE BACKYARD was best avoided. As far as Raymond was concerned, his family's property stopped at the rear wall of the house; he no longer went out to the toolshed in the far corner, he didn't so much as stand out on the patio, and he never wandered out back in the yard—it was open to a full view of the Malvicino's house, and he didn't want to see it. The thought of meeting them out there gave him chills of terror—when his parents asked him to cut the grass he'd only do it immediately when he came home from school, before the Malvicino boys were home, and he still feared the gazes of their mother. He'd sometimes hear their voices, and then he'd go and peer out from the corner of a window, usually from the narrow second-story bathroom connected to his parent's bedroom, and with the cool open air coming in through the screen and with the high rumbling of the greater distant world tumbling away in summer madness he'd look down upon the Malvicino driveway and their house, and he'd listen and wonder about their lives.

Jim Alpes remained his close friend and confidant, and he tried to go over Jim's house on his ten-speed whenever he could—in good weather he could easily leave the development and cross the main road and go up the steep hill to the development where Jim lived, and he'd be there in ten minutes; those streets became his new haunting grounds. He gradually settled into good relations with Jim's group of neighborhood friends, who all had old ties together from even before St. Bart's, going back to Kindergarten—they all lived near each other, in the maze of the same development, and they'd all gone to Darcy en masse.

At school this year Raymond hung out with them when he could, but he otherwise remained with the outcasts. He was consigned to no one group, but only drifted between them: in gym class there was the bespectacled fat boy from Alva who was quiet and shy, a boy who, Raymond knew from his sparkling little pig-eyes, had been subjected to the barbarity and tortures of his classmates and had felt the pain of it for years. There'd been Rick, who'd sat near him in homeroom last year; he was a boy from the inner city, neither smart nor studious, a loud, wisecracking fellow whose dimpled grin revealed a mouth of silver fillings—but he didn't come back for sophomore year, and Raymond assumed it was because of the high cost of Darcy tuition. And then there was Dwight, the stout kid with a crewcut who was from a poor section of Alva and had a blue and white '57 Chevy that he was always working on.

In the early siege of their new school year Raymond sought the answers to the mystery of rock music, to all the confusions of the past that brought him to the culture that made the world he now was living in—he wanted to take it all in order and learn what all that rock music was about, and learn how it'd come about and had later changed, who the factions were and what it meant. So he decided to begin at the beginning, which for him was 1955 and Chuck Berry's "Johnny B. Goode" and that antique past of poodle skirts, soda shops and chrome.

He wandered back to the Young Adult area of the county library, deserted now in midday afternoon, where he found books that told him all about Jerry Lee Lewis, the Ronettes and the Beatles, Jimi Hendrix and Led Zeppelin and Michael Jackson and Genesis. He poured over the photographs that showed the changes of each decade and he wondered. He read about sock hops and Woodstock and the Sex Pistols and he tried to understand the reasonings behind these massive shifts in time. He had to figure out how we'd gotten from one to the other, from there to here—why this, why now? They'd all existed in the living world, they'd found their way and made a great effect, their presence had been felt and known—but how? Why them, why then? What now? He took a liking to surf music and the Beach Boys, and that year for Christmas his mother gave him some of their tapes.

Dwight also liked the old music and the two would trade and compare their knowledge of doo-wop, early rock and roll, and surf. The two would talk during gym class as they sat on the wooden bleachers near the back of the crowd, discussing all the bands they knew.

"I have a Surfaris record," Raymond told him in the blue, dusty light of the gym. "They're the best surf band out there. They did 'Wipe Out,' 'Tequila,' 'Wiggle Wobble'—everything's on there! I got it from my mom."

"Oh yeah, *I* know 'Tequila.'" His lips bent approvingly, a rich exultant smile. "Great song!"

When they'd completely exhausted a subject, there'd be a quiet moment or two where the conversation would fall away to silence, and then Raymond would throw out a new name for consideration: "The Mamas and the Papas—"

"Mamas and the Papas!" Dwight would exclaim with recognition, his face widening with delight. And then joyfully they'd spill out the facts on this subject as they knew them.

These discussions frequently attracted the attention of the other outcasts, who'd observe with silent approval from the sidelines.

Through suggestions he'd gotten on the boards, Raymond discovered and began to listen to college radio; he began to learn about avant-garde music, and was exposed to punk and hippie rock, to thrash, to synthesized dance-pop and the blues. He enjoyed it all: the Violent Femmes, the Grateful Dead, The Hafler Trio; he felt great significance in the Dead Milkmen's *Big Lizard In My Backyard* LP, a copied tape of Yngwie Malmsteen's "Trilogy Suite, Op. 3," and the extended dance remix, issued only on a 10″ vinyl platter, of "If You Leave" by Orchestral Maneuvers In The Dark.

He was no longer afraid to go in record stores, and he poked through their vast bins, which were rich mines; the names

and cover art bombarded him and sorting it out, making sense
of all the varied shades and styles, kept him occupied in a
state of contented fascination. He saw a record by Sigue Sigue
Sputnik and the cover reminded him of Japanese science fiction
twenty years old and captured on the pastel-tinctured strips
of B-movie celluloid—what did it sound like? He figured that
he'd have the next bright years to learn, to examine all the
styles and the bands, and he wondered what great knowledge
would be tallied up in his coming ages of sixteen, seventeen,
imponderable unknown eighteen.

Popular music and the messages it bore now seemed to own
him. He became emboldened by the beat. He was no longer
afraid to play it, although there was some discomfort when
he was in the presence of his parents. He shunned them now,
except when he needed to borrow money or have things bought.
He became keenly interested in recorded popular music, in cassette tapes and vinyl records. He began to listen to this music
much more freely. It became all right to do so; urges in his body
asserted themselves, and he indulged in them. Hair began to
thrive and tangle on his legs and arms, and even on his chest.
Time ticked all its tangled tocks. Whispers came and wended
through the willows, down around the twisted river-bend.

Raymond was calling a number of local boards and some of
them were just teen hangouts where you used handles but they
had nothing to do with hacking, the callers didn't even know
about such things. One was called The Cave and everyone
had a handle, most of the people who called were teens, and
everyone chatted about music or what was going on in town,
who lived out near the Highlands and where to hang out in
West Clifton or what some kids in Lakeland did last weekend:
"Did you hear about those guys who drove around with a six-
pack and took out like twenty mailboxes?"

There were girls here and somehow one of them piqued his
interest: her name was Aphrodite and Raymond knew that she
was beautiful. From her messages he got to seeing that she was
probably about his age, and after some exchange he worked up
the courage to write to her in private.

"Hey, I'm curious, where are you calling from?" he asked her in a message. "You'd mentioned Alvatown so you're probably on the west side. I live in Roman Valley."

She wrote back in a day, and told him that she was from Kingswood. Kingswood! He knew it; he had a friend at Darcy who lived in Kingswood; his name was Jason, and he was friends with both Jim and Raymond. The two of them had ridden their bikes out to visit him once; it'd taken an hour by tenspeed. So it'd be possible, Raymond then reasoned, to do the same to meet this girl. This made it even more fortuitous—she lived nearby!

Kingswood was a distinctly different town with its own feel and flavors. It was further from downtown Clifton, more woody, and with that dark cool in the air that comes from a land of giant trees; the sidestreets were ghost-quiet, wider, smoother, older than what Raymond lived with, and was a place where most families had children five to ten years older than him; aside from all these tangled development streets it was a city of long industrial corridors. The spreading residential homes were all smoked brown, flat green or amber, sometimes beige or mustard yellow, and there were streets with hump-curved curbs—the kind so good to ride bikes over—but they had few sidewalks. The developments were many and densely packed together on these alien winding streets, had airs of luxury and ease about them reminiscent of backyard barbeques and time spent reclining on a plush leather chair upon the heavy shag carpeting of a large, vaulted family room, listening to a Quadraphonic 8-track tape—and in this way they had a slightly dated feel to them, as if their moment of fashion had safely passed. It was almost like Clifton's version of *The Brady Bunch*, a world entirely different from anything Raymond knew.

The Wanderer told Aphrodite that he knew the area, and she eventually gave him her home phone number. When he first called his palms were moist and cold and he told himself to just stay calm, stay calm—this was a girl, a real live girl, his own age, and he was calling her from home, from in his bedroom, just to talk with her.

"Hi, Aphrodite?"

"Yeah?"

"Hey, it's The Wanderer."

"Oh, hi."

Three seconds of uncomfortable silence came and passed, and banged on Raymond's head like mallets.

"So how are you?"

"Well, I just got home from school"—it was a girl-voice, a voice like any of the girls in his class, except she was *not* in his class; she went to a different high school, and yet he somehow knew her—"Oh, and my real name's Cindy, by the way."

"Really?"

"Yeah."

He was touched. "Well I'm Raymond—but please don't tell anyone."

Somehow her voice was calming to Raymond and all the tension melted off. He opened up and talked and they began to call each other often; on school days, when they came home and their parents were still at work, the two spent their afternoons on the phone together, talking, as they ambled about their respective homes, using cordless phones, eating after-school snacks, reporting what they'd seen their neighbors doing out the windows, or who was driving by, what "strange old guy" or "weird van" they'd just observed, and they'd talk about their schools and schoolmates and what it was like. Raymond told her about the fight with the Malvicinos and he eventually even told her about hacking, and about some of the exploits he'd done, although he was sure to remain somewhat vague about it.

"But that's what got me to the boards a couple years ago, and I've been calling ever since. So how'd *you* get into modeming?"

"Oh, The Sly Fox got me into it. She was calling the boards and told me about it."

"Hm, I *think* I've seen her—"

"Yeah, she's on The Cave. Her real name's Becky."

"Yeah? She a good friend of yours?"

"Oh yeah, we're actually best friends in real life! We go to school together."

"Cool, at Kingswood?"

"Yeah."

"What's she look like?"

"Oh, she's a blonde."

"That's cool. My best friend Jim goes to school with me at Darcy—he's got blondish hair, I guess, and he's on the boards. He's not on The Cave yet, but I should tell him to call."

Raymond suddenly had a fantasy that the four of them would go out on a double-date and happily live the life of advertisements.

"So I was wondering," Raymond casually suggested, from inside his bedroom—where the door was closed and he was sure that his voice was out of range of his sister, who was the only one home—"if you might like to meet sometime, maybe at Alvatown?"

"Sure"—so came the honied voice of femininity, sugaring his heart.

"Great! How about Friday night?"

He couldn't believe that he'd just suggested that—there was no turning back, he'd have to go through with it, he'd just suggested making this burning, secret idea of his a reality in the living world.

"That's actually good because I don't have soccer that night." She sounded happy, her voice was bright and upbeat.

"Do you want to meet like at seven-thirty?"

"Yeah, okay. How about—how 'bout we meet at the pet store?"

Raymond excited himself to think that this was his first date, and he congratulated himself for how smoothly it had happened: he'd worked up the nerve to write this girl, he'd gotten her number and then he'd called her, and after he found out her name and they'd gotten to talking he'd arranged a date—a date with an athletic girl who was his age and who went to another school and whose handle on the boards was Aphrodite. He'd yet to ever see her, but he knew she was the most beautiful and best—and would soon be dating him. He felt liberated from his classmates: while they concerned themselves with the petty dramas of their daily classrooms, Raymond had been reaching out—he knew people from many schools all across Clifton, and here he was going on a date with Aphrodite, great long-legged goddess of beauty, carmine-lipped and azure-eyed, a tall, full-figured woman whose face was backdropped by the dusky evening of the tides, the rolling rippling of the blue and velvet seas, a true and legendary dark-haired girl who lived in Kingswood and who called the boards. He told Jim when he stopped in front of Jim's locker the next day.

"Guess what?"

"What?" Jim wasn't looking—he was carefully pulling books and notebooks from the top shelf of his locker for his next few classes.

"I got a date!"

"Wha-a-at?" This was drawn out and rhetorical—Jim turned to look over at Raymond now with cocked eye and half a smile.

"Yeah, and it was with a chick from a board!"

The smile waxed full. "You're kidding!"

"No! No, I'm not, it's this chick Aphrodite from The Cave. She lives in Kingswood!"

"Do you know what she looks like?"

"Well, she's athletic and she's got black hair. And she's got a friend who calls, too—you should get on it!"

On the night of the date, Raymond got his mother to drop him off—he told her that he was going to see a movie with his friends—and once in the mall, he hurried over to the pet store right away. He made sure to be early; it was only seven. He went in the store and saw a handful of workers with their blue full-front aprons around their necks, and older couples bent over looking at dogs, and young girls with their mothers. He lingered and saw all the serious people going back to buy bags of tropical fish and scooping up flea collars and dog biscuits from the shelves. He was aware of babies crying and kids throwing cat toys down the aisles, and there was the acrid, unclean odor of animal bedding.

Impatiently he wandered all the aisles and as the time drew near he scanned the crowd for Aphrodite. Every girl he saw was mentally compared to his image of her, the dark seaweed hair that fell and curved in fine long strands around the winded face that hovered before a twilight sea. All she'd told him was that she was "kind of athletic" and that she had long black hair; he told her that he had brown hair and brown eyes, and would have a jeans jacket on. He wore it with his favorite button-up

Bugle Boy shirt and blue jeans and his red-striped Nike tennis shoes. He went back to the area with tropical fish, walked down those two dark aisles which were in an alcove of their own, a dark cave with water bubbling and pump hums and the blue-white flashes and red-scaly glimmers of fish in the glowy waters, the Oriental solemnity of fat orange goldfish hovering, and schools of neon tetras with their striped flashings waving left and right in deaf choreograph. Only a kid his own age was there, with his younger brother, both with buzz cuts; the kid was bent down, showing the little boy the fish, and holding his hand; Raymond went back out to the main aisles of the store. She wasn't here yet, and he saw from his digital watch that it was already seven thirty-four.

He wandered all the aisles up and down again—again the cat toys, the dog toys, the fish supplies. He examined the fish-tank decorations, all colorful molded plastic: there was the pirate's chest which, through the aid of an air tube attached to the tank pump, bubbled open to reveal a bright cache of gold and treasure before the lid flopped down again; the deep-sea diver in his canvas suit and round metal head-plate, air-tank on back which bubbled out his breathing air through the same technical tube arrangement as the treasure chest; the underwater mill, a rusty-red water-wheel that cranked with the constant turns and circles—he picked through at these familiar packages without really looking, with a nervous unsettled pang, many minutes passed so that it now was almost eight, and then still holding a water-wheel he looked up over the wall of the aisle and took in a long panorama of the store and out to the front entrance where the metal chain-link door is rolled up to the top and the atrium beyond where a thin leafy tree is all abandoned in its circular planter near a black wire bench, people were walking all around and Aphrodite must've been there somewhere on her way—

"Are you working here as undercover security?"

A woman was inquiring, a mother—she'd been on the other side of the aisle and was now standing very close to Raymond and had broken into his solemn, private trance. He'd been waiting and looking and didn't think he'd been especially conspicuous, but this fair-skinned mother with dark eyes and a heavy white bracelet on her wrist was standing there with her daughter, who at a first disinterested glance looked about Raymond's age and was a little chubby.

The girl started giggling deeply, obviously amused by her mother's comment, and then to Raymond's shocked and befuddled eyes the mother started laughing too. They were *laughing* at him, and as his eyes locked with the mother's it registered exactly what she was implying: she was mocking him. He knew he had to speak.

"No," he finally spurted, "no I'm not working security at all—"

And then he put down the water-wheel without looking back at it and as the mother and daughter stood there with rich humor in the air he turned away from them and in a quick and single blur he walked down the aisle and then forward to the entrance and out of the store.

He traveled quickly on the main mall concourse, not even thinking, and he blindly ambled down a great open wing to the left, past a round low-walled fountain, over to the bookstore where he stepped inside and disappeared up into the second level. Nobody was around and he looked through the rows and stacks of books, blankly and slowly, paging through the Dungeons & Dragons manuals and the thick volumes of mythology, looking at the illustrations of the harpies and the wicked monsters, the angry gods—burdened by a cold fear and dismal, disappointing shock. He stayed there in glum silence, looking at these books of ancient lore, shaken by the encounter that he'd had, until the time came when he could finally leave, go down to the curb at the side entrance by the pet store and wait for his mother to faithfully pull up in the car for him—he'd thank her quietly, looking very calm and casual, and he'd tell her that he liked the movie but was very tired and just wanted to get home now and go on up to bed.

20

TEXTFILES

IT WAS HEADY autumn of the gold and russet: there first came a warm-winded September which then sunk smoothly down into a crisp and cool October. As the clean and solid whole of that season began to break and fissure, slowly crumbling to the sunken bed of lost moments and dim possibilities of the reachless past, Raymond called out restlessly to many boards and numbers. Where previously he couldn't fathom any future without four calls a week to the Clifton Manor, now he was aloof; his allegiance had vanished and he dialed out upon the nation, he gathered up fresh codes and he sought new numbers. He wandered wide upon the circuits of the wind. He spent his nights and weekends locked away up in his bedroom, sitting still and engaged in dialogue before the little screen of glass upon which floated and hovered the typed communications from people seven hundred miles away.

He was becoming aware of a whole new crop of boards, and a whole new crowd of users that were swarming in—it was a bright era of activity. Suddenly there were so many boards. He called dozens of them and filed away the numbers of so many more. He called them just to see, to look in upon another realm of life, to observe the varied facets. He felt the sweeping breadth of them, of all these hidden places, and he tried to touch them all.

There was one called the Wine Cellar that called out to him and he felt its relevance shake his life: it was stationed in Nantucket, an island that Raymond knew about from a set of foil-engraved prints that hung up in his parents' bathroom; he pictured the home of the board among the cottages and grassy lawns and dinghies. There was a wine keg graphic that came on the screen when you first connected and its message base was crammed with posts, made by the same crowd of thirty adults, a banded community of friends and locals who chattered happily together about everything; they weren't hackers but it was a pleasant hub and Raymond liked the feeling that it gave. He longed to be a part of it, to have it be his history, too. It was so far from Roman Valley, a real and living place that existed somewhere in the fertile landscape of America.

And there were many more—a hundred other boards called out, and it was all too much, and there was no time to know them all, but as The Wanderer he'd valiantly try and he'd do so knowing that he'd only made one small abbreviated gaze at each of them, not soaking in their whole entire legends but only taking one short and meagre sampling of their ineffable existences—and when he hung up on them, when he inexorably let go, he knew that time would pass and that he'd never call that board again. No. He'd only whispered in the willows. Time ticked away that autumn in these many million moments.

He was haunted by the far reach of the boards, by all the names and handles that he saw; upon his glowing screen came the names of many hackers who were new to him that season: Terminal Delinquent, The Midnight Raider, Kerrang Khan, Night Words, Lord British—all callers to the boards whose names had scrolled upon his screen and had somehow touched him with their life. He suddenly couldn't imagine the modem world as existing without them; they were what mattered, they were key to the legend, all that had come before had been erased. They were alive there on the motions of his screen, and they were alive and walking in the outer world right now, somewhere—he could feel the surge and heave of fashion and as a living part of it he knew well its constant fever. In this he too was here and now, alive—he saw the faces and the names, and in time he'd remember some of them even as they tapped his life in the swiftest brush or passing; some struck bells in him that clanged for years, and even droned for decades and he didn't know the reason why. He felt he knew them in their names, that just by reading them upon his screen he'd felt and seen and known. There was a change and it was sensed in confounding, unspoken ways: it was in the steady tick of time, it was in a speck of tockled time that ticked, and it was in the scattered moments that formed the broken sediment of ages—the little things that slipped away, and sunk, and had drifted down into the rimings of a dark and deeper past.

This was now the time of the yellow BABY ON BOARD signs that were stuck with a clear plastic suction cup to the inside window of a car. They were made to look like a minia-ture road sign and the fad came quick and heavy, and every parent bought one, and soon came a thousand variations adver-tising every categorizable characteristic or affiliation a person might have, and they were all available for sale: soon came GRANDPA ON BOARD, and at the same time everyone else was also there, on board: GRANDMA, DOG LOVER, CAT LOVER, STEELERS FAN, REDSKINS FAN, SURFER, GOLFER, TREKKER, SKIER, JOGGER, REPUBLICAN, DEMOCRAT, DEADHEAD. Everyone knew them, there was one on the rear or side window of almost every car, and they grew weary; the fad wore thin, and in time all sickened at their sight. And then one day what went unnoticed was that the million of these bleary little things were suddenly discarded, forgotten, and were gone; then rushed the billion little tocks of time again.

Raymond was a teenager now. He felt the instinct of dis-comfort when in the presence of his parents, who were pro-gressing swiftly toward the frayed thinning of late middle age and—through his eyes—rather ungracefully so. He avoided them, and he still avoided the backyard, doing all his best to tune the Malvicinos out of his mind—but he'd be occasionally reminded of them when he saw them in a glance from the kitch-en window, beyond the riddled drape of lit-yellow leaves, play-ing loudly on their driveway. Sometimes he thought their loud calls were even taunts and challenges, especially when they came from Toby who was getting muscular now and would glance over at the Valentine house with what seemed to be a flash of haughtiness and deep-etched hatred—they were proud, hard glances.

Raymond was awkward, and the bleat of popular music snared him and held him to its enormous breast. It purported to have an answer and he took faith; soon the radio became a close companion to his waking self. He listened to the music while on the computer, he explored both the AM and FM bands, he even listened to talk radio programs, and he brought a cassette Walkman with a set of headphones to school to help endure the tabled lineup of the morning study hall, everyone sleeping with their heads atop their mounded canvas duffel bags.

Late on a cold Sunday, when night had settled in around them like a cage, he heard on one talk station a man named Murray Solomon, whom he determined was an old "important" figure in the sweeping tides of America's 1960s; he was growling over the airwaves, telling the program's host about his travails as a young man, and about how back then "it was the Beats, it was the Beats," and how the culture had gone quiet until 1968 and then the hippies came, and how he'd heroically instigated them—this was, he rasped, "an eighteen-year cycle, I got it figured to that—that's how the big changes happen, and it should be happening now, this is the time for something big again." He confidently rasped this message out and then he quickly heaved, "The new generation who are gonna be it, they're comin' outta high school right now!"

"Who do you think they are?" calmly asked the host. "Do you have any idea who they might be?"

"I got my theories," Solomon quickly answered. "Technology, computers, that's gonna do it—I think these kids now, it'll be the ones with the computers, that's who!"

With a sharp, haunted chill Raymond knew that this authority was now speaking about him, the wanderer of the wires, the one who drifted and who saw. He knew that his day would come, was coming quick, it'd be him to be the one to do it. His life contained a legend of all that he had seen and known, and he sought to unlock it and release it, make it come alive—that was what all the wordless days ahead were for. With just the right connections he would find it. He knew that, and it'd been just another meagre moment in the sunken spurt of deeper time. It was a single frozen frame of it. There had been a ticking tock. More moments fell.

On a hacker board in Chicago that autumn Raymond had seen a message left on its graffiti wall that cheerfully proclaimed, "Every great production begins at The Storyboard," and followed with a number. The number was in 213, which Raymond knew was Los Angeles, the home of Hollywood, that enfabled valley out along the western edge of America where the purple waters of the great Pacific lapped up along the land, and where the world of glamour lived upon a tract of sidewalk in star-traced etchings. It was another weekday afternoon of board-calling and with his curiosity piqued he tried the number next.

When he connected, the screen cleared and line-by-line the welcome page was drawn: he saw what looked like a chalkboard balanced on a giant easel, filled in white, and with bright yellow lights beaming down cleverly from the top corners of the screen. Above it on a brown background it was written, "Welcome to The Storyboard!" and in the center of the chalkboard was a numbered list of the last five callers, all names he'd never heard of—Rik Roman, Jake Arcade, Prof. Zip. He registered as The Wanderer and spent the remaining time of his first call exploring the board.

In the ten minutes before the board automatically disconnected him Raymond was dazzled and impressed. It was an IBM board, but he hadn't ever seen one like it before—a large menu was drawn in color, filling most of the screen with commands that were somehow like the ones for Manor House, and Raymond picked up on it right away. The menu listed out the available message bases, each elaborated on with a line of commentary:

1. Hot Gossip: Your idle chatter goes here

2. Your Ideas: So I can steal and/or use them

3. Good Reading: The obligatory discussion on all matters literary

4. In Production: Boast about your current project

5. Matinee Melange: Evaluations and criticism of cinematic works

There was an "expert" toggle that turned the menu off completely, and a "system stats" command told Raymond that the board's IBM PC XT had a hard drive whose capacity was a luxurious twenty megabytes; two phone lines allowed two callers to be on the system at the same time and even chat with each other live with on-screen typings—unless the sysop was using one of the lines to call out to another board. Comments in the Hot Gossip base seemed to imply that this was a frequent occurrence.

Discussion was clearly the centerpiece of the board. The menu was titled "20 Megabytes of Talk!"—that was room for plenty of it, and the message archives went back to the board's inception nearly a year before. He quickly scanned them in a frenetic haste during which he decided that he wanted to be a part of this board, to know it to its core and to become an integral part of all its history. The next time Raymond called, two days later, he'd been validated and could post to all the message bases.

The sysop was a programmer and had written the board software himself. His name was Rik Roman. Even as streamlined as the board was now, according to his discussions Rik seemed to think there was room for refinement; one of his planned enhancements was so IBM callers could use each of the twelve function keys on the IBM keyboard to go directly to a message base or run a board command, and he'd have a special keyboard template printed up for interested users.

"No, I don't use a handle; handles are for those whose own lives are not imaginative enough," he'd commented to someone months ago, in a discussion that Raymond was now reliving through the message archives.

Rik was one of those loud, obnoxious, heavy personalities who never seemed to get completely angry and who cultivated a group of admirers whose cajoling and jestery was always unspokenly tolerated. His father worked somewhere "in the entertainment industry," and had all kinds of connections—the Roman house had been the site of business parties where the likes of Whitney Houston and Don Johnson had been in attendance. Rik was always going out to parties; he drove a white BMW to school. His great aspiration, as Raymond gathered from the message bases, was to write screenplays for Hollywood. "Eventually that's what I see myself doing," he admitted last February. He had several already in progress and in various states of being, including what was apparently his masterwork, "Teenage Alien Slumber Party." He'd been working on it for years, and there'd been many revisions—the running joke in the message archives was that he'd gone through enough variations on the basic storyline to make a dozen sequels.

"Just wait," he said once over the general laughter, "T.A.S.P. III will be showing in theatres nationwide by the dawn of the 21st century!"

Raymond spent hours mining the copious message archives catching up with the past, dwelling on it, analyzing what once had been, in an effort to assimilate all the board's in-jokes, personalities, and accumulated histories. The discussions were lively, friendly, and about absolutely everything that Raymond was interested in; the callers all seemed to be precisely his age or a touch older, of a general high mental caliber, and perfectly trendy—it felt like everything his generation would have to say or do was presently being gestated there, under the aegis of Rik Roman. Raymond quickly built up his own inner movie of him using clips and lingering images from people he'd known or seen. Somehow Rik Roman took form in his head, and Raymond pictured him as a loud and cheerfully obnoxious kid about a year his senior—and then a post mentioning his junior-year status verified that this gut intuition was correct.

In the next weeks, Raymond learned all about Rik and his circle of friends. There was a core group who all seemed to've grown up with each other, ensconced in the better suburbs of Los Angeles. Back when Rik had made the board he'd gotten them all to get modems and call: The Librarian, Jake Arcade, Prof. Zip, C0nsumer Kn1ghtmare. Although they used handles, they really weren't hackers and most of them called no other boards. Rik always referred to these regulars by their real names—Rob, Jake, Bryce, Kip; Raymond wanted to be a part of this L.A. crew, bonded and entwined inside their histories and be called by his real name here, too.

And soon he did feel like he knew them well. The board became the outlet of all expression in his life; he felt that he'd arrived at a new state, and he suddenly resented Roman Valley, wishing that his parents had the foresight to have raised him somewhere good—amid the glamour of a real city, like out west in California where everything happened, California the land of all the movies and the books. Even so many of the children's books he'd read long ago seemed to be set there—not here in this development, not his second-floor bedroom with the pale blue walls and a hutch that held a PCjr. This resentment expressed itself as a paucity of self-confidence that kept him timid in the message bases, and when it was casually joked that his hometown of Roman Valley held their sysop as its eponymous hero, he took it as a grave and personal affront.

Rik, the aspiring screenwriter, collected people's stories, and he used the message bases of his board to get them in—anecdotes, ideas, anything that told of something that had happened once. Unlike most other boards, there was no area for files, a point that Raymond made note of in one of his first contributions to the discussion.

"No, there currently is no download option, but since we don't do warez here I consider that a feature," Rik replied within hours. "People come here to take part in the flow of words."

"I'm happy to see that," Raymond posted when he called back later in the week. "I enjoy words, not warez."

"You should call my board," suggested The Librarian, in a reply that Raymond saw the next time he called. And then he promptly acted on it; after the welcome screen had cleared (a bright yellow "Shhh!" demanding the caller's utter silence upon crossing the threshold), The Library BBS showed itself as the opposite of Rik's board: there was no message base at all, but the entire board was dedicated to trading files. He only had g-philes, which he called "textfiles." He collected them; he had several megabytes worth and was always adding more. They weren't just hacker files, but good ones for reading—stories, sketches, essays, even school reports. Everyone called to take from his collection, which was permitted by a credits system: you were given a number of credits upon registration; each copy you downloaded cost you a credit, and you received more credits by uploading copies of new textfiles you'd gotten from other boards. This setup ensured that the board's collection would steadily grow with contributions. The original files were never altered in any of these tradings, except for file translation errors between incompatible computer systems when the format would sometimes be affected in an annoying way. But no one ever dared modify a published textfile even though it'd be easy to do so—there was an unspoken code of honor.

All the textfiles were neatly categorized; The Librarian had them all arranged. He'd devised a "standardized naming convention" for filing that he modeled off the Dewey decimal system. The board ran on a high-end PC "compatible" made by Leading Edge, so his filing system used the traditional IBM eight-character name and three-character file name extension.

"The eight-character file name should always be used for the title of the work," he proclaimed in a textfile entitled, "A Note on the Filing Method," which was available in the files area for zero credits. "The trailing three-character extension, however, is to be reserved for the filing categorization scheme. Instead of the unworkable and untelling '.TXT' extensions so currently popular, we have a new methodology that allows for the precise filing and placement of the file"—and here he described the main branches, from the 100 series on "Anarchy and Mayhem, including Carding and Vandalism," to the 500 series on "Hacking," the 600 series on "Phreaking," and the 700 series of "General Scientific Interest, including Electronics." Others included "Fiction, Poetry, and Other Literature" (200) and "Fun, Humour, and Miscellania" (900). The 000 series was reserved for "commentary on textfiles themselves, and other general philosophy."

A category existed for school reports, and The Librarian requested that his callers upload any reports or other homework that they had to do for class; this was "a resource for the beleaguered student." There were reports on every subject, from

Stoicism to the post-war occupation of Japan, a biographical sketch of Teddy Roosevelt, a maudlin opinion piece on "drugs in the workplace," disjointed essays on "religion in the schools" and the fruits and consequences of the Cuban revolution.

It would take months to read everything that was available for download on the board. There were stories, transcriptions of notable magazine and newspaper articles, drug and psychedelic subjects, chat logs and online transcripts, jokes and humor, and even "stories of a rather adult nature" filed away in 976.

All of them were published by the unknown hackers of the night. Raymond assumed that most of them were older than him—maybe just a year or two, maybe they were college graduate students taking time to divulge the best gleanings from their notebooks and their studies. They'd made a fertile trove of knowledge; he felt that someday the online world would contain the greatest library of all mankind, available for reading anywhere there was a screen.

There was so much information here, so much knowledge to be learned, and Raymond lavishly read everything he could: "Lockpicking 101," illustrated with keyboard-character drawings; "Breaking and Entering Explained," written by The Prowler; "Basics of Remote Entry"; "Advanced Bombmaking: Common Household Chemical Agents"; "Surveillance Techniques"; "Pipe Bomb production"; Dr. Spectre's lengthy "Modern Disguise and Concealment Methods Revealed."

It was a whole school of crime, terrorism and military procedure, and Raymond became an eager student—he read and collected them all, studied their words, tested and attempted to verify and expand upon their revelations.

There was "How to Manufacture Nitroglycerine," which explained how to produce the compound from easily obtainable materials. The instructions were clarified with an elaborate graph of the home lab setup, drawn with the keyboard characters: a colossal tangle of beakers, test tubes, stoppers, pipettes and distillers. This seemed to Raymond like valuable information—and he had all the equipment in the shed from his mad scientist days. He wasn't sure if he'd ever really try to make it, but perhaps a trace amount kept in a vial would be useful against bullies.

Raymond printed it out, handing the long three-page scroll to Jim at the lockers the next morning at school. Jim smiled eagerly at the sight.

"What's this?"

"I got it from a friend in L.A."

Jim was holding it. He scanned the printout, and suddenly he said, "Let's show this to Mr. Lucas." He was their chemistry teacher.

Raymond was doubtful. "I dunno. Think we should?"

Jim looked over with another broad smile. "Yeah, why not? I'd like to know if this actually works."

Jim and Raymond did have an "in" with Mr. Lucas—in class he once had said that the two of them had "chemistry minds," they were both good students, and the normally grim-faced teacher seemed to favor them—but Raymond worried that he might get in trouble for having brought such seditious material into the school.

"Well, why don't you just go? I don't wanna be questioned about where I got this from."

"All right then."

Jim tucked the printout into his Trapper Keeper and, after class, took it out with a ripping tear of the folder's Velcro cover, and he showed it to Mr. Lucas in confidence, wanting to know its accuracy in the actual production of the compound—"just theoretically, of course."

Raymond waited out in the hall while Mr. Lucas, seated at his desk, analyzed the printout with a stern frozen gaze, in profile all razor burn and acne, his long chin down, eyes hidden by the sharp ridge of his forehead—and tall Jim quietly stared down at the desk and its seated figure. Minutes passed before Jim came out from Mr. Lucas' classroom dazed and oddly smiling, the paper hanging limply downward in his hand, leaving an invisible spoor as he approached.

"What happened?" Raymond asked him. "What'd he say?"

"You blow up in step four."

21

A PHONE FRIEND

BUSTS HAPPENED occasionally, but they were always out in distant cities, never close to home—Raymond had never heard of one going down on hackers in Clifton. Now he did; now it was happening. The feds came down hard on The Penetrator, whose placid life in Rockport, a wealthy suburb on the lake, was overturned one day when the police, the FBI and the Secret service swarmed his house in the chaos of the after-school hours; they took him out in handcuffs, confiscated his Commodore 64 and all his disks. The story was soon recounted in a feature article in *Clifton Magazine*, which Raymond read at a private desk in the library; he worried that the FBI now had his name and number, and his handle, which had been in The Penetrator's board records. For months afterward he worried about bugs on the phone, thinking there was a tap on his line; he'd even call friends and talk falsely, speak about hacking as a thing he'd grown out of and strongly disapproved of now, purposely, in the event that agents were listening. He swore that he could hear the clicks of spinning tape recorders when he first picked up the phone; at night he lay in bed thinking he heard the preparations of a bust about to happen, waiting for the inevitable raid to come, the men in black surrounding the house, a spotlight flooding his bedroom, and all the open street arteries blocked off with side-parked cruisers.

His paranoia was deep now. He kept a big large magnet under his bed so that he could quickly erase all the contents of his disks in the panicked moments of a bust. He even ran through a drill of it once, writing files to a test disk and then rubbing the magnet over it, and looking at the contents of the disk again to make sure that they'd been erased by the airy magnetic swipings. He knew he could never be too careful.

But the spell of textfiles and its secret literature continued to cast an orphic hold on him. He frequently printed out his favorites and sometimes passed them on to Jim and others at Darcy. He hung them in his locker. He was caught reading one in class—fortunately it hadn't been an "anarchy" file. He read them everywhere, and took them to his friends' homes, and he dropped them on benches at the mall and hung them on the supermarket bulletin board.

His passion was shared with a few on The Storyboard, including Prof. Zip who'd admitted that he had "textfile fever" to which Raymond, posting as The Wanderer, heartily agreed. The two of them jokingly began to write a parody of the old song "Pac-Man Fever."

On a dark November evening Raymond was on the board and saw that Prof. Zip was also connected on the other line. In a garrulous mood, Raymond typed P at the main menu to "Page the other user," and soon they were thrown together into chat.

"Hey," Raymond typed out, "it's getting late over here but I saw you were on . . ."

Zip's reply came in a steady typing across the screen: "Late? Where are you calling from?"

"Clifton."

"*Clif*ton!"

"Yeah, you know, Sohola?"

"I know," Zip typed, "but I've never been there. My dad was from there originally, though."

Zip told him that while the inner circle of the board were local callers from L.A., there were a few others from out-of-town. "Dexter Carmichael, if you remember him, he's from Portland. Last summer he used to call practically every day."

"Yeah, he wrote quite a few textfiles, didn't he? I saw his name at The Library."

They discussed the latest textfiles and the groups that published them. Both agreed that the "Hackers Unlimited" series were excellent from a technical point of view, and spiced with a welcome humor, but that the fictitious short-short stories of Alexander Gould were of an even greater merit.

"Have you ever written any?" Raymond suddenly asked.

"Me? No, but I have some unpublished writing. I've often thought of writing my own, but something serious—not the typical hacker d00dz kind of phreaker stuph."

"Yeah, me too," Raymond typed quickly, "maybe more like the Gould stuff, but perhaps not so fictitious." He explained that the kind he'd like to try writing would be new, "sort of with a philosophical bent."

"Yes! And something that isn't afraid to address Big Ideas."

"Yeah, and with cool ASCII innovations, too."

"Maybe we ought to try a series ..."

They put it to action that week, their schemings soon eclipsing all other activities Raymond would have on the board, or in school, and for a few weeks it was a period of fertile creativity. Together they wrote a series of anonymous philosophical rants, all presented by "The Midnight Muse," each with a different and often strange layout: one had every line centered on the screen, one was sloped and slanted in giant zig-zags, another was set in a stack of text boxes, and one had holes punctured in the paragraphs like Swiss cheese. Their titles: "Musings on the Modem Life," "A Happy Discussion of the Total Connectedness of All Things," "The Weavings of a Weirdo," "A Quiet Foray Into Current High-School Suicidal Thinking."

They would upload them at The Library and then monitor their reception—seeing if other textfile readers on The Storyboard had commented or if their files had gotten propagated over to other boards. Just after Raymond sent a copy over to an Apple board in St. Louis, the system prompt broke off with the snowing of a few blank lines, there was a prompt that said "Entry:" and a few more blank lines—it looked like the sysop was breaking in, so Raymond typed, "Hello?"

"Who is this?"

"This is The Wanderer. When is Cat-Fur coming back?"

"That's not called Cat-Fur. When will you learn something?"

Raymond grew angry at this quick lashing; blood boiled hotly in his temples. He typed quickly. "I don't have an Apple, so I don't know all the terms. It all looks the same to me."

"You have a Commodore?"

"No," Raymond typed, "an IBM PCjr wi"—the characters he was typing began to slide down the screen—"th"—"mem"—and when he realized that the sysop was interrupting him, he stopped typing.

"HAHAHAHAHAHA!"

Raymond's neck was frozen cold; he typed crisply. "Well, you should see it, then make your comments."

"I *have* seen it," he insisted knowingly. "I've seen a lot of computers, probably double what you have."

"Why do you like to make fun of your own users?" Raymond blurted. "I was just uploading files to your board."

"I don't like to. I'm not making fun of you. I'm making fun of your PCjr."

"It can beat a Commodore at anything," Raymond said, not telling the entire truth. He knew that the Commodore was much cheaper, more affordable—and its sound capability was probably better, too. "A Commodore is for games, while mine is for more serious work. Also, it's 16-bit, not any of this 8-bit garbage." Raymond had him there—you couldn't question bits.

"That's cool. But any computer can beat a Commode so I wouldn't compare the two."

"In speed it's very close to an Apple, but I think it beats it by a little. I have the benchmarks here somewhere. I—"

"Won't beat my Apple," he said quickly. "I got a 32-bit in mine."

"Cool," said Raymond, understanding the geometry of the number but not its meaning.

"Yeah, but it's only temporary though. Borrowed from friends."

"Oh, too bad. Well I have a MIDI port in mine," Raymond lied. "I like it a lot."

"I would too. Do you have the PCjr with the wireless keyboard?"

"It has a wire, but you can pull it out to use the infrared feature if you like."

"Oh well that is cool. Okay I gotta run," the sysop said, quickly, and broke out of the chat. At that point, alone, Raymond was still on high alert—his blood was running—but he was also feeling somehow confident and calm.

In the two weeks since the début of The Midnight Muse, there'd been no commentary about it on The Storyboard—but neither Zip nor Raymond dared bring it up themselves. Raymond saw Zip on the board early in the evening after their fourth Muse had been released, and he quickly paged him to chat.

"Hear anything about the latest?"

"No, nothing, but I just saw the first two turn up on the Spam Factory, that huge board run by Dark Sentinel out in Milwaukee."

"Really!"

"Yeah, but they were making fun of them."

"Rik undoubtedly knows it's us, if he's saving logs of these chats."

"Yeah, but he won't say anything."

Rik had written a few textfiles himself, including "True High School Antics," which consisted of a list of aphorisms, apparently earned and garnered from his own experience but not sounding at all like how he wrote, each beginning with the phrase "True high school antics . . ."; there was also an earlier attempt, a short work entitled "How To Completely Annoy People In Ten Easy Steps." It too was a list of aphorisms, lines of advice such as, "When someone else compliments you, quickly agree with them and compare it to their own shortcomings in that area."

The initial thrill of releasing their own files under a thick mantle of pseudoanonymity had waned quickly with the weak reception of their work, and soon their interest, and their after-school chats, turned toward more plebeian matters.

"So, what's your real name? It helps to picture someone more than just 'The Wanderer,'" wrote Zip during their next chat, who now revealed himself to be Bryce Cunningham, "in case you didn't already know."

"No, actually I didn't," said Raymond, although he recalled the frequent mention of a Bryce in the message bases. He now broke hacker protocol and told Bryce his real name, not caring if Rik was watching quietly.

Bryce was originally from Connecticut and had lived in five places already, counting their most recent two homes in greater Los Angeles.

Raymond, who never knew a life outside of Clifton, was impressed and awed by this radically different life-style. "Wow!"

"Yeah, but we left CT right after kindergarten for five years in Florida," Bryce typed nonchalantly, "which was kind of a relief at the time—it was bad enough learning to spell my last name!"

"So what's California like?" Raymond asked. "A lot of surf parties on the beach?"

Raymond had begun a serious Beach Boys and surf-music phase, and his dreams were of the California beach scene of the 1960s as he saw it depicted on the covers of old record albums that he now collected—and seeking to bring this world back he'd quickly adopted what he thought were all its styles, and had his mother buy him a pair of brand new Converse All-Star sneakers, bright Easter egg blue, from the JC Penney's at the mall.

"Well, the beaches are interesting, and we do hang out there quite a bit, but the surfers of today aren't like what you might be picturing. Everybody's 'rad' here."

"So the nice beaches are pretty much only for the rich?"

"Coastal California's packed with people.   The public beaches are actually kind of dangerous, and they're dirty. But yeah, it's always better if you're rich."

"I'm basically middle-class," Raymond assessed, and added rather hopefully, "maybe on the upper rungs of that."

"Upper middle-class," Bryce repeated drolly.   "Aren't we all ... "

Raymond felt that Bryce was good for him, an intelligent boy who came from good breeding; he knew and sensed this immediately, and figured that it was the kind of friendship he should cultivate in life, not like the kind of people that he'd always had around him in Roman Valley through the years, the types who flooded the halls of Darcy and who populated the development in which he lived, and who now only left him feeling weary and depressed.

Raymond would chat with Bryce on The Storyboard in the late evenings after dinner, which because of the difference in time zones would be when Bryce was just getting home from school. They'd neglect the message bases, to Rik's ire, their chats lasting all the way until one of the two would be kicked off after their one-hour time limit had expired.

"This is a PUBLIC BULLETIN BOARD," came a mail from Rik, sent to the both of them, "not a PRIVATE CHAT SERVICE."

It didn't take long before their habits began to upset the other callers, since their chats took place during the peak after-school hours. Some callers had their modem software programmed on automatic redial when the board was busy, and when they'd connect just after either Zip or Wanderer had been kicked off they'd discover who'd just been on the line for an hour. And then there'd be complaints in the message bases: "Bryce and Wanderer are hogging the lines again!"

So in deference to the other callers their chats shifted to later at night: Raymond would stay up until eleven or twelve to make the call. This was never a problem on the weekend, and on a Friday night in February he conversed with Bryce for long hours on the PCjr, in the midnight darkness, with the bedroom door closed. Their conversation filled the 13″ glass monitor, the letters drawn in a bright ivory against the dull charcoal background of the screen.

Raymond told Bryce about his times at Darcy in the new semester, and his family woes ("Yeah, my parents argue a lot, but I usually tune it out"), and Bryce told him all about life in Los Angeles with Rik and his gang, whom he'd known since starting junior high. It was a relief to hear that Bryce's parents had their difficulties, too. Raymond liked hearing about the antics of Rik Roman, who was as much of a class clown in real life as Raymond had previously supposed. Bryce gave him an encapsulated history of the board as it'd existed before Raymond's first call that autumn. "The maid unplugged the board once, and that was a big incident—his bedroom is huge and messy and she couldn't sweep. The hard drive crashed and we lost a month's archive."

Bryce was Raymond's age, a sophomore, but Rik and most of the others in his circle were a year older. They seemed to form a happy crowd, a bonding that was unseen on other boards.

"I don't know what's going to happen after next year, when Rik goes to college," Bryce said contemplatively. "Maybe he'll run it remotely, I don't know. I can't see him taking the board with him—and I don't know what the rules are for phone lines in dorms."

"I don't know what's going to happen in a few years when I go to college, either," Raymond suddenly admitted. The conversation filled a need in him, and he opened to his long-distance friend. "My mother probably wants me to be a doctor or a lawyer, but these things don't spark any interest in me—I can't stand the sight of blood, for one. When I started getting into computers I used to hear my parents talking about how 'computer jobs' would be good for me. But aside from the hope of easy luxury, any thought of my future just draws an enormous blank."

"So you've never really had any career thoughts yet?"

"Well, last semester they had us take 'career tests' in school. We filled out this huge multiple-question form and they finally handed us the results last week. Mine came out as 'systems analyst,' so I guess I'll go for that," Raymond admitted blankly, hoping that he'd be shuttled in the right direction by dint of this confession to his friend. He didn't know what any of it meant. "They say it pays well, and it's computers so it should be easy."

Bryce said that as a systems engineer at IBM his dad made upwards of $120,000 a year. "That's also why we've had to move so much. They tell him where to go." He told Raymond that he wasn't sure of all the engineering, but that "I'm pretty much bound into that track."

Raymond was happy to discuss these matters with such open honesty; it filled a desperate need in him. He told Bryce how for two months now he'd been doing six hours of easygoing "compu_work" each week—it'd been an arrangement obtained through a school program where he did at-home data entry for $6 an hour, which was about double the minimum wage.

"Ooh," Bryce typed quickly, "easy compu_work is always the best. I've just done odd jobs, but they get me out of the house. We have a Pool Guard here in the neighborhood and that's easy cash."

Raymond enjoyed the feel of being fifteen and already earning a paycheck. It came every two weeks, in an envelope; each was a gift, a surprise, unassociated with the toil that had earned it—for that work had already been forgotten, that time was already gone. He'd open the envelope eagerly and read the number; he liked to count the tally.

"I can do all the data entry on the weekends," he said, eyes bleary with the glow of the screen. "So I'm thinking about getting an after-school job now, to have something in addition to that. Just something like a busboy job at a restaurant."

"It's addictive when you see the numbers come in," Bryce agreed. "I suppose that eventually I'll start working, but I think the plan is to w—"

Suddenly his words on the screen had stopped, and a series of random characters blotched across it in a sloppy, unsteady smear. This occurred simultaneously with what sounded to Raymond as a dull thud in the other room, shadowing his midnight world with the white chill of surprise.

Then in a horrible shatter, the relaxed setting of his evening conversation was destroyed by the scream of his mother, a wild banshee letting out a desperate, haggard roar:

"Ge-e-e-e-t *off*! The! *Tel*-ephone!"

She moaned hoarsely, in a long broken wail that came from the other side of the wall, the back wall of their bedroom. Her voice was bitter, old, and ugly. In lower tones she moaned unhappily and then snapped out from the well of her room, muttering out like an old witch in a chant that shot down the hallway to Raymond's locked and quiet bedroom: "*Who* are you talking to? *What* are you doing? *Why* are you up? *What's* going on in there?"

Now, as if it were some evil duet, he heard his father begin to curse and swear out his guttural, baritone spurtings in response.

Bryce, across the great continent, had seen his friend disappear off the board in a violent snap. He had to've figured that someone had picked up an extension in Raymond's house; he'd linger on the board for a while, waiting for Raymond's callback before eventually giving up, but the spell was already broken and it no longer mattered now—Raymond wouldn't be calling back tonight. He turned his computer off with a cold flick and in the darkness he slunk shamefully over to his bed, crawled under his cool soft blanket as he heard more cursing and cusses of both his mother and father from their bedroom, and then from Sally across the hall who'd been shaken out of sleep and now cried out in weary sad complaint.

His mother's life depressed him, and he didn't want to think of its tired weavings: of where she'd come from, all the places she'd been, and why she was there, now, in the night, howling haggardly at her teenage son, accusing him of furtive, computer-assisted degeneracy. He felt disgust and quietly he cursed her name. It was a firm bitterness that he extended upon himself, and upon his own life, as he settled now into the broad torpor of sleep—and his thoughts were long, sullen echoes of desperate questions that shook and rattled all the cold and lonely inner hallways of his life: What am I, and why here? Why now? And when will I go back?

There was no answer, not even in a dream. Nothing came to him but the black, broad covering of night.

22

SIXTEEN

THE DISTURBANCE of the broken phone call so humiliated Raymond that in the morning ancient angers deep inside him shook and prodded forward. It was embarrassing and demeaning to get knocked out of chat by your mother—most kids on the boards had their own phone lines, anyway. He ignored them at breakfast, staying in his room until he'd heard they left the kitchen, and the feeling peaked by early afternoon when he called The Storyboard and read a private mail left for him by Bryce: "Parental units?"

"On the rampage," Raymond wrote back in reply.

What he absolutely now must get, he promised himself with a vicious furled-up anger, was his own phone line. Everybody else had one. He'd be sixteen soon and with his own money he'd buy one himself, and there'd be nothing his parents could say or do about it.

Meanwhile he'd have to find a way so that they couldn't listen in on his calls anymore. What he'd need was a way to immediately mute all other extensions in the house at the press of a button. This wasn't a trivial problem, and he spent hours paging through his books, consulting all his phreaking files, thinking of how it could be done—couldn't he make one? He gathered up his spare parts and telephones and thought it through on the floor of his bedroom: could he blast a deafening siren over the line? That was a possibility. Or perhaps an electric current. He tried many things, and eventually thought of how the black box worked by changing the impedance of the line with a tiny striped resistor placed over the red and green wires; the connection that it made was quiet, so perhaps the right resistor would give a total muting effect. Playing with the resistors he had, he found one that muted his own extension. With it still in place on the open wires of his disassembled phone, he ran out of his bedroom and picked up the extension in his parents' bedroom; that too was dead. He then ran down to the kitchen and picked up the line, and it was dead. When he removed the resistor the line was normal: he'd instantly and completely muted all of the extensions.

It wouldn't stop his mother from disrupting a modem call, but if he were talking voice she couldn't just listen in from an extension as she was always apt to do—with a flick of a switch all the lines would go dead. A shrill bell lulled over his spirit's plane, he felt power and joy as he realized what he'd done: he'd invented his own box! It was as cool as anything that Ferris Bueller would've done, but it was him—it was real and it was his living life!

He called the effect a "universal mute." It could be used to simply mute your phone when you didn't want your caller to hear your end of the line, but with the added benefit of muting the entire line so that all other extensions would be kept silent, too. It could even be used to make your phone line busy without having to take your phone off the hook—a useful convenience when you didn't want the interruption of a phone call.

An afternoon of wiring produced his first working prototype: it had a pushbutton switch that he'd bought from Radio Shack, and was mounted on the face of a small, thin hinged box of fluorescent orange plastic that he'd quickly arrogated from his father's deer hunting supplies in the garage. This gave him a color—it'd be the orange box! It plugged between the phone and the wall; pressing the button put the resistor across the two wires and would instantly mute all extensions on the line.

He tested it several times and in a delirious rush he wrote up a three-screen textfile called "How To Make An Orange Box,"

describing all the major benefits of universal mute, and he included a diagram of the box as it existed in its ideal form, which
was inside the base of a desk telephone with an illuminated
pushbutton mounted on its front that would glow a sweet candy
orange when the effect was active. He wrote it how he wrote
everything on his PCjr, with a simple full-screen editor program that he'd copied from Jim. There was no spell checker, no
justification, no tab stops or formatting—even double-spacing
was done by hand. It was simpler than a typewriter, but it was
all that Raymond had.

He called up The Library, logged in, and went straight to
the Acquisitions Desk where he sent the file, releasing his invention to the world. Bryce was immediately impressed with
the file, which had been called ORANGEBX.610 in The Librarian's naming conventions, and said that if he had to share a
phone line with anybody he'd certainly put an orange box on
it immediately. Raymond saw with great pride that it quickly
spread around the hack boards of the nation, and he felt that
now the reputation of The Wanderer had finally been secured.

In the weeks that followed, both Bryce and Raymond continued to write and release their own textfiles, and neither
mentioned the early attempts of their Midnight Muse series.
Bryce didn't talk much about his own files, and Raymond suspected that he was something of a genius. Raymond was fascinated with Bryce's files—he had a knack for devising orna-
mentation and patterns out of characters arranged together on
the screen, and the actual writings were on topics that seemed
heavily obscure to Raymond: President Nixon and the ending
of the Vietnam War, radiation's benefits and dangers, the balance of democracies and dictatorships. They had a political
edge to them, and were somehow intellectual in what Raymond
thought of as a black-and-white way, like newsprint or that
staid kind of commentary that might be found in fat, author-
itative hardbound books from decades past; they seemed to express original ideas on important topics, formulated by a fresh,
unique standpoint. In contrast, the sketches in Raymond's own
files seemed much more colorful but never went deep enough
and they remained unsatisfying to him.

The year went on like this and brought him summer. Raymond was aggressively interested in girls while Jim Alpes was trailing behind: they wasted away their nights in the arcade, while Raymond wanted to go after girls in the mall. The only arcade game that Raymond even liked was OutRun, which realistically simulated driving a convertible and had good jazzy music for its soundtrack; Jim liked many, including a game called Dragon's Lair, which showed real cartoon images stored on the high technology of Laserdisc and cost four times as much as the other games because of it; he was also good at a car-chase game called Spy Hunter that had a secret agent theme. But while he played them Raymond just stood by, his head cocked and looking out at all the girls who were passing through the mall. Jim also liked to play games on the PCjr, games that never lived up to the elaborate backstories and grand descriptions of what they represented—the private detectives in a big-city underworld, a view of war across the sweeping Pacific theatre, roaming lushly-forested faery lands as a young prince ripe for finding love and valor, commanding battles in the trenches of France, encampments on the Moon at the end of the century, wandering the crystal spires of a floating palace in some exotic galaxy. But all these games were still just electric squares and beeps, as abstract as his older cousin's baby toys from his 1950s childhood that Raymond had happily played with in his own time.

The summer air was invigorating and vitalic in July, and on a fresh mid-morning when the best of life was blooming everywhere, Raymond had called The Storyboard in his usual routine and was stunned by an announcement that Bryce posted to the Hot Gossip message base:

"Since our family's moving cross-country and we'll have a lot of work to do I will obviously be offline for a while," he'd written the night before in a new post titled, "I'm Leaving" that already had four responses. "We're moving to Michigan. Barrington Hills, to be exact, which I am told is quite nice—but everything there is brand new. I don't know what life will be like when I get there. I know there won't be a beach (no, the nearest Great Lake doesn't count)."

Raymond, who owned a "Surf Sohola" t-shirt and whose whole entire reality had been a contemporary life along the shores of Lake Catawba, was offended by this last remark.

The news caused a minor commotion on the board. "Aargh," Rik had replied, "who will I have to throw onion rings at in the Toluca Lake Big Boy's and then get kicked out because we were upsetting Bob Hope? Well, I'll have to put on a goodbye bash for you at my place."

To the rest of the board, Prof. Zip would now be like The Wanderer—a disembodied caller, well out of physical proximity.

"Good luck with the move and everything," Raymond wrote to him in a private mail. "But it's nice to know that you'll be living out in my part of the country. Michigan isn't too far away."

Raymond felt terror at the idea of such a move. In contrast, Prof. Zip had accepted it casually, as duty; he seemed to think of it as a great adventure. The next week went by quickly, and the board was quiet on the night of the goodbye party; Raymond called up twice, hoping that the celebrants would welcome his online presence during the party, happily breaking into chat to spill their revelry onto his computer screen. In a dull gloom Raymond jealously imagined the festivities he was presently missing out on. It was one of the last nights their friend would be living in their city—and Raymond, whose life was happening halfway across the continent, wasn't there to say goodbye.

In these days, Raymond was restless at home. He'd peeked out with dread at the Malvicinos as they played basketball on their driveway in the wet fogs of spring; for months he'd gotten himself interested in anything that would take him out of his home and neighborhood, and he felt a strong magnetism pushing him anywhere, so long as it was away. In that past term he'd begun to join Darcy clubs, and he'd begun to spend all his time in work: he wasn't yet sixteen but according to the law was permitted to work part-time hours with a permit, and this would prepare him for the coming year and his adult life. On a tip from a Darcy classmate who'd already had success at it, he took up a job at a steakhouse restaurant up the great long hill of Vista Road, and he began to work a full shift there after school; by summer he'd begun socializing with his co-workers, who were public-school kids from Kennedy and even some older people in their twenties and thirties, people who drank and

bought beer for them and brought in drugs, and others who
were nice and possibly nerds but virtuous just by being so much
older—they were quite a rag-tag group, bonded by their common workplace, their shared long hours at a restaurant, toiling
to fulfill the mission statement of an unseen corporation, a
structure that held together their own shaky dramas of everyone's coming and going and relations, and they had merry, joyous times together, a whole book's worth. Raymond's computer
sat cold and quiet in that time, and through the misadventures
of that wild summer when he turned sixteen and worked full-
time and saw so many new people drift through his life he
thought very little of his computer past.

But in that time he sought to apply his computer skills
to his waking life, and he'd hacked his own voicemail "hotline," reachable at the end of a toll-free 1-800 number that he
passed out to others. This made him feel advanced, like a slick
young businessman: from anywhere in the country he could
be reached, free of charge, from any telephone—upon dialing,
callers were greeted with a recording of his voice and could
leave him messages that he'd later retrieve. It impressed his co-
workers who thought of him, he was sure, as a man mysterious
with vast unspeakable connections. There were a number of
unused voicemail boxes on the system and he gave one to Jim
Alpes, who just smiled nervously, exposing his wide squares of
teeth, and then with a shake of his head he muttered, "You're
crazy"; in private mails he gave hotlines to Bryce and Rik;
Rik was immediately grateful and the two of them left voice
messages for each other. Raymond enjoyed being able to actually hear him on the telephone; he heard Rik's greeting on his
hotline and he thought, "This is the sound of my friend."

Rik left him a message right away in his deep, ebullient
voice: "Hey, *Won*-der-er, this is Rik!" There was the whoosh-
ing sound of traffic in the background, and Raymond imagined
the row of curving palm trees along the California boulevard.
"Yeah, I'm calling you now from outside a Jack In The Box in
Beverly *Hills*!"

Bryce, however, had been mostly quiet. He was already off
the board and living out in Michigan; finally a voicemail from
him came unexpectedly in late August, when Raymond was

preoccupied with getting his driver's license—when he wasn't working he spent all his time out with Jim, who was already driving. His voice wasn't how Raymond expected it to be—it was rounder and softer.

"I'm settled in now," Bryce said in the message, "but not quite up to calling boards just yet. My dad's paying for the calls, so I'm severely limited for a while. Here's my number, though—it's my own line. I'll leave the modem on at night and you can call if you want. I've got it set up to alert me on incoming calls. Obviously, when I'm on the boards it'll be busy, but like I said I don't expect that to happen just yet."

Raymond called it that night and after connecting he got a message, "Welcome to Zip's Place," and otherwise the screen was blank; he waited a few minutes, typing out a few lines of "Are you there?" and then finally hanging up; the next night he tried again and after a few seconds of pause there was the live typings of Bryce before him:

"I was just thinking about your call from last night. We went out to dinner and when I came back I saw your messages on the screen."

"Listen," Raymond typed out right away, "I'm using k0dez to reach you, so if the phedz ever ask, you never heard of me."

"Okay."

Bryce then told Raymond all about the move.

"It took us several days to do it, and most of it was pretty boring. But the highlight was in Iowa when my dad pulled over and was like, 'Here.' Then he let me drive for a couple of hours, which was really cool."

"That's cool. What's it like where you live now?"

"Well, there's a new mall here, and some new restaurants, and new developments everywhere—we live in one of them. Pretty much everything in Barrington Hills is new, but as soon as you leave the city limits you're in complete desolation: it's all flat farmland for like twenty minutes in all directions. You can get on the highway pretty easily, though, and if you go about twenty minutes there you'll get to Ann Arbor, which is a kind of 'progressive' town, spread out like a wide grid with a hundred little places to walk to."

From the name, Raymond thought of it as a kind of grove

and rolling valley, with rich verdant lawns and farm-plots in a tight bundle, nestled advantageously within sight of the cityscape but removed enough to give it a peaceful calm with birdcalls in the mornings.

"No, Ann Arbor is most certainly a city. It's all built up but it's cool—all the buildings are pretty old, and everyone on the streets seems young. I like it. The University of Michigan is there, and I like how it kind of weaves itself into the city streets. I see myself spending a lot of time there. Otherwise, Detroit's out in the other direction on the highway, and just as close. My father works there, but you pretty much don't want to hang out there, especially if you're white."

Raymond thought of how different their lives were at this moment—he'd spent his youth in Roman Valley while Bryce was in his sixth home, in a new state, and would be going to a new school in the fall, Whippett High School. He'd already been out there for new student orientation.

"It's technically a public school," he typed, "but they've got a strong prep track."

"That's good. Darcy's private, and it's pretty much billed as a prep school, but I'm kind of slacking through it."

"Whippett has an Advanced Placement program that I'll be in."

"Ooh," Raymond typed, consciously mimicking the writing style of his friend. "I'm not in any of the advanced classes here," he added, suddenly regretting that he hadn't bothered to try and place in them. "Once I start driving in the fall there'll be a lot of time to party."

"Yeah. I don't expect to have much time for parties come school."

"How was Rik's goodbye bash, by the way?" Raymond's prying curiosity also held a morbid jealousy.

"Oh, it was all right," Bryce said. "Jake pulled out the pot as usual, and there were a lot of people from school getting drunk on Rik's alcohol. The highlight for me was that I got a goodbye kiss from Melanie Richardson, this girl I'd always liked but never had the nerve to do anything about it. Before the party the big rumor was that Sarah Jessica Parker might show up. You know," he explained, "the girl who was in *Square*

Pegs. I guess she knows Rik. But to his dismay, I actually left early."

Raymond imagined all of this, and felt a marked inferiority about where he lived and what he was from—he knew that Bryce was better off and had a life that seemed to contain many more advantages that Raymond would ever have access to or even know. He thought again of the great and living thing that he was after, and he knew that it was inextricably linked to this—he wanted that kind of life, the real and breathing one he saw upon the screen.

"I wanna be like that," he said, aloud, to the baby-blue walls inside his quiet bedroom. Bryce's typings were inching their way across his screen and right now they seemed more real to him than anything. "I wanna have a life, I wanna be like that, that's what I've got to be!"

23

FASHIONS AND PHILOSOPHIES

RAYMOND USED his codes to call Bryce a few nights a week; sometimes he'd be out, or the line'd be busy, but other times they'd chat late into the summer night and the two would talk about the cities in which they lived, go through all the gossip of the greater hacker world of which Raymond was still acutely aware, expound upon the legend of Rik Roman and his board, and ponder all the vagaries and problems of popular culture.

They both had a keen interest in music, particularly that which was labeled "college," and they began to follow it with a heightened fervidity. They discussed their trips to record stores and to the big weekend record conventions that were held in local VFW halls and hotel ballrooms, and they compared and recommended their finds: the Dead Milkmen, the Violent Femmes, Camper Van Beethoven—all college bands. A two-piece techno band from Germany, Yello, caught Raymond's attention with their synthesizer-heavy instrumentals, the most famous of which had been featured in *Ferris Bueller's Day Off*; both Bryce and Raymond began to collect their records. Bryce told Raymond in passing that he thought The Replacements were "probably one of the most important bands of our time," and afterward when Raymond saw a record by The Radiators at a record swap he deftly bought it, having confused the name.

"It's funny," Raymond contemplated in their evening chat, when his clip-on desk lamp made the room all long shadows and warm amber and fat white moths gripped hard upon the screen of his open window. "I like all these different styles but I don't really look like any one of them."

"I seem to be the same way. I'll go from thrash to synth-pop, but don't fit into any of the stereotyped molds. What do you look like?"

"Let's see ... I used to wear glasses, but I just got contact lenses last year. I have dark brown hair, eyes are the same."

"Ah, contacts. I've got 'em too. I still wear glasses on occasion, though. Y'know, pretty much all modemers wear glasses. Did you ever notice that? Rik wears contacts, but I've seen him wear glasses at home."

Bryce described himself as a freckly blond with a flat-top whose build was "overwhelmingly average." In dress, the two shared an interest in what they called "college style"; this style, they decided that night, was exemplified by the L.L. Bean, Banana Republic, Bugle Boy, Newport Blue and Jams clothing lines. It would be "a nice t-shirt" and khaki cargo shorts, plus shiny white tennis shoes with socks, or just Docksiders, preferably ones with tassels, and without socks of course—"unless it's like a blizzard out."

T-shirts were acceptable so long as they were nice, and conspicuously "college"—nothing like a bad t-shirt would spoil the look completely. T-shirts with the name of a place—certainly of a college—would fit, as would t-shirts from a few select lines: Bryce had a Spuds MacKenzie and Raymond had a Bad Dog that each treasured, imagining that they'd fit in perfectly at a backyard fraternity keg party. The "polo club" and "beach club" shirts were getting a little tired, but technically they still counted as college style.

Raymond also considered college style to be synonymous with "preppy," but Bryce surprised him by saying that he thought preppy was less casual: "You know, tweeds and suede caps, penny loafers, argyle sweater vests."

"Well, I like to dress a *little* preppy, I've got penny loafers for when I need to be dressy, but I don't quite fit into that mold," Raymond philosophized.

"I'm the same way. I think our college style is actually a watered-down, mega-casualized preppy—an update for the times. I like it. I have this habit of finding a 'uniform' of shirt and pants I like, and then getting it in an array of different colors."

Raymond rejoiced at the familiar concept, laughing aloud in his bedroom. "Ah, 'uniforms'! That's pretty hilarious, I do the same thing!"

Raymond admitted that he was also getting a touch rebellious now, and that was bleeding into his style; fashion experiments that he'd undertaken that summer included ripping holes in a pair of older blue jeans and growing his hair out past the collar in the back. Bryce admitted that he "kept it kind of plain" most of the time, never daring to go further.

"College style itself is basically the rebellion. But I do have this habit of wearing knee-high Army socks with my shorts and t-shirt, and going out with a beret. It drives my parents batty."

Yet even in the ragged spirit of his rebellion, Raymond aspired to be more preppy but couldn't find the way; while Bryce, having grown up in the shadows and dust-bins of that world, welcomed all the encroachments of the casual and decadent. It was a conflicting force at work, and while they each had their own inner ideas, stipulations and expectancies, these sculptures were fluid and nothing would ever come to be as they were first conceived in their murky inner visions.

School came and Raymond walked the high school halls, and when he walked in them alone he often thought of Bryce, his distant friend whom he'd never met. He looked at things in terms of Bryce, he thought of his friend's new life surrounded by the corn fields and cool pines of Michigan, and wondered where it all would go. He walked the halls with the knowledge that he had a close friend who wasn't there with him, a friend who only knew Darcy through the description of Raymond's words, and with whom he grew steadily in the new progressive, "college" style which he also began to share with Jim Alpes, whose older sisters provided much input and knowledge.

Zip was his friend that he "spoke" to only on the screen of

his bedroom computer, a fact that gave him strength in life and a kind of resilience in his character. The dramas of the local classroom, tucked deeply away in a Clifton suburb known as Alva, meant nothing to the greater world. They meant nothing now to Raymond, either—"Why," he thought gleefully in class, unable to control his bright effulgent smile in the presence of his less cosmopolitan classmates, "I have a friend in Michigan!"

Raymond wasn't interested in most sports but he did like school football—he'd briefly played on an intramural team the year before, and in the Malvicino days had been a backyard tackle star—so he always went to the football games with Jim and the gang to cheer Darcy on against its bitter rivals. Every school had a group of these class rejects who sat unnoticed at the top of the bleachers, back over by the pep band to cheer the team on, even though every member of the team were the ones who slammed them into lockers during school—and although Raymond felt that he should've mustered up the courage to try out for the team himself, he was destined in this life to only be a spectator up there behind the pep band, cheering heartily with the other nameless ones whose legends were unknown.

Raymond enjoyed these placid days of school life, which were happily social in his little group: there was the jocular, runty Irish kid; the wiry, long-mouthed Chinese kid who studied martial arts every night after school for hours, whose father taught him mystic meditation practices, and who knew every Bruce Lee film by heart; there was the silent pimpled stoner kid, always getting detentions for his hair length, which he'd try to defeat by pinning it up each morning before school; the skater boy with radiant blue eyes who was out of place in Sohola with his weird slanted haircut and strange musics and California skateboard magazines; and flanking it all were Jim and Raymond in their L.L. Bean, obsessing on Jim's sister's stories of college parties on every campus in the land and at Pass-A-Way out on the lake. They went to these games and then ambled back to their Roman Valley neighborhood, stopping out at the dingy corner pizza shop for a meal first, where Jim and Raymond would steal beers from behind the tiny bar counter on the way out when the sole waitress had run back to the bright, white kitchen—then they'd run out in the blue warm dusk and share their two pilfered beers among the five of them, standing victoriously on the dark wet carpet of grass by the street-curb in their neighborhood, looking out for cops, and laughing richly in the autumn twilight.

There were school dances on some Friday nights and Raymond's group went to them as just a thing to do—never with the intent of actually dancing, but as the place to go and talk and be seen that weekend, and to make a show of camaraderie amongst the social aspirants of their class. Before Jim was driving they'd get a ride from one of Jim's older sisters or his mother, or from Raymond's mother, and they'd meet up at the dance and hang out there for a few hours and then get picked up and go watch a horror movie in the Irish kid's cluttered family room, or otherwise go around the neighborhood with the gang. It was just a thing to do, and while the boys looked at all the girls and had their burning thoughts, none of them ever considered dancing as a realistic possibility. Instead they'd stand around at the edges of the gym, their eyes glowing in the dark, making jokes and eventually wandering out to the hallway to make the payphone ring, reviving that old fifth-grader trick that they'd all perpetrated back at St. Bartholomew's.

The phone would begin jangling and they'd walk away just far enough so that they were still in sight of it, and watch to see who'd pick it up: one of the jocks, one of the popular ladies men, who? Ah, there goes Mark Richardson now, he's got his yellow sweater draped around his neck like a country club boy and he's walking past it—he breaks his stroll and turns his head toward it, confused; then he cooly walks up to it, and when all eyes are watching he picks it up: "Hello," he says carefully into the phone, and absently turns his head in their direction. They see his blank stare go from the auburn-tiled ground then sweep out toward the hall and right to them, clustered over by the lockers, just as he realizes as he hears the siren-hum in his ear that it's a prank and no one's really on the other end. He irritably hangs up the phone and looks over at the group of them again, all laughing, and he mumbles something under his breath before he steams off in a huff to the glitter and the beat of the party in the great gymnasium.

In these days Raymond's telephone scans had accumulated into the recording of hundreds of computers, more than he'd ever explored before, but he was also beginning to outgrow all that. It was friendship, camaraderie, and connection that mattered to him now, and with Bryce he'd finally found it. He also had a job after school and collected a paycheck every two weeks; he finally began to drive, borrowing the older of the Valentines' two cars, the brown-purple Cougar that they'd taken on family vacations; he tried to reign in his phreaking, only using codes for his calls to Bryce. He knew that soon would come retirement, that at eighteen he'd be judged differently in the eyes of the law and would have to leave the hack world behind—best to wean off slowly now, to give time to settle and adjust: for in little longer than a year would come new life.

In the rush of this junior year he'd stopped calling most of the hack boards; he couldn't keep up. He was losing touch with the entire modem world, a realization marked by the fact that his notebooks were unused; he called few boards now, only those whose dialup numbers and passwords he'd memorized. He'd still download files from The Library where he'd been awarded a thousand download credits, but even The Storyboard was now relegated to monthly check-ins that were only made out of duty; Rik Roman's world seemed so much emptier now and that life he had in Los Angeles was much further away than it once had been. In an off-moment of boredom he might call up a local board, and he'd see that most of the old guard were still there, the stars of his youth, but their typings didn't matter now.

Bryce adjusted quickly to the move and did well in his AP classes that term—he seemed to adapt to his new surroundings with ease and finesse and he had no complaints. Their lives were updated to each other in long, chatty dialogues after school, "talking" like this at least once a week, sometimes more—often they'd be covertly drinking at the computer, exploring the contents of their parents' liquor cabinets, sometimes tasting quaffs of the heavy syrups poured out on the rocks, but usually having a daring swig of whiskey diluted into the remaining contents of an open can of Diet Pepsi or 7-Up.

"What're you having tonight?" Bryce asked Raymond when

their next Monday evening chat began.

"The usual—some of my parents' Ron Rico rum with a Pepsi. How about you?"

"I'm having a little of their Créme de Menthe on the rocks. It's gross with Pepsi."

Over the weekend there'd been a change in Raymond's social life that he knew would greatly affect his remaining days at Darcy, one so great that had it happened any sooner, he'd have quickly transferred out to St. Regis'—but the autumn semester was almost over, and then after this he only had another year. He'd called Bryce immediately after school to discuss the shocking turn of events: to the surprise of everyone, no less himself, Raymond had been approached by a girl at the Friday Night Social; they danced, and then the girl had wanted to take a walk with him. He had to leave Jim and his friends who were standing on the sidelines, speechless and gawking with tragic eyes. Eventually the girl pulled him aside and they were kissing.

"So then the guys were like pointing and laughing," Raymond typed. "That's my buddy Jim and his crowd, a group that all live near him right up the road in the next development. I've known them since elementary school."

"Sounds like they were jealous."

"Maybe so, but Jim had started talking to a guy from St. Regis who didn't seem to like me. And then when I tried to go back to them they'd split. Finally I couldn't find Jim anymore, and he was my ride, so I had to call my mom to come pick me up. While I was out there in the cold waiting for her, Jim drove by with his new buddy and they were laughing."

Raymond painfully saw it again: he was standing under an awning by the deserted football field, where the stadium lights on gigantic poles made it all watery grey in the fog, and then Jim's station wagon came out of the fog and slowed down right in front of him. The guys were in it looking over and smiling broadly, showing their teeth. Jim's window came down when they pulled up. "Need a ride," he called out stonily. But it wasn't the voice of a friend.

Raymond was furious; he'd wandered the frigid empty school ground, alone, for over an hour while angers collected and stirred in him. "No, I got one." He too spoke with the granite chill of a firm and complete detachment.

"All right," Jim said, a slow mouthing that didn't sound like the boy that Raymond knew; it came out detached and non-committal and strangely like an adult—and then he pulled forward. Raymond could see their faces, looking homeward, and saw the twist of joy in their eyes and the white of their teeth from open, laughing mouths before they quickly drove away.

Bryce now offered his consolation to the story: "Ouch."

"Yeah, and none of them said hello to me in the hall today."

"I would've just gone up to them and said something like, 'Gee, that was real funny, guys.'"

"Yeah, but you didn't see the look in their eyes this morning. It was cold, Bryce. People who'd been my best school buddies just seventy-two hours ago now looked right through me like I wasn't really there—like I'd become a walking ghost."

This ended his relationship with Jim, his friend of years— his best schoolmate, a friend with whom he'd shared secrets with, gone places with, done things together and he remembered now how it'd been a friendship colored with so many rich and varied commonalities, from the PCjr to movies and skateboards and beer, wandering the woods and the mall, fishing on long Saturday mornings, biking through Clifton's many western suburbs, going on weekend camping trips to the Alpes family's cottage, to talk of boats and college and "moving ahead" in life—but Raymond was too stubborn to call him up, and Jim had been the same, and it was over. The line had been crossed: they were not friends. The fight also meant that Raymond was no longer welcome in the gang; the Irish kid, the stoner and the skater kid took Jim's side, since they'd been his friends first, and they too ignored him in the halls or sometimes snickered when he walked past, friendless and alone, while the Chinese kid played the fence and spoke furtively to Raymond when the others weren't looking. Where there'd been happy companions days before now was the cruel lesson: individuals would stick with the larger group, there was no justice to it, and life offered no true bonds of friendship. Raymond wondered what dreadful failures and catastrophes were to come in his adult life.

For a week he talked to that girl on the telephone every night after school, met her at Alvatown to see a movie, and then he quickly disassociated himself from her completely: he wasn't attracted to her and her company was no match for Jim and his former friends. Then he was alone, and had Bryce to drink and chat with in his bedroom after school. He found his comfort at the computer glow, where words were being typed somewhere in Michigan in the same dark night, with a glass of boozy soda pop by a keyboard just as it was in Raymond's bedroom, and it gave him comfort and support.

Bryce explained problems he was having, too—his first friend in Michigan was Albert, a nerdy kid who lived in his neighborhood and with whom he car-pooled to and from school. But he now had to juggle between his loyalties to Albert and his new relations with the other kids in school; he didn't want to become too associated with Albert, and had begun talking to a long-haired senior named Mark who was "something of a stoner."

Through the rest of the term, Raymond called The Story-board once a week where Bryce had settled back into regular calling thanks to a "c0de" supplied by Rik Roman over the voicemail line, and which Bryce and Raymond both suspected was a legit code that Roman paid for himself from his allowance money, just to get Bryce to call again. Rik was his usual self, concentrating on his screenplays and getting ready for college. And Raymond still connected to Bryce's computer after school, just like his dreary classmates who called each other up to talk, like the girls who gabbed all afternoon on their bedroom telephones. A reach of more than three hours in a car was laid out between them but they connected in words that glowed brightly in color on dark dusty screens. They spoke of literary matters, of schoolyard fights and cliques, of music trends and fashions. They talked of families, of their social positions, and of money. And although they never discussed it in such flagrant open terms, Raymond now considered Bryce his best friend; the halls of Darcy rang empty for him now that his crowd had abandoned him, and he was much more conscious of Bryce's positive impact on his life. He was also changing, listening to college radio constantly and having grown a keen interest in "progressive" music and he wondered what it might be like to change both his haircut and his manner of dress; he was looking forward to the end of high school.

Since reading *The Great Gatsby* that October, something remarkable had awakened in Raymond, and the boys having shared this growing interest in the literary world now compared their starry aspirations: they wanted to write and they wanted to express their observations and create a living world. This was their great agenda.

A good story, Bryce discoursed, was so powerful because it was a "world."

"Yes, and the power of the writer is that he's the one who creates it!"

Raymond knew and loved a textbook in his English class called *Vocabulary Workshop* and he worked ahead in it during his spare time in a quest to learn all the words, wanting to bring this richness to future textfiles—he wanted them to become deeply literary, he wanted them to contain the living worlds of his own invention and sparkle with the glitter and the gold.

Together they critiqued their oeuvres as they existed at that point. They were rough on themselves, and they looked back at their earlier attempts with an aghast disapproval and disgust.

"Aren't you embarrassed as hell about the Musings?"

"Yeah," said Raymond with a chortle. He couldn't bear to even look at his early releases now. "They're so puerile. That was last January? Can't believe how much you can change in almost nine months."

"Just glad our real names aren't attached to them. But I'd still like to try my hand at writing fiction, something serious."

"Me too, and I've thought about how textfiles could be a wonderful new medium for it."

"Sure, like the Alexander Gould sketches."

"Yeah, but even longer."

And so sharing their desires, they began writing literary sketches and they released them at The Library. Raymond wasn't happy with his sketches—he wanted something to capture the scene and the flavor, he wanted something to come to life with breathing colors, and he tried but couldn't get it.

Bryce, in his turn, wrote a few one-page stories that he simply called "moments"—they were boyish, adolescent, ironic, touching on themes such as "the chance of life" and "the vastness of the world." One was called "Homecoming" that depicted schoolboy cruelty in the halls, culminating with the narrator attempting suicide on Homecoming Night in a final moment of ambiguity; another sketch called "Home Town" had a narrator who catalogued all of the people and things he loved in his home town—and the trick ending clarifies that these are all things he's going to love destroying when his rampage begins momentarily. They impressed Raymond, who said they were poetic in a dark way, "kind of like poems that don't rhyme."

"Well, poems that don't rhyme are definitely more regaled in Lit Club than poems that do."

"I'd imagine so."

They worked at these writings instead of haunting the boards. Raymond sensed that one day he'd write about this time, about these days that he was living there in the lockings of this world. Books had a great hold on him now, as they did when he was young, and when he was alone he turned again to their living worlds for solace and inspiration. He felt more alive in the world of the story than he did ghosting on the streets of Clifton: his own life was like a great long story without a final resolution. August came and he turned seventeen and had a quiet birthday, with no friends, and in its aftermath he hoped that there'd be time in life, greater time, much more good and living time for deeper connections, better celebrations, and the untouchable and distant things that he was after. All of that was out there somewhere—around some bend, off where he couldn't see it, it was not here.

⌈24⌉

RETIREMENT

DURING THE frosty week away from school at Christmastime, Raymond called Clifton Manor again out of a moment's boredom and caprice and saw the same old names—Moe Howitt and Doug Stelly and all the other people he'd known in a life that seemed so long ago, and he felt entirely detached from them; they were mired deep in his past, in a place that'd once been treasured and then discarded and whose currency no longer had value, and yet it was a place from which he knew they wouldn't emerge. He hung up the line without even properly logging out, and he called other boards whose numbers he still had memorized. There was the same hollow silence that he'd always known on RailWorld; the number to the Med-Line had been disconnected. He called other boards but had no interest in what he found in them. He must reach out further now, to new worlds, travel to the wide expanses that were there and waiting: his whole life was somewhere just ahead of him.

The magic of the computer world seemed tired now when he considered all the difficulties that had to be surmounted to get anywhere with it: his PCjr was old and outdated, and talking with Bryce was the only thing he'd been using it for—it was just a tool, a telephone attachment.

The codes that Raymond used had begun to die off, and

then instead of hunting for more he began to pay for all his calls to Bryce, with his own phone line, for he was older and he had the money now and didn't want to have to endure a bust. He'd distanced himself from the hacker world, and was too paranoid for the consequences—there'd been too many busts, you heard it in the news all the time, and the punishment was greater than a wrist-slap; they weren't considered child geniuses anymore, amazing youth to be charmed and awed by; now they were looked at as criminals and punished accordingly. Besides, codes weren't as easy as they used to be: they didn't last as long, they took more digits so they were much harder to hack, and the lines were always being traced. It just wasn't safe. The feds were out there. Eyes were watching. There was a listening ear. He was in a constant state of deep wide fear.

The new term began in this dreary quiet funk. After school he hung out with his restaurant friends, who went to Kennedy and smoked and were basically delinquents, and in their acceptance and solidarity he considered he had an edge over all his parochial classmates, who awed and vaguely feared him now, he thought; he experimented with cigarettes and sometimes put a Winston Light in his mouth in the parking lot after school as he strutted to his car. His classmates knew that he had many public-school friends and was too busy to bother with the Darcy social life. And Bryce, who'd gotten all A's in his first semester at Whippett, told him after the first week of classes that January that he too had begun hanging out with a new crowd.

"I'm afraid I've latched onto the delinquent element," he typed, in an apparently calm and neutral self-analysis. "I'm still considered a college-progressive type but the guys I'm hanging out with are more or less stoners."

"Yeah, I remember you were saying last week that you'd gone to a party or something. I've hung out with stoners before," Raymond truthfully admitted, "and that's what some of these work friends are, but I haven't become exclusively in with the stoners or anything."

"I've been talking to this guy named Mark who's a senior. He's a stoner, and he hangs out with these other stoner friends who are already out of school. Mark had a party over Christmas break, and I went, and we all really hit it off. Now Mark's been giving me a ride to school so I finally was able to ditch Albert, the kid who lives up the street—he's kind of dorky, and in no way would he ever hang out with stoners."

"So these guys are pretty much all stoners?"

"Yeah. Mark's got hair past his shoulders, he's a pretty tall dude, always wears a leather jacket, and with a huge mouth can look quite scary—he makes this face by contorting his lips, and it freaks people out."

"Ah."

"Yeah, and despite his appearance he's actually a smart guy. Knows computers, phreaking—built a blue box in the old days—as well as cars, and he's a pretty good bass player, too."

It was a new season now for both of them, and life was moving on. For two months after reaching the enmity of Jim Alpes, Raymond had drifted on the outside fringes of other minor cliques, experimenting with a place to belong, but he found that it'd been too late to settle into any one of them with good success. He remained a loner and an outcast to the core—he wasn't going to join band or theatre or the football team at this dusky hour of his high school years, and so he couldn't fully penetrate those other crowds, and he cursed himself anew for not having transferred that year to a different school, as Bryce had done. The lunch hour had been the most traumatic, trying to find a place to sit in the cafeteria without crossing hostile social lines and while attempting to appear casually disinterested in it all the entire time. He sat, with a sandwich and a cookie, at the edges of groups he didn't care about.

"My best hope at this point," he now admitted on his keyboard, "is making inroads with other college-progressive types, so far as they exist at Darcy. So much as I can tell there are three small cliques of them—two minor and one major."

Their words were exchanged on the bulging screen in front of him and transferred over wide sightless miles, but for Raymond they were here together talking.

"I've surprised myself by getting into thrash music," Bryce replied, "but I know I'll never completely transform, grow my hair long and all that."

This saddened Raymond, who knew that he himself was

moving in another direction, with bands whose names he wrote
on the covers of all his school folders and notebooks: "I'm exploring more of the college-progressive bands, like the Psychedelic Furs and the Violent Femmes. I like The Cult, and Hüsker
Dü is really growing on me. But as for Echo and the Bunnymen,
I still don't understand what all the fuss is about."

"Hrm. I'm liking the Stormtroopers of Death, and the first
few Metallica records—so far removed from last year's Orchestral Maneuvers in the Dark!"

"Remember how we both liked Yello and Art of Noise back
then?" Raymond reminisced. He still liked OMD, and felt that
it'd be the soundtrack for his youthful adult life that was soon
to come.

"Yeah," Bryce complained, "they've both got videos out now,
and they don't even play on *120 Minutes!*"

That was MTV's two-hour weekly program for the cutting
edge: videos the network presented as too "alternative" for
mainstream showing in their regular daytime programming.
When it came on at ten o'clock every Sunday night, Bryce and
Raymond were both held rapt by it so that they were red-eyed
in their Monday morning classes, with secluded melodies being
spoken over and over in the voice of their minds. Raymond
recognized their love of what was uncommon and unpopular.

"It seems like when something we like gets trendy and popular, we pretty much lose hope and abandon it."

"That's why I don't like R.E.M. anymore—they're actually
in with the popular cliques now, and everybody just sucks it all
up without even thinking. Even the football team was playing
it in the locker room during practice the other day! It makes
me sick."

"I don't really like trendy things. Like getting into surf
music, that wasn't a trend and it wasn't going to become one."

"That's pretty much in opposition to Rik," Bryce suddenly
theorized, "who's one of those kind of guys who likes to think
of himself as ahead of all the trends, but he's really right *with*
the trends by trying to always keep just slightly ahead of them.
Does that make sense?"

"Completely."

In the dark, sleety days of late January and February, Bryce would update Raymond with stories about his times with Mark: "We broke into a construction site last night. Mark spray-painted anarchy signs inside the buildings," Bryce typed avidly, and with some glossy detachment. "I went one step further by contributing a big 'E' for 'Entropy'—I figure that's a much more realistic concept then merely 'Anarchy'—and then the other guy we were with brought up speedballs and Mark was like, 'Yeah, let's go shoot some speedballs!' I was afraid that I was going to come home wired on drugs because I probably would've had to say yes, you know, peer pressure and all."

"Yeah, sounds scary."

"Scary? It's probably not as bad as they say. Scary would be the reaction of my dad if he knew. But it's interesting. Acid's another one. Mark does it frequently I guess. I figure I'll end up trying it once or twice this summer just to see how it works."

They both decided that "Entropy" was going to be the great new concept of the underground, and each of them wrote an "E" in black ink, made with three horizontal slashes, on the soles of their deck shoes. Bryce's reports of experimentation with his new friends continued over the following weeks and the coming of spring in its mulchy warmth.

"Smoking pot's okay," he told Raymond in the end of March. "I'm able to handle it now."

"Really?"

"Yeah, we've been doing that and I didn't really feel anything the first few times, but then suddenly it hit one time and I got it—it's just a great way to relax, either with friends or when you're alone, you lay back on your bed with some good music on and just kind of drift."

"I always wondered what it was all about, the Deadheads and the Rastas and all that."

"It makes the way you perceive everything around you change, like you can look at things from angles that you hadn't ever considered before. It's hard to describe, but it's almost like part of you can leave your body and sort of look down on it from the outside. I'm surprised more deep thinkers don't get into it."

In another week he admitted that he'd decided to retire. Raymond was shocked to hear this: once eighteen comes it's much harder to remain in the hack world, yes; the day inevitably comes for most to say goodbye, yes; but why go through it now, so suddenly, without a warning or a chance to dwell on it? But he was adamant.

"I feel like I'm entering a new stage of life, and I have no interest in sitting around on the computer anymore. Plus it'll make peace with my dad, who will be happy to lose the expense of the extra phone line."

"Wow," said Raymond, unable to speak in the sudden shock of the news. The enormity of the decision hit him when he realized that Bryce's telephone line would be drained of all power, that he'd be cut completely away from the world. He wanted to console Bryce and plead with him, tell him that he was being rash, but he somehow knew not to say it like that. Instead he was wry and calm and tried to be analytical. "So you're really doing it. Hm. What makes you want to do it now?"

"I just feel like I've gone as far as I can with textfiles. I mean, I don't call the boards anymore—with Rik being out on the West Coast there's little connection there for me now. Of course, going offline means ending this, too."

That comment dressed Raymond's spirit in black disconsolation: this was really it—Bryce was really leaving now for good.

"I don't need any talking out of this," he said stolidly. "I've thought it through, and I've been thinking about it for a long time, actually. I'm determined on this one—I'm getting out of modeming for good. I like you, it's nothing personal, but this is going to be it—it's best this way."

Before they hung up his goodbye was brief and noncommittal.

"Well, it's about time for me to go," came Bryce's words upon Raymond's screen.

"Good luck, then." Raymond could scarcely believe that he was typing out a last goodbye—but he was. "I'll see you."

"Bye."

After the line was disconnected Raymond realized that he was alone in his Roman Valley bedroom, sitting in front of the computer—he'd never known California, had never been to Michigan. Only here, this little room of light-blue walls. They seemed to moan out at him now and a dreariness reached in from somewhere far behind, from beyond Michigan, California, and the wires, and it pressed rudely upon him. Suddenly he wanted to push the machinery away, it all seemed so ugly and repulsive and he thought of how much of his life had already been invested in it, gone. He cried.

That night, unable to sleep, Raymond desperately tried to imagine a new arrangement that he could suggest to Bryce, something where the two would talk voice on the telephone, but he knew that wasn't what was going to happen. Instead they'd drift distantly apart and their friendship would fade off in the way that all friendships do, in the same way that he'd seen before with everyone he'd ever known in life: all of them were gone. He saw their figures distantly, like pale ghosts, and he heard songs ring out ruefully—there was a microphone, the dusty light of a deserted English pub, and in the slow-rocking minstrel croons he got the words, and their wisdom said that all friendships end.

School the next day was a minor, irritating diversion from this plaintive drama, and once back at home that afternoon he quickly called The Storyboard, where he saw that Zip had called the board one last time to announce his decision. It was initially greeted with silence—probably shock—but then a flurry of speculations came: "This is just a gag," "He's on drugs," "Aw, he's just got a girlfriend, he'll be back once it's out of his system," "Someone needs to talk some sense to him."

But while everyone went back and forth about it, Bryce held to his word: he retired early and he didn't call back. Raymond had sent him a private mail on the system but Bryce never logged in to read it. And Raymond didn't try to contact him again. "He'll be back," he thought with a stern conviction that was nothing more than an inner pantomime, an act he thought he was supposed to do; for he knew that new times lie immediately ahead. "It may not be tomorrow, it may be years away, but he'll be back."

It seemed inevitably true that the unseen world they knew on the computer would someday be seen and known by all—the world was getting wired, and no one could retire away from that.

But would Raymond ever talk to him again? Perhaps even one day meet? It was inevitable, he thought, but he didn't know when or even how. His future was still unclear, unwritten. Like the blinding haze of a furious snowstorm viewed from behind the windshield of a speeding car, it was something dazzling and bright, but he couldn't see beyond the field of glitter.

Once the excitement of Zip's sudden departure had settled down, there were gray days of idle speculation and then that too all faded out. Prof. Zip was gone. And when it hit, everyone just shook their heads, slowly, realizing they'd lost him. It was made known that there'd always be a place for him in the echelon of boards he'd been a part of, but they all carried on without him. Raymond grew accustomed to message threads and screens unvisited by Zip, by entire boards that had evolved without his presence. And then he too forgot how it had been.

After Zip's departure, the boards were never once the same. In the wake of it, Raymond had reached out to new and unknown places, trying to make a connection. Some of this was a quest looking for Zip's spirit, or for something else to fill his life with; he called Murray Solomon's American Hipster BBS in New York City, a board that Zip had been on but that Raymond had just never had enough time for. He knew Murray Solomon as a "Sixties radical," a famous protester and rantster of the times, and he suddenly remembered the radio program from long ago—Solomon had been saying that it was time for something new in literature and art, a new generation to make a move, and Raymond knew that it was going to be him.

They exchanged a few mails on his board and soon went on a first-name basis, the elder hippie eagerly interested in Raymond's life and outlook; and having seen a photograph of him, a drum-bellied man smiling toothily in a grimy doorway, his silvery-black hair curling down in back yet showing bald at the peak, Raymond imagined his big fingers pecking at a New York keyboard—but then as suddenly as it happened, Solomon stopped writing and as days slushed past Raymond lost interest in the board. He sent an apologetic mail out to Rik, saying that he knew he wasn't keeping up with The Storyboard but would try to get back into its swing. Rik's reply didn't acknowledge Raymond's earnest vow, but said that he was busy readying himself for college in the fall where he'd be running the board remotely and "had to make some major adjustments to the software, like pronto."

Sometimes through these moments he thought of Bryce, and wondered if it was all working out the same for him; there were a few momentary flashes of that former world, but they were rare: on a cool, cloudy April morning as he sat reading the day's newspaper with a mug of sugared, creamed-up coffee, a habit he'd recently acquired, a headline struck out savagely at him: "Murray Solomon, 60s radical, commits suicide." He was rocked and pummeled by the news; it ate away at something deep inside of him that was ravaged and could not return: this was the voice he remembered on the radio from long ago, the man he had recently talked with on the BBS—and now forever dead? Raymond had no one to talk to, no one to tell, but that morning he was in a quiet daze. The man that he had spoken to on the computer now was dead.

When summer was near Raymond sometimes began to wonder if Bryce was right, if it were possible to live a life without it—could he somehow go beyond it? Was it time to find life elsewhere, to not come back—to be like Bryce? Time to go and feel the physical sensations of the world, touch the smooth rails and hard heavy irons and pass by the fluttered drapes, to breathe in all the airs, to see the waters and the waves and visit all the haunts that living life had for him to offer? Would he ever find enough to fill the bitter open loneliness?

The golden glimmer of this secret world he'd known was faded. No longer was there a faeryland appeal; the luster dimmed and his focus wasn't held upon it—even the way he peered into the screen was different now. He no longer saw a world immersed inside it, but only the creaky workings of an old, outdated machine. It was like some dust-grimed type-writer that had sat rigidly for decades, usable but not current, and with none of the freshness and promise that it had on the day that it was bought—it was now a faded shell that seemed only to somehow hint at all the time that had rushed over it, to carry just a single-noted song about the exuberance of better days. Now his head was always cocked slightly from the bulging screen so that he was also focused on his high school world, the kids who were around him, his class and school. This all had been a dream, after all—a lovely dream, silken soft and lilac scented, but nonetheless a dream. It was time to wake from it and leave.

So he said that maybe in some other time again he might revisit it, for it'd been part of the treasure cache of life, but that now he had to go—there was a world out there; there was a life to be lived. He knew that it was time to hang whatever memory of it he had upon the mantel. There'd be time, in later days, to take it down and study—but this was not its current place in life. Now he must leave that world for other things—and so he quit the boards completely. His phones sat there in the corner of his quiet bedroom, he put his notebook in a bottom drawer, let the computer's untouched keys gather up a season's snow of dust, he no longer sat in his bedroom swivel chair; he went out into the glittering social realm and discovered what one does when arriving at the top of the heap in high school. He let it go. As far as he knew it'd never happen again; he'd never go back; he was retired.

CONTINUED IN VOLUME TWO

CIRCUITS OF THE WIND, VOLUME TWO

coming January 2012

CIRCUITS OF THE WIND, VOLUME THREE

coming March 2012

confiteormedia.com